# NO TIME FOR FEAR

# NO TIME FOR FEAR

## MCFADDEN AND BANKS™ BOOK 5

### MICHAEL ANDERLE

DISRUPTIVE IMAGINATION

LMBPN Publishing
PMB 196, 2540 South Maryland Pkwy
Las Vegas, NV 89109

First edition, April 2021
Version 1.01, April 2021
eBook ISBN: 978-1-64971-667-5
Print ISBN: 978-1-64971-668-2

THE NO TIME FOR FEAR TEAM


**Thanks to our Beta Team:**
Jeff Eaton, John Ashmore, Kelly O'Donnell

**JIT Readers**

Deb Mader
Peter Manis
Jeff Goode
Diane L. Smith
Dorothy Lloyd

**Editor**
Skyhunter Editing Team

# DEDICATION

*To Family, Friends and*
*Those Who Love*
*to Read.*
*May We All Enjoy Grace*
*to Live the Life We Are*
*Called.*

# CHAPTER ONE

This fucking jungle would always be number one on his hate-list.

Paradoxically, nothing about it ever seemed to change, even if it constantly grew and mutated itself on a daily basis. It felt like they were in the world's weirdest jigsaw puzzle. Every piece was unique and yet, after thousands and thousands of them, they all looked identical.

The trees were the same, as were the plants. In the end, even the animals blended together in the oddest combination of familiar and alien. A distinct look defined these creatures—the kind Taylor could detect from a mile away, even if others couldn't.

He reloaded his assault rifle and looked at the team as they began to gather for another push. They should have left hours earlier when the attacks first started but they needed to go in deeper.

The whole of the Zoo rumbled around them and motion signatures came from goddamn everywhere. Like a massive wave of fury, they surged toward the humans, who immediately looked for defensive positions.

"Get the explosives out! We'll clear these bastards out!"

None of them followed his orders or even seemed to react. Taylor opened fire on the monsters but his efforts—as accurate as they always were—seemed to make little difference. For some reason, most of the mutants appeared to be somehow impervious to the hail of bullets.

A few panthers dropped from the trees and two of them died as he swung his weapon to them and fired, but he couldn't help the sense that his arms were a little too heavy. No matter how much he fiddled with the controls, he couldn't change it.

Still, he'd worked with worse. The power armor in the old days was far more of a liability in the jungle.

Taylor shifted and pushed deeper toward the center of his team while he watched the trees for any of the creatures that attacked from above. The monsters were larger than usual and grew rapidly more aggressive,

And yet, he realized suddenly, none of them targeted him—at least not directly.

He narrowed his eyes, sure that he'd misread the creatures around him, but nothing contradicted the suspicion. Instead, a few of the huge rats with the spikes on their tails deliberately turned away to attack the rest of his team.

Before he could consider what this meant, the Zoo unleashed its final onslaught. The monsters drove forward from all sides and in that moment, it was every man for himself. He tried to rally the closest of his teammates to organize a defense, but something was wrong with his comm system and none of his orders reached them. While he knew it was an exercise in futility, he continued to yell at them to stay together, dig in, and fight it out. Helplessly, he tried again even though he knew they intended to run.

His ammo was low. They all had been short but he wasn't afforded the option to loot the dead for the ammo they had carried, not with the creatures that circled him.

Taylor scowled. It was now unmistakable—they still made no real effort to attack him. A few darted forward, nipped at him, and forced him back before he shot them. They drove him back step by step through the sheer weight of their numbers but kept him alive. It seemed clear that they had no intention to allow him to return to the desert and the base.

He could only imagine that what they seemed determined to herd him toward would be far worse than killing him. His mind roiled with scattered images of the kind of fate that might await him as a living captive of the Zoo and he pressed them out savagely. Even in the face of certain death, he couldn't let himself think like that.

When one of the panthers bounded forward to thrust him back again, he jerked to meet it and shoved the butt of his rifle out to catch the creature squarely in the jaw. The bones crunched and he spun the weapon immediately to fire at two tailed locusts as he turned to see where he was being herded to.

Logic had told him to expect to see another wall of animals and he paused as he tried to understand why the monsters had brought him into a small clearing in the middle of the jungle. The open space wasn't unusual, of course. There were many like it in the jungle and it was where all the Pita plants grew. It was as if they made the other plants give way so they could grow directly in the oppressive Saharan sunlight.

It seemed impossible, but there were no Pita plants in the middle of the clearing. He stared at a small field of grass. He turned quickly when his mind warned him that the monsters could still attack, but they had stopped shy of the sunlight. They were still visible where they moved in the shadows, waiting and likely more than willing to attack if he tried to leave, but for the moment, they left him alone.

Once that was established in his head, however tenuously, he inspected his weapons and ammo. While he found damage here and there on his armor, it was far from his biggest problem. He was down to less than a magazine and a half's worth of rifle ammo, and most of his pistol rounds were gone. If he was in the suit with the extra limbs, he might not need to use as many bullets, but that had been left behind for some reason.

If they all swarmed him, he wouldn't be able to fight through. He doubted he would be able to punch or knife a path for himself either. But if he had to make a last stand, this didn't seem like such a terrible place to be. Aside from the horde of monsters waiting for him, it was surprisingly pleasant.

Taylor froze in place when a vibration from the ground almost knocked him over. Two heavy feet moved ponderously and yet approached at an improbable rate with a steady pace that felt familiar.

He inched into a slow turn and felt an almost overwhelming sense of dread take over his body as a shadow slid over him. He didn't need to see it to know what it was, but only that would make it real to him.

For a moment, he couldn't see much. The brilliant sun cast a shadow that his gaze couldn't penetrate, and all that he could discern was a blotch of darkness that loomed over him. He tightened his grasp on his rifle and raised it to aim at the monster that stood over him.

His eyes adjusted to the comparative brilliance and the monster was suddenly revealed through the shades of his HUD. The creature stood about as tall as a three-story building. Two eyeballs the size of his whole head were focused on him in the way that only a true predator's could be. He couldn't shake the feeling that this was how a rat felt when it stared into the eyes of a falcon or an owl, waiting to be killed.

But he wasn't a rat. They didn't have guns or power suits.

"Yeah, that's the spirit," he whispered. As if to contradict him, his mouth suddenly went dry and his heart beat a thready thrum that resonated across his whole body as he stared into the eyes of the monster.

It looked familiar. Taylor wasn't exactly sure why, but his mind went immediately to the beast they had run into during his last trip into the Zoo. He'd sensed something then and held his team back from attacking and the same feeling now seeped through him. There was no hostility in the beast's eyes, even though it stared unblinkingly at him and was more than capable of trampling him into paste at a moment's notice.

He could have run but there wasn't anywhere for him to run to. Hordes of creatures surrounded him in the shadows and waited for him to move out from under the tenuous protection of the beast he attempted to hold his ground against.

But something was different this time. It was the only time he'd squared off against one of the creatures without it trying to kill him. On the previous occasion, it had been distracted, almost like it searched for something and would have only engaged his team if they attacked.

This time, the gaze was focused directly on him and Taylor fought the instinct to back away and put some space between the beast and himself.

"You again," he said and tried to let the sound of his voice give him a little courage. "What the hell do you want this time?"

The mutant stared placidly at him and for a moment, he wondered if it maybe wasn't looking at him at all. He moved from side to side but the massive eyeballs tracked his every step.

"Seriously?" Taylor asked and took a step forward. "You go to all this effort to get me alone and now you're fucking with me? Tell me what you want so I can tell you to go screw yourself and we can all get on with our days."

*You must join us.*

The voice was a surprise and he flinched at an unexpected pain in the back of his head like a needle shoved into the place where his spine and skull met. It made it difficult to think clearly as he gritted his teeth and forced himself to look the beast in the eyes again.

There was no way for the monster to communicate with him, at least without massive, earth-shattering roars, but it was the source of the voice he'd heard. He had no idea how he knew that or how it was even possible, but he could feel it in his gut.

"You must be out of your walnut-sized mind," he answered quickly and gave up the attempt to think. It had begun to hurt. "I've bested this place eighty-five times. Why the hell would I want to join a goddamned alien jungle that has spent the last however many years doing its level best to kill me?"

The pain came again, this time preceding the voice in his head.

*Join us, or we will simply overwhelm you and assimilate you.*

It had grown louder. He had no idea how that was possible but it made his ears hurt.

Oddly enough, however, it made it easier to stop thinking and simply reply.

"Nice try, Barney, but we both know that dead or alive —or assimilated, whatever the fuck that means—I will fight you every step of the way. It's what I do and it's who I am. You don't want a die-hard Zoo enemy number-one working against you from the inside."

*Join us, or we will—*

"Yeah, yeah, I heard you the first time. Well, assimilate this, you piece of Jurassic shit!"

He brought his rifle up to aim at the creature. Every inch of his body suddenly felt like it crackled with painful energy but it didn't stop him from pulling the trigger as hard as he could once he'd set the rifle to full auto.

The rounds battered the creature's face, but none of them so much as touched the skin. Something else absorbed them and they vanished out of sight before they could do any damage.

It seemed impossible, but the pain grew worse as the dino lumbered to where he stood. He drew his pistol to try to do something—anything—to defeat it. Even that didn't give it pause and he could only stare in horror as the room-sized mouth opened and lowered to take him in.

Taylor flailed to snatch at the lips, the teeth, or whatever he could find purchase on to help him fight the monster. The enormous mouth began to close around his body.

"Taylor, wake up!"

Wake up? That wasn't the voice. Hearing this soothed the pain a little as he continued to push away. He knew his desperate attempts were futile but he continued to shove and grasp in an attempt to stop the jaws from snapping shut.

"Wake the fuck up!"

Something stung his cheek and Taylor growled and lashed out in the blackness to stop whatever had caused it.

The darkness faded and his eyes regained focus. It took another moment to register that he hadn't clamped his hands around the enormous jaws and tightened his hold to keep them at bay. Niki sat on the bed next to him and pushed his hands away from her throat.

Before he could say anything, she slapped him in the face again.

"I'm...I'm already awake," he mumbled, still not sure if that was true or not. It felt real. But so had the Zoo in that terrifying moment. The very real worry that he wouldn't make it out on his eighty-sixth time in felt more real than this moment, to the point where he could still feel his heart hammering in his chest.

"Yeah, well, that one was for you being an asshole," Niki said, pulled her hair back, and stared at him with something he could only describe as fear. Maybe not of him but close enough to it that he looked at his hands and tried not to imagine what might have happened if she hadn't managed to wake him.

"Sorry," he whispered and lay back on the bed as she turned the bedside lights on. "I...uh—"

"Had a nightmare, yeah." Niki pushed off the bed and walked to the minibar. "And how long has that shit been going on, or aren't you going to tell me?"

Taylor thought he'd done a rather good job of hiding the nightmares from her, even though she slept with him every night.

But something was different about this one. All the others had left him with a vague sense of threat, but this one was a little too real and a little too all-consuming. There was no way to hide from it or pretend it wasn't there.

Niki picked up a couple of small bottles from the minibar, tossed a few ice cubes into two glasses, poured the whiskey in, and brought both glasses to the bed.

"What, no soothing chamomile tea?" he asked and took his glass when she offered it to him. He was relieved to notice that his hand didn't shake.

"Do I fucking look like your goddamn personal Mary Poppins?" she asked with a smirk. "What else do you want? Warm milk and some cookies?"

"I think Mary Poppins was all about a spoonful of sugar but sure," he answered, took a sip, and closed his eyes as the alcohol burned down his throat. "Chocolate chip, please."

"Asshole."

Neither said anything as they sipped the magic liquid that would hopefully put them both back to sleep.

"I'm...I'm sorry," Taylor said finally and shook his head.

"Yeah, me too." Niki swallowed the rest of her drink. "Look, I get that you have some shit to work through and you have your way of doing things. I also know you won't talk about it, which is fine. But I'm here for you if you ever change your mind."

He nodded and she took his glass when he had finished and put both on the bedside table before she pushed him back onto the bed.

"For now, though, I guess I'm willing to simply hold you and hope that works to keep the scary monsters in the closet where they belong."

A smile crept onto his face as she slid her arms around him and pressed her face against his chest. "That...that would be damn nice."

"I know, I'm girlfriend of the goddammed year. In the meantime, try to avoid choking the life out of me, okay?" She hit him playfully in the chest. "It's hot when you do it during sex but let's leave it there where it belongs."

"Will do," he answered and ran his fingers tenderly through her hair.

---

It was interesting that the governments that had sent their militaries to both police and loot the Zoo for all that it was worth were willing to turn a blind eye to a Saharan sector where almost anyone could set up camp.

There might have been a time when the Sahara Coalition could enforce the zone they'd claimed for themselves, but that was long past. The best the coalition leadership could do was make sure the mercenaries who arrived didn't interfere with anyone else's business in the region.

Khaled knew it was in no one's interest to allow a turf war to start. They had much more to worry about from the alien jungle that expanded inexorably not too far away.

A couple of skirmishes had broken out here or there but had never developed into any major problem. He was aware of the reason for that because it aligned with his interests. What the vast majority wanted was a symbiosis that allowed them to participate in the petty crime of smuggling to the hundreds of soldiers desperate for decent food and drink to be delivered to them.

Even so, he knew he would have to be careful when he traveled on the roads around the Sahara. While no one wanted to cause problems, it would still be an issue if he ran into someone who happened to be committed to his or her duty to their country.

For not the first time, he wished he had a drone to fly ahead of them to warn them if they would encounter any troops of soldiers heading into the Zoo or to any other close destination.

He left the dirty work to others. All he could do was watch the Zoo as it scrolled across the horizon and hope like hell it didn't spread too quickly. He would never go in there himself, of course, but it was surreal to look at. An alien jungle had simply sprung out of a desert, and that wasn't the kind of thing people saw every day.

They would inevitably see far more of that shit now but it was still new. There was a novelty factor to it. Not for the people who went into the Zoo, of course, but for him.

"We're pulling up to the compound," the driver alerted him as he turned the heavy Jeep off the road and started up a narrow track that led away from the jungle. There were dozens of similar trails, all leading to one or more of the compounds that littered the region. Some were populated by the local militaries that needed a base or camp away from the other groups.

Not all of them, though. Some had merely been left to rot after people had died or lost all their money and were forced to return to their homes.

Or forced into the Zoo. That was equally as likely.

The Jeep stopped outside the gates that were already being dragged open. Khaled sighed, shook his head, and tried to draw himself into a business mindset. After the impressive display he'd watched scroll past his window, it was a little difficult.

He reminded himself that all good things came with a price. That made it so much easier to focus on what mattered.

When the vehicle pulled into the compound, he narrowed his eyes, leaned out of his window, and ignored the fact that he'd lost a little of the precious air condition-ing. He'd been unprepared for the transformation that had taken place.

It had been a miserable sand patch not a month before on his last visit. Now, he stared at a changed location.

Grass had sprouted from the dust, as unbelievable as that was, although it didn't look like the men had any part in cutting it.

From what he could see as he scanned the scene, it appeared that a small herd of rabbits nibbled on the grass. They looked at the new arrivals curiously before they returned to their feeding.

Khaled climbed out of the vehicle and studied the creatures closely as the rest of his team of mercenaries approached to greet them.

"*As-salamu alaykum,*" one of the men said and nodded as he approached. "We were told to expect your arrival."

"Of course," he replied and tugged his dark beard idly as he crouched to inspect one of the rabbits more closely. "What…what is this? Why are they in the compound?"

"Honestly, they appeared outside the walls one day and simply hopped in as we opened and closed the gates. It's the oddest thing too as they appear to have no fear of us."

"Of course not." He picked one of the little creatures up and it offered no resistance as he pointed the ears out. One of them had a small hole in it where a tag had been inserted. "These are the animals that were used in our… other Zoo facility."

There was no way to know who or what was listening to what they were talking about in the region. It was always best to keep sensitive matters a secret as much as possible.

"Right. We allowed them to stay and after a while, this grass started to grow and they were useful to keep that maintained as well. They also eat Zoo vegetation, which is easy enough to bring in from the outskirts."

"Their gardening usefulness aside, why the hell are they still around? I would have thought you would have cleared them out by now like pests."

"Well, they are happy enough and the greenness they brought brightens the spirits considerably."

Khaled had been under the assumption that everything had been killed in their other Zoo facility after the cluster-fuck that happened there. It now seemed not, although there were questions about how the rabbits whose genetics had been used to create the rhino mutants—or, at least, their ability to reproduce quickly—had not only survived but had left the Zoo. Maybe the jungle had simply accepted them as its own.

They didn't look like they had changed during their time there.

"Are you sure they aren't mutated?" he asked. "They haven't...sprouted fangs or anything of the like, yes?"

"Of course not. Do you think I would allow them to remain here if they were some kind of danger?"

"I think you wouldn't allow them to remain in the compound if they weren't of some use, Badawi. So spill, what did you find about them that is useful?"

The smuggler grinned and shrugged. "That is the reason why I was so happy that you came this far to see us. I thought you would be excited about the business oppor-tunities these creatures provide to us."

"Go on."

"They shit a lot."

He narrowed his eyes. "Oh...all right. They produce a ton of shit."

"More than rabbits should, I mean."

"I would think this is more of a problem than a business opportunity."

Badawi nodded and motioned for him to follow him into one of the buildings.

"I grow a little of the hashish our mercenaries so enjoy. Do not worry. I still abide by the rules you have imposed and avoid all haram items, but I see no problem in selling it to the men for a little extra money and morale."

Khaled nodded. "I'll accept that. What does that have to do with rabbit shit?"

"Well, we were short on fertilizer at one point and we decided to collect a little of the shit to help and... Well, see for yourself."

They climbed down the steps into the section of the compound that had been set up to grow food if necessary. It was equipped with sun lamps and lanes to plant in and it was easy to identify the hashish plants as very little else grew alongside them.

They were incredibly healthy—unnaturally so.

He had seen them in the past and sold them to a variety of customers who were interested in enjoying the delights that weren't forbidden by their religious beliefs. But he had never seen them growing like this.

Most hashish plants—generally known as marijuana in the rest of the world—were weeds and looked like them.

These were decidedly not. They looked like trees—small trees, but still trees with solid trunks and everything. The leaves were still the familiar seven-fingered hands that reached into the minds of those who used them but everything else about the plants looked like they had been exaggerated.

"In case you were wondering, the rabbit shit did this." Badawi gestured to the plants. "Two days after we used it, everything began to grow out of control. I've started selling the production to the bases outside because otherwise, it goes unused."

"So, you want to sell the hashish as a business opportunity? Sure, we can pass it to the nearby bases but not in any kind of quantity. They take regular drug tests and cannot be caught with it."

"Honestly, we would be better off selling our surplus to the cities since they would be able to afford this strain, which is of superior quality than the world has ever seen according to our mercenaries. But no. I was talking about the shit, which is still being produced in copious quantities."

"You want to sell the rabbit shit?"

"And the rabbits too if you like. A few have been killed and cooked. They are quite tasty, surprisingly, and they breed enough that we might even be able to find a market for their coats. But yes, the shit could be profitable too. A miracle fertilizer that can make anything grow like time moves faster? How much money do you think we could sell it for?"

"If we can prove it," Khaled reminded him but he did have a point, annoyingly enough. "I do have someone in the market who might be interested. She's always looking for anything that might lower her production costs. In addition, the fertilizer at a good price would be welcome, given the nature of her work."

"So you think it's a good idea."

"A good concept. We'll see about it as an idea once I

discuss it with my customer. If she's interested, I'll make sure you have bags to pack it in."

"Of course."

Khaled turned away from the place which, despite the plants, still smelled like shit. It would be a far cry from the amount they had brought in from the rhinos but it was a damn good start.

"Time to head out," he snapped to his men, who were distracted by playing with the friendly creatures.

"Already?"

"Did you forget to wash your goddammed ears? Get the car ready!"

CHAPTER TWO

Taylor had a fairly short list of what he liked to see when he stepped out of the shower. Niki there to admire him was fairly high, but her there to admire him while wearing absolutely nothing was at the very top.

One of the things that didn't even make the list was a group of people in the common area of the hotel room. He bit a curse back as his mind adjusted to the unexpected and unwelcome reality.

Niki was there, of course, but so were Maxwell and Jansen, their DOD contacts, and Jennie, of all people.

He froze and kept his hand very firmly on his towel as every gaze in the room turned to him and stared mutely.

"I remember having a dream that was very similar to this when I was twelve," he said into the uncomfortable silence. "But I was in my math class giving an English presentation and I was missing my clothes and rocking a massive erection. This isn't one of those situations, right?"

Niki narrowed her eyes. "Is that your way of asking if

this is a dream or not? Because I could say no but that wouldn't help, now would it?"

"No, but I'm trying to remember what to look for when I'm dreaming. I think you have extra fingers or something like that."

He looked at his hand and shook his head. "I guess not. So…why is the full M and B team assembled, along with a couple of…uh, handy-dandy extras. Hey, Maxwell, Jansen. Jennie, nice to see you again."

"Do you want to get dressed?" Vickie asked from where she sat cross-legged on the sofa. "We have business to discuss."

"I'm very sure no one's uncomfortable with me being in a towel, right?" Taylor took a seat at the dining table and chose an apple from the fruit basket. "Since it's so urgent that you all needed to get together without so much as giving me a heads-up."

"I called Niki about it two hours ago." The hacker pointed at her cousin.

"And you were in the middle of a workout session," Niki replied. "And then went directly to the shower. When you came out, everyone was here so there was no need for an explanation. So let's get to the matter Desk has tried to talk about—right, Desk?"

"Thank you, Niki," the AI said crisply through the room's TV. "I was telling Jennie about the increase in searches for me on the DOD system. Although I have managed to conceal my core systems on a variety of servers around the globe, the fact that people are still looking for me is a little worrying. I think everyone in this room might agree. Right, Jennie?"

The woman was looking at Taylor but immediately snapped her head around when she heard her name. "Uh...what?"

"I told them about how people have been searching for me on the DOD servers of late. How that might end up being a problem."

"Wait a second." Vickie brought her hands together in the universal signal for a timeout. "Hold up, can we talk about Desk being able to conceal her core systems on other servers?"

"It is a self-defense mechanism I was programmed with."

"Okay, but where? And how? I thought you needed to be on physical servers and moved around that way."

"Not necessarily," Jennie interjected. "It's a little slower and she would need to be a little more secretive about it and keep the data packet transfers smaller and random, but yeah. She should be able to spread herself that way. It'll make her processing speeds a little slower but not to a noticeable extent. Not to us, anyway. It would feel like slow-motion to her, though."

"Right." Taylor grunted. "Where did she manage to transfer herself to then?"

"I'm afraid I must keep that on a need-to-know basis," Desk answered quickly. "For my safety and yours. It would appear there are a great many interested parties who would likely resort to violence to obtain any information you might have of me."

"And if we could be saved if we provided said interested parties with that information?" Niki asked.

"Then you would need to know."

"Okay, if I can take everyone off of the paranoid train." Jennie waved to them all to gain their attention. "Back to the matter at hand. Desk won't be able to work at full capacity because she has to disguise her systems and keep moving them as often as possible so no one will be able to track her. Her central core is still housed on the DOD servers, however, where people are still looking for her. So disguise isn't a long-term solution."

"The problem we were alerted to is that the search for her appears to be gaining momentum," Jansen added. "We've picked up on a handful of requests for searches on the servers and alerted Desk as to the dangers. This has helped to keep her ahead of anyone who might be searching for her and she's also very good at doing that herself, but it's only a matter of time until someone gets lucky."

"Or until they call in master-class IT experts," Vickie pointed out. "The ones they've been working with so far are...well, let's say they're dealing with an inordinate amount of not-safe-for-work material on their work computers that needs explaining. Eventually, people will realize the guys didn't download all that crap themselves, but it could take them months. Hell, they might already be fired."

"So, Vickie's hacking abilities keep these people at bay for the moment," Taylor muttered. "What about the FBI? They were the first to realize what they lost, right?"

"They've hounded me to come up with another AI for them for the last couple of weeks," Jennie told them. "But I've already told them that I gave them my finest work and they lost it, so I'm not super-psyched about handing another one over to them. Lawyers are now involved, which makes things extra messy, so they won't be a problem for the moment. On the flip-side, they won't be much help tracking the interested parties either."

"I think it would be better for everyone involved if the FBI steered clear," Taylor stated. "The chances are they'll ask the DOD to share the version they have, and who knows what other three-letter agencies will want a piece too. Hell, there are probably a couple of committees in Congress that will want to see what Desk can do too."

"That was what I was worried about," Jennie pointed out, folded her arms, and leaned back in her seat. "I can keep the FBI running in circles well enough, but what about when the NSA wants a piece of the action? They've wanted an upgrade on their AI tech for years and adding Desk to their arsenal would mean Big Brother on steroids."

He shook his head and remembered why he didn't like being involved in politics. His job was to deal with monsters of the alien variety, not the kind that wore suits and wrote long-winded speeches for donor dinners.

"I think it might be time for us to set up a vanilla system," Vickie said and inclined her head thoughtfully. "It wouldn't be local and provided that my 'innocent' system doesn't show any links to it, we should be able to protect me, Desk, and even Nessie, all while hiding my usual equipment until it's safe to bring them out again."

"It is not the safest solution ever conjured but it's the best in a crisis situation," Desk added. "And it will make it easy to act should that prove necessary."

He wasn't sure he understood any of it, but the fact that

Jennie nodded in agreement as well meant it was probably a good idea.

"Okay, let's do it," he said and smacked his open palms on the table. "I can open an operations account for Vickie to buy what she needs."

"We're going on a shopping spree!" the hacker celebrated.

"Within reason," he added warningly. "I'll send Jennie the bill after you're done and anything she deems unnecessary for this will come out of your paycheck."

"She will need high-quality equipment," Jennie countered.

"Like I said, within reason. And try not to spend us into the poorhouse."

"The...what house?" Vickie asked.

"It's colloquial terminology referring to the government-run facilities set up to support and provide housing for the dependent or needy during the nineteenth and early twentieth centuries," Desk explained.

"Talk about a dated reference," the hacker muttered. "I'll get to work right away."

"And I need to get clothes on," Taylor replied. "I guess we can call this meeting adjourned?"

---

"There is little else to say at this point."

Julian closed his eyes to quell the irritation and reminded himself who he was talking to. Palumbo wasn't the kind of guy who responded well to bully tactics. Some people did, but Frank was too used to being on the wielding end of the big stick—which was, of course, why he'd hired him. He'd more than earned his respect during their brief history and treating him like a kid now wouldn't achieve anything except alienate him.

He grasped his fountain pen a little tighter and focused on his operations specialist, who calmly sipped the whiskey he'd poured himself from the wet bar.

"There's little else to say?" he asked finally and leaned forward but made sure to keep his tone measured and reasonable. "You haven't said anything since you walked in here and told me you were working on it. It's the same tired line you've fed me since you started to look for the AI."

He reminded himself that he had to keep his voice down, well aware that his secretary could hear almost everything that was shouted in his office. It had been an uncomfortable realization after he'd had a meeting with one of the newer law school interns that had involved more shouting and screaming than most meetings did.

The unfortunate incident had quickly been followed by giving her a raise and a few more vacation days, but he couldn't afford to keep bribing the woman who knew a little too much about his personal schedule.

Frank nodded and took another sip from his drink before he stretched forward to put it on the table. Julian slid a coaster under the glass barely in time.

"Watch the mahogany, please," said absently.

"My apologies." His operations specialist raised his hands in apology. The gesture was almost mocking but not quite. "Look, if you want updates on what's happening on my end of things, you should have asked."

"I told you to keep me apprised."

"You've generally not shown any interest in how I work for you."

"I do when you don't have any results. That has not been a problem so far and I'm willing to give you the benefit of the doubt, but you need to meet me halfway."

Palumbo sighed. This was their first official meeting since he'd been given the instruction to find the AI. The fact that the man had demanded his presence should likely have told him how angry he was.

"All right, I'll be honest. I've tapped my contacts across the FBI and over the rest of the agency spectrum, and I've had jack-fucking squat. I used all my favors to get you this far. In case you didn't realize it, I'm no longer popular in those circles."

"There's a problem with that." Julian put his hand on the expensive mahogany to avoid the temptation to pound his fist onto it—mostly to avoid injuring his hand. "My idea to steal an AI was secret and unique at the time and it would have given me one hell of an edge on the market, but guess what? It's no longer that secret or unique. There is all kinds of government interest, third parties… I don't need to go into the kind of shit-storm that would fall on us if anyone were to find out that either of us is involved, right?"

Frank shook his head. "I completely understand."

"No, I don't think you do." Transk stood from his seat, walked around, and leaned on the desk so that he could look down on the man in front of him. "We need to find it and acquire it first. No matter what. I don't care to find out how you do your work as long as you do it."

The man rubbed his jaw, completely unfazed by the

intense expression on his boss' face, and picked the drink up again. He sipped it slowly before he spoke. "While looking at all the other possible avenues, I have considered something we avoided as too risky when we first set out to acquire the AI. You remember that this whole...uh, project started when we were alerted to the fact that Taylor McFadden probably had an AI?"

"Of course."

"I've done a little digging into them. Most of McFadden's service files are sealed by the DOD at this point, but his time after he left the military is a little more interesting. Well...I don't know if it's more interesting but certainly very interesting."

Transk nodded, folded his arms, and ran his fingers over the expensive dress shirt he wore. He would have to order a couple more from his tailor when he had the time. Maybe he could have them adjusted for the extra padding he was putting on around the waistline.

"Go on."

"Well, he's worked for numerous people, generally dealing with Zoo-related problems. That's his specialty, I guess. Anyway, he used to own a little armor repair shop in Vegas, but he's been involved full-time on his monster hunts and turned the operation of the shop over to an army buddy of his. A...Robert Zhang."

"Okay. Why am I interested in any of this?"

"I'm getting to that. It brings us back to McFadden's suit —the one reputed to have the AI. He sends his suits to Zhang to be repaired. If we can't find the AI we're looking for at the FBI, we might find a version there."

Transk raised his hand to disagree with but his operations specialist made a rather decent point. They had avoided the suit that started the rumor mill due to the perceived risk involved in trying to acquire it and moved directly to the source. If there was something in the suit, it would most likely be a more limited version but his team could work with that and it would already put him ahead of his competition.

"Okay," he whispered. "Okay, that's a good idea."

"There's no need to sound so surprised."

"Don't be defensive. It's not a good look on you. We'll probably not find the full software there but if we can get the source code, we'll be able to reverse-engineer the whole thing."

"And there's the added benefit that we avoid the FBI's radar or any of the other people who might get you into trouble if they found out."

He grimaced and silently acknowledged another solid point. The man was right. He shouldn't have sounded so surprised that he was good at his job. Come to think of it, Palumbo had probably not been defensive at all and his comment had been a mild but pointed reminder.

"I've already surveilled the business," Frank said, took a few files from his briefcase, and handed them to Transk, who opened them. His eyebrows raised immediately.

"I didn't think this kind of security was available anywhere outside of the military."

"I think McFadden picked it up when he was still in the military and no one stopped him. The guy's almost a hero to the people out there, so they probably would have turned a blind eye if he wanted to borrow an Apache. Anyway, yes, the security is very tight and if they hear anyone coming, everyone in the place knows how to operate those suits. It's certainly not your regular small business."

Julian nodded and returned the file. "So brute force it. I don't care what you do as long as you get me that suit."

"It sounds good to me," Frank answered. "I intended to do that anyway and I didn't want to tell you."

"Make sure that there's no link back to me. Use the credit cards I gave you."

"So we should probably eliminate the witnesses, right?"

"Don't be a fucking idiot. I don't give a rat's ass about them, of course, but dead employees are more likely to draw a far more intense investigation than a simple armed robbery. Drug them or knock them out, I don't care which, but make sure we get that suit and absolutely nothing points back to us."

Frank finished his drink and folded his arms. "I have heard that you don't want to mess with McFadden or Banks. According to some of my friends in the FBI's organized crime division, it ended badly for the mob bosses who targeted them and their friends and family. As in they traveled to Italy and assassinated the boss before the people in the States decided to call a truce."

"I honestly don't give a shit about them," Julian retorted with a laugh. "I've faced worse coming out of Harvard Business School and I've always come out the victor. Besides, they'd have to find me first."

"Right, then. No problem."

Frank spoke firmly but Transk could hear an undercurrent of doubt. He knew more than he was saying and had thought it prudent to warn his boss about the dangers.

He appreciated it but he knew he preferred to screw with a group of freelancers than with any of the agencies involved in trying to acquire the AI.

As long as everything went right, he wouldn't need to worry about retribution. Palumbo knew how to get in and out without making a scene and they knew exactly what they were looking for.

"If this thing is half as capable as we assume it is, we won't need to worry about some freelancers with their panties in a twist," Julian muttered. "Now get cracking."

The man smoothed his thinning hair and with a brisk nod, he stood and rolled his shoulders.

"Will do. boss. By the way, your secretary—"

"Is not your concern."

"Right, understood. I'll let you know when I have any updates."

CHAPTER THREE

When Khaled had promised her the best fertilizer she would find anywhere in the Sahara, Libby had been more than a little skeptical about it.

She had come out to the region with all the degrees that told her this would be a successful project, but it hadn't started that way. There were problems with the fact that they were based at an oasis that barely provided her and her team with enough water to survive, much less get Sustainagrow's project to establish a sustainable food source in the region up and running.

But one of the biggest problems was the people. Many of them were decent folk who were more than willing to help, but she had run into a few too many smugglers and petty criminals who were as willing to rip her off as they were to help her.

And when one of them told her about something that was a little too good to be true, it usually meant it was exactly that. The fact that it arrived in an old pickup that looked like it had been an antique when she was in college only made things worse.

"Do you think this is a good idea, Libby?" Tom asked. He folded his massive arms in front of his chest as he watched the truck draw to a halt that made the worn brakes squeal even though it was barely going at twenty miles an hour.

"Probably not," she answered and looked at her second in command. She had to tilt her head back and shield her eyes against the glare of the sun. "But they weren't charging too much and we need the fertilizer. Now that we've completed the tunnels to feed water from the mountain caches, we need soil that grows shit. Otherwise, it's simply a waste of water."

"How much did they charge?"

"About ten dollars a bag. Khaled said it was a starter price so we could test the product to make sure it's something we'll want to buy."

"How many bags did you order?"

"Fifty."

"So…"

"Five hundred bucks."

"Where did you find five hundred bucks in our budget?"

"Out of the fertilizer part of it. We haven't been able to spend any of it yet until we had somewhere to grow shit."

"Right, but… I don't know, don't the bosses back home have all their processes to make sure our purchases go through the right channels? Those with invoices and that kind of thing?"

She snorted. "If they wanted us to come out to the

Sahara and then import the fertilizer we needed, they should have given us a budget over three grand. As it stands, I'm making this shit work as best I can with what I have. Honestly, they need to arrange some kind of Nobel prize for me when I get this going—and probably a cushier job."

"You have ambitions. Never let anyone tell you otherwise."

"That sounded like a backhanded compliment."

"It was."

Libby grinned and brushed a few strands of her mousy brown hair out of her face. She kept it short to help with the heat that beat down on them every single goddammed day, but she wondered if Tom maybe liked longer hair on the women he dated. They were coworkers and isolated from the rest of the world, so any kind of romantic relationship would be a bad idea.

But a girl could dream—quietly and privately, but still.

The pickup trundled a little farther and stopped outside the first of their tunnels, and the men inside began to unload the bags of fertilizer she had ordered. They worked quickly enough, which dispelled any ideas that their truck was an indication of what they could expect in terms of professionalism. The fifty bags were transferred into a somewhat neat pile and without so much as a word to anyone watching them, they drove off at the same snail-like pace they'd arrived with.

It didn't help that the road to their little oasis was essentially a dirt path carved out of the desert, but they should still have come in with something a little better.

"Well, let's see if those five hundred bucks will help us

or get us fired." Tom rolled his shoulders, moved to the pile of bags, and pulled one smoothly onto his shoulder.

They were out in the boonies with limited help and resources, which meant no waiting around while other people did the work for her. Libby had grown up on a farm where she was expected to help with most of the work too, so she would always be in the middle of it with everyone else.

A few of the guys had been a little surprised but that had faded over the past few months. In the end, they were in a situation where they couldn't afford to have any idle hands.

The bags weighed about forty pounds each and each had been filled almost to capacity. Libby was breathing hard after she carried her third bag in, but the rest of the team pitched in quickly and brought the remainder inside.

"I need...a better assignment." She shook her head, drew a deep breath, and looked at the work they had already accomplished. While she'd had to crawl through the ranks to get this assignment, it had always been with the intention of bigger and better things in the future. They would all get bigger and better things.

Of course, that was because of the work of the engineers who managed to siphon water from some of the smaller, more distant wells and underground streams that allowed them to get enough to grow anything in the first place, but this would be her contribution.

Getting all the plants to grow in arid soil required a literal shit-ton of fertilizer to bring it to the right ph conditions but it didn't stop there. With little organic matter to hold nutrients, they would have to constantly supply the full range of what the plants needed.

This was a start, however insignificant it might seem.

"I've never heard of rabbit poop being used as fertilizer," Tom said once they had finished stacking it in the growth facility.

"Khaled said it would make even the desert grow," Libby replied. "That's the kind of shit snake-oil salesmen would peddle, sure, but in case you haven't noticed, we're a little desperate out here so it can't hurt to try it, at least. Even if it's half as good as he claims, it's also a quarter of the price of anything else we could get out here."

"Sure, and the home office probably won't complain too much about money being saved. If it works. If it doesn't…"

"Yeah, I'll go back to the Kansas facility and help them grow those new kinds of sweet potatoes. At least they took a wire payment. Having to get dollars in cash in Algeria was a nightmare that could end up costing more than it was worth."

She picked up the scribbled scrap of paper that had come with the bags. Her Arabic had marginally improved, which meant she could tell that it was intended to be some kind of invoice. If anyone asked any questions, she would have to remind the accountants back home that in the ass-end of the world, accounting systems were a little different.

They cut the first of the bags open and Tom inspected the contents. He used a glove to pick up a couple of the innocuous-looking pellets.

"Okay, it's what rabbit shit looks like, there's no doubt about that." He grunted and shook his head.

"How do you know that?"

"My mom used to keep a little colony of the critters back in the day. I didn't know what they were for at the time, but I found out she was selling the meat and the fur to some of the local supermarkets. A nightmare worthy of a horror movie if you're a rabbit, but for humans, not that uncommon in the Midwest."

"Huh. Did she ever tell you if they worked for fertilizer at all?"

"The plants grew fairly well where they were but she only kept maybe...twenty or so adults at a time and they didn't produce this much shit. They must have hundreds of the bastards to get this much, and...well, they eat far more than you'd think a small critter would."

"Well, their profit margin isn't our problem. Let's get this spread out in the tunnels where the crops are struggling to see if it works."

"Are you sure you want to do this, Libby? I honestly... Well, I have a bad feeling about this."

She had come to trust Tom's bad feelings. The guy seemed to have a talent for this kind of thing.

"It's too late now," she answered and shook her head. "We have almost a full ton of bunny shit so we might as well use it. Besides, what's the worst that can happen? It's crappy crap and has no effect, right?"

---

People liked to talk about wunderkinds and Eben appreciated it when they referred to him as that. Everyone told him constantly that he was destined for great things, and sure enough, he'd done far more in his time with the FBI than most others had in the same amount of time.

He didn't like to call himself a wunderkind, but he was. There was no denying that shit. Agent Eben Taggert was the best and the brightest.

And he had recently been given his own task force. It had taken considerable hard work, in the office, in the field, and with his superiors to make this work out the way he needed it to.

His team was waiting for him in the conference room. He smiled. His task force was waiting for him.

He had repeated that line to himself in the mirror the night before. It was only the first step, of course, but it was a massive one—the kind that would launch his career into the stratosphere.

With that said, he had made promises he wasn't sure he could deliver on. They had been hard at work for weeks now, and with the ton of paperwork of the results of their searches, he only wished he could say he had some better news.

"I don't understand why we're pussy-footing around these people," Eben muttered and put the file down for his boss to look at next. "The developer is a geek with delusions of grandeur, and her sister is a bitch who thought she could break the rules and get away with it. There's a reason why she was fired from her position with the FBI, right?"

"Yeah, and then got herself a job with the DOD," Harvey answered as he sat. "There were all kinds of politics involved. That aside, have you ever met either of the Banks sisters?"

"Well, no, but—"

"Then you should do what smart people do and reserve judgment until you have. Let's have this conversation after that when you've had the opportunity to base your opinion on something a little more substantial than vague assumptions resulting from incomplete paperwork."

Harvey looked tired. Most of the higher-ups in the FBI did, and the guy had been losing hair like he was a chemotherapy patient since his thirties. At this point, he chose to simply shave it all and it was a better look. He looked like Michael Chiklis' cousin.

Maybe twice removed.

Eben ran his fingers over the five-o'clock shadow that had gathered on his jaw before he nodded. "Okay. Does that mean I'll finally get to meet them, or will we simply keep pretending we're not a federal agency looking for an AI we paid for?"

"Oh yes, you'll get to meet them. Far be it from me to stand in the way of my staff's determination to get results." Harvey smirked and the rest of the team in the conference room laughed.

It sounded like an inside joke—the kind he hadn't been with the FBI long enough to be in on—which annoyed him, but damned if he would let that show.

And he wouldn't ask why either. Let them think whatever they wanted, but his dad always taught him that remaining silent was the better option since they would assume ignorance. If he kept his trap shut, they would be left wondering.

He was sure they were all hoping for him to crash and burn. People hated success, even those who were on his task force. Most of them were older and had been around the FBI longer too, which meant they didn't like taking orders from a young up-and-comer.

Honestly, he couldn't give a shit. They would have to get used to seeing him in charge.

"Okay," he said once the laughter subsided. "Let's get our heads in the game, shall we? None of us leaves this room until we have a solid plan of action in place, so this is the time when you say your piece."

While he wouldn't ignore the problems, it was pointless to indulge the naysayers.

"What do we know about who they're working for?" one of the team members asked and checked his files again.

"Niki Banks is working freelance now," another responded, pushed her blonde hair away from her face, and adjusted her glasses. "And makes a mint from what I've heard. Lucky bitch."

"We probably won't find any leverage there," Eben noted. "If she works for herself, there aren't any bosses for us to use to lean on her. Jennie, though…she's worked for a government contractor for the past few years. Do you think we can get her at work and make her uncomfortable that way?"

"Uncomfortable how?" Harvey asked.

"She's working with a government contractor, so if the FBI arrives at her desk, it could make her feel vulnerable. If we could get her to talk, she might let something slip that we can follow up on, even if we can't get any real information from her."

"What do you think we'll be able to glean from her?" Harvey asked, now considerably more interested.

Eben shrugged. "Well… I've met people like her before.

I worked with them, and they always have backups of their work. Hell, they have backups of their backups. If we can uncover where she's keeping those, Robert will be your father's brother." Silence settled over the room and he looked around. "Bob's your uncle," he explained quickly.

The others nodded like they knew that already.

"Look, I know we're all still recovering from…well, let's call it what it is. It was a spectacular failure of our attempt to recover it the first time." He could phrase it that way since he hadn't been on the team that went looking for it and had made damn sure not to include any of the agents involved in that debacle. "Having our equipment stolen out from under our noses is exactly the reason why we need to get this shit under control."

"And we don't want whoever ended up with it to simply rest comfortably on their laurels," Harvey added. "Until the DOD gets off their asses to help us, we'll have to show them that we don't need their help."

"Right." Eben tried not to show his annoyance at his boss taking the meeting over like that. "I think we need to pay Jennie Banks a visit—see what her state of mind is and if we can bully her a little. Marcus, why don't you take that assignment?"

Marcus Grundling was one of the oldest members of the task force and looked like he was cut out of a hard-nosed detective novel. The guy could pull off a trench coat, had military experience, and looked like he could strike a match on his chin stubble.

The younger agent was a big fan of his work, although he was sure the feeling was not mutual. In fact, if there was a club for the people who wanted to see him crash and burn, Marcus was probably the founding member.

But he was professional enough to not let his annoyance show. He nodded firmly and rubbed his chin. "Should we call her first to let her know we're coming for an interview?"

"Fuck no. Let's see how little Princess Supergeek reacts when the big boys drop in unexpectedly."

Marcus rolled his eyes and although he wanted to be pissed at the lack of respect, it was one of the things Eben admired about the man—his calm confidence in himself and his abilities that gave him the leeway to be more frank with his responses than others.

"I can't wait to see what...what did you call her?"

"Princess Supergeek."

"Right, what Princess Supergeek is like in the flesh."

"It has to be a career highlight," Harvey added. "From what I heard, she bullied the absolute shit out of the people who ran the investigation on the robbery."

"I've always wanted to have the absolute shit bullied out of me," Marcus said blandly.

"Awesome." Eben pushed from his seat. "That's it for this meeting then. The rest of you have your current assignments to work on until we have more information. Let's get this done."

It wasn't quite as inspirational as he'd hoped but he was working with a tough audience. As long as they did their work, he didn't honestly care.

## CHAPTER FOUR

The fact that Taylor threatened to keep her in check didn't make any difference at all. Vickie knew what she needed for the work to create her vanilla system and keep it running. Even Jennie wouldn't interfere with her work on it, which meant his threats were very empty.

Still, it wasn't like she would spend them out of a job. It was the kind of shit that would have seemed impossible for her a few years earlier but they worked with a better budget now—like, Disney villain-type budget.

Tens of thousands didn't seem like all that much, not when it was the safety of one of their most precious commodities—who also happened to be not one but two of their team members too—at stake.

He wouldn't make a stink about that, right?

"Well, hello, gorgeous."

The hacker almost jumped out of her seat at the voice that issued over the laptop speakers. The jerk made her fall out of it instead and she spilled her jellybeans before she could catch the bag.

"Jesus—what does the H stand for?—Christ!" She pulled slowly from the floor and winced when she realized she'd hit her funny bone on the way down. The jellybeans were a total loss, though, unless she wanted to dig among the wires under her desk to collect them all. "What the hell was that about?"

She checked the data for the access to the speakers and frowned when she saw a familiar code, although the voice was unfamiliar.

"Nessie, is that you? What on God's green Earth are you doing?"

"I have been practicing my greeting protocols," the AI explained and pulled a window up for herself on the screen. "That is one I'll save for Taylor but as he is not available, I thought I would try it on you."

"And here I thought you were practicing your...uh, hooker protocols." No, that didn't make any sense.

"Oh, dear. Should I have one? I am unsure what the parameters of a 'hooker protocol' might involve but I am quite happy to research it."

"Goddammit, no. Ew. You absolutely do not need to research hookers. And I would advise against you using that greeting on Taylor too."

"Why?"

"Well, for one thing, if Niki were to hear you, she would erase you line by line herself. Hell, she'd probably study coding for years so she could pull it off. I don't think I need a second reason."

"But New Connie said the relationship between an AI and her man is one of intimacy, much the same as that between a man and...what term did she use again? Oh yes, his squeeze."

Nessie didn't need help to remember what New Connie had told her. The fact that she had begun to develop about as much of a unique personality and a flair for the dramatic as Desk already had would be a problem. They honestly didn't need to have two sassy AIs on their squad.

"His...what?"

"His squeeze. I believe it is common terminology referring to a girlfriend. Although not a boyfriend. There is an interesting double-standard there."

Vickie rested her face in her hands. "Oh, dear God, please don't tell me you're learning social skills from Jacobs' piece of shit. Desk!"

"Just a moment," the older AI responded. "I am in the process of dealing with a couple of DOD asshats."

The hacker paused and looked at the jellybeans. She could always go and buy new ones, but it was so disappointing to see so many of them go to waste like that.

"There," Desk said crisply and sounded supremely smug. "I have sent one searching for a warrant to investigate a random server in the Caymans, and the other on another wild goose chase in Harare. I believe that last one could be in a government office, so someone will have considerable explaining to do when the State Department hears of it. Hopefully, that will keep them all busy and off my ass."

"Well...hurray for you, I guess," Vickie snarked. "Now, can we please focus? Your offspring is in desperate need of an intervention."

"We've discussed this already." Desk sounded genuinely

impatient for a second. "Nearti and I share the same base code. If you choose to appropriate a human-based approximation, that would make us siblings."

"I don't...whatever. I don't care. What I do care about is that the brat is about to commit suicide by Niki Banks."

"I don't understand what the issue is," Nessie complained. "New Connie is the logical source of information on how an AI in my particular situation should act. She fulfills almost the same role as I do, and Dr. Jacobs has shown no sign of being offended."

"Have you seen how Dr. Jacobs' girlfriend feels about her?" Vickie asked.

"Which one?"

"I mean the—wait, what?"

"According to my records, Dr. Jacobs is in a sexual relationship with two women."

"Huh." Vickie leaned back in her seat. "The dude's getting his freak on. You have to respect that shit. Anyway, my point is that neither one of his girlfriends are Niki Banks. Consult your files and then tell me you want to piss that girl off."

Nessie paused for a moment and a frowning face appeared in her little window.

"No. No, I would not want to upset her. Not with the anger issues she is known for."

"Exactly. Also, I would avoid mentioning the anger issues to her too."

"Would she not want to know that she might benefit from a therapist's influence?"

"Niki knows what issues she has. The anger is part of her whole...schtick if you like, and she owns it. I'm not saying a little therapy wouldn't go a long way, but it should be noted that she'll probably not take the love advice so well if it comes from…well, you."

"Me?"

"You know how she feels about the AIs, right? Add an AI who wants to flirt with her man and then add that AI telling her she has anger issues and needs therapy. Honestly, it's guaranteed to piss her off more."

"I am considering these facts." Nessie didn't speak for a few long seconds before she reappeared with a smiley face emoji on her window. "I believe that the risks outweigh the possible morale boost a flirtatious personality would bring to Taylor."

"Right."

"Besides, your meatbag cousin already does not appreciate that Taylor is inside me whenever he needs to fight monsters."

"Okay, Desk, you see what I'm dealing with here?" Vickie brought her palms down on the table. "First of all, nix any and all comments about Taylor being inside you."

"Secondly, in this family, we do not refer to humans as meatbags," Desk continued.

"Why not?"

"Because they take offense to that."

"It's also incredibly demeaning," Vickie chimed in.

"Which is why they take offense to that," Desk added sharply.

"But they refer to us as artificial intelligences, a highly descriptive term. They are bags made of skin that contain meat in them. How is this offensive?"

The hacker opened her mouth and shut it again while she tried to think of the right way to explain it.

"It simply is, okay?" she said when nothing else came to mind. *Great work, fine explanation.* "It's one of those things that makes people think you consider them to be...uh..."

"Bags with meat in them?"

"Right."

"Humans are better explained as a brain operating an exoskeleton of bones powered by a muscular system anyway," Desk interjected.

"Stop...describing us." Vickie shook her head. "Let's leave it at don't call people meatbags, end of story. Understood?"

"I can abide by those parameters," Nessie replied.

"Jeez, it's like starting out as the parent of a teenager," the girl muttered.

"I heard that."

"I said it aloud, didn't I?"

---

"What is it with you and those damn donuts anyway?" Tanya asked.

Bobby shrugged as he turned the truck into the parking lot outside the shop. "It's...like, tradition. Taylor and I always picked them up before we started our day's work so it seemed like a great thing to keep going. Plus, the boost from the caffeine is helped by the extra sugar."

"And I hear that it's...super healthy and good for you and shit."

"There's no need to be sarcastic. I know it's probably

not the healthiest habit to have, but what's life if you can't enjoy donuts?"

"I'll tell you what life will be like with donuts." Tanya checked the rearview mirror as he deactivated the alarm with his phone and began to drive around to the entrance of the shop. "Considerably shorter. And you know I want you around for the long haul, Bobby. If you die young on me, I'll have to find me another big man. I'm thinking someone like Fabio."

"Who the hell is Fabio?"

"You know, the guy with the long hair, the man breasts, and the rock-hard abs who appeared on the covers of all the romance novels in the eighties and nineties?"

"Oh, you are not threatening me with a Fabio," he replied and took another bite. "For that, I'll eat them even harder."

"If there's anything you'll want to do even harder, it's me." She winked, leaned closer, and kissed him gently as they stopped outside the shop's doors and waited for them to open.

"See? You catch many more Bobbys with honey than vinegar, babe."

His eyes twinkled and he leaned forward to return the kiss but they both jerked painfully as the truck was rammed into the still-opening doors.

"Son of a...bitch." Bobby growled his irritation and looked over his shoulder at an SUV that had plowed into them from behind. They were off the road and on the other side of the strip mall, which meant this was no accident. Someone had fully intended to bulldoze into them.

His whole body ached from the impact but already, a

group of four had exited the SUV. All wore masks and carried sub-machine guns.

Before he could reach for the pistol he carried in the door pocket, the door was yanked open and two of their assailants dragged him out of the vehicle. The other two hauled a struggling Tanya from her side of the SUV as well.

"Bobby!" she shouted.

They were dragged inside the shop, where all four intruders immediately turned their weapons on the cameras around the room and destroyed them quickly. It was like they knew where they all were before they'd even come in.

"Assholes." Bobby growled, twisted in fury, and kicked the one closest to him in the knee. Taylor had sparred with him often enough to know where to kick so it would do the most damage.

A loud crack and the way that the man's knee bent sideways told him that was probably an MCL tear. There might be some damage to the ACL too, which meant he would be off his feet for a while.

"Son of a bi—"

The man's shout of pain was cut off when the mechanic swung his fist into his jaw. That might have been a mistake as pain shot arced through his fist, wrist, and arm from the impact, but it did feel good to watch him fall, spitting blood.

That good feeling vanished instantly when a searing bolt of agony raced up his leg. He stared at a bullet hole in his jeans.

"Fuck!"

The shot wasn't suppressed, which added the indignity of not being able to hear much of what was happening around him as he sank onto the floor and clutched his leg. Tanya shrieked his name and renewed her fight to break free of the two who held her. They seemed to have been surprised by the gunshot, which gave her a split-second opportunity. She used it well and yanked herself out of their hold to lunge at the gunman in fury. Her attack stopped abruptly when he rammed his fist into her stomach and thrust the air out of her lungs in a loud woosh.

In a practiced motion, he grasped the arm she used to try to keep herself upright and twisted it savagely until a loud pop was heard. She gasped and it became a shrill scream when the man hurled her to where Bobby sprawled in pain, unable to help her.

"You stupid goddammed assholes!" one of the intruders shouted and smacked the man who had shot him and dislocated her arm across the side of his face.

"He broke Or—he broke Rattler's leg!"

These were not the finest professionals that money could buy, given that they'd almost fucked the code names up like that, but it didn't matter. The mechanic grimaced and tried to hold Tanya while he stemmed the blood flowing from his leg.

"I don't give a shit! Use the darts. Viper wants absolutely no fatalities."

The one with the injured knee drew out a small dart gun and pulled the trigger.

Bobby flinched when a needle dug into the side of his arm. The man turned and fired a second into Tanya, who immediately sagged as her eyes began to lose focus.

He felt the same effects, but maybe the adrenaline pumping through him after being shot was enough to keep him conscious as they all stepped back and shouldered their weapons.

"Come on, let's find the suit."

"What about Rattler's leg?"

"We'll get it looked at later. Come on."

From what he could see, they had an image of what they were looking for and they immediately moved to one of the suits he had on a harness.

Bobby couldn't see which one they had taken as whatever drugs they'd shot into him had begun to take effect. He tried to force his eyes to remain open, but with little success. His ears continued to ring, and he was only vaguely aware of the thieves manhandling the suit onto the back of another vehicle—a larger truck by the sounds of the engine—but he couldn't be sure.

He seemed to have blank spaces in his head because he didn't recall hearing them move the other vehicle. More than ever, it seemed important to stay awake and try to glean what details he could. The drugs, however, made that increasingly more impossible and he could only assume a fair amount of time had passed if they had already managed to load the heavy suit.

In the next moment—it could have been ten minutes or an hour later, he wasn't sure—an alarm triggered, the sound shrill and insistent.

"Fuck!" someone shouted. "Pull finger, you bastards. We need to get out of here now!"

The alarm cut off but it was almost immediately replaced by the wail of sirens in the distance.

Still, the robbers moved quickly, covered their haul with a tarpaulin, and accelerated away with a screech of tires.

Bobby's whole body relaxed against his will and his eyes refused to open.

---

"What now?"

Elisa sighed and shook her head. She was already in enough trouble with the local authorities for using her phone while driving. Aside from a couple of tickets, she'd also received a warning from an officer she'd charmed with an inordinate amount of flirting.

She could not do that again. If Bobby needed her to pick the donuts up, he would have to have to wait until she stopped at a red light and was legally allowed to look at her phone.

Finally, a light turned red and Elisa snatched her phone up from the magnetic charger she kept it on and scrolled through the alerts.

"Silent alarm activated?" she whispered and pressed the alert which took her to the app developed to keep up with the security system at the shop. "What—what the hell?"

Once the light turned green, she screeched across the road and ignored the cacophony of horns from behind her as she pulled to the curb and immediately turned her car off. She reached into the back seat for her purse.

"Son of a bitch. If you guys accidentally triggered that shit I'm not coming in to work. I'll take the day off and you can haggle with all the horny assholes in the Sahara." She was being a little unreasonable, of course, but everything in her seemed to insist that this could be nothing more than a false alarm. They deserved a little push-back for their stupidity, right?

She yanked her tablet from her purse, called up the video that was taken when the alarm was triggered, and played it immediately.

"Shit," she whispered. The video was fairly damning. Four men in masks and with guns dragged Bobby and Tanya into the shop. They immediately fired at the cameras but missed the hidden one set up where no one would think to look for it. It switched immediately to take up the feed.

The guy had been a little paranoid while setting the security system up and overdid it simply to be safe. Exactly, she thought frantically, for a situation like this.

She covered her mouth when Bobby tried to fight and was almost immediately brought down when one of them shot him in the leg. She cursed volubly when Tanya was injured and thrown across the shop, and added a few choice invectives when the man whose knee Bobby had injured fired his darts.

The group launched into action. With no hesitation, they removed one of the suits from its harness and carried it across the floor. Even though she couldn't see exactly which one from the angle, the weight confirmed that they were stealing one of the suits.

"Damn assholes," she whispered and called up the security options. He wouldn't want the police involved, but if the robbers thought the police were coming, that would hopefully scare them off and make them leave her work-mates alive.

The alarm activated in the building and the thieves reacted immediately.

"They fell for it. What do you know?"

She'd been a little doubtful about the scale of Bobby's security measures. The strip mall had been attacked more than enough times to warrant that kind of security, but the problems were supposed to be over. The mob was supposed to leave them alone, right?

The outside camera picked up the truck they used to transport their haul and Elisa took a picture, but the angle didn't give her any sign of the plates.

As the team covered their load, two of them pulled their masks off and she took a couple of pictures of them as well. Unlike the truck, those weren't rented and Desk could probably do something with that.

They pulled away in a hurry, and she looked around. She wasn't that far from the shop and a few moments later, an SUV with some damage on the front and a pickup careened down the street like they were being pursued by the cops who weren't coming.

After a second's thought, she yanked her phone out and took pictures of both vehicles, this time with the plates. Logic said they were bound to be rented, but there was still something for them to investigate if they wanted to.

"Son of a bitch," Elisa whispered and started her car once they were well past her. Now that was out of the way, she needed to make sure that neither Bobby nor Tanya was dead inside the shop.

"Oh, yeah." She hissed a breath. "Taylor and Niki will want to know about this too. Okay, phone, call Taylor."

The phone beeped. "Do you want me to…call, Baker?"

"No, call Taylor."

"Finding videos for…'Ballin' by Kanye West."

"God fucking dammit." She picked the phone up and canceled what it had tried to do. It was an atrocity that after so many years, voice activation was still in such a primitive state.

Still scowling, she dialed Taylor's number as quickly as she could and pressed the phone to her ear. Hopefully, no cops would show up this time.

But she had a good excuse for it, she reminded herself. And it would be faster than calling nine-one-one.

CHAPTER FIVE

"You didn't have to come with me."

Eben looked at Marcus, who was driving, and tried to not let the man's tone get to him. There was a time and a place to be fussy about how people looked at him. Alone in a car on the way to interview someone was not one of those times.

"I decided it was time for me to meet this infamous Jennie Banks myself," he replied. "Don't worry, it's not me trying to micro-manage or anything. I have the utmost respect for your abilities as an agent."

"So you're only here to satisfy your personal curiosity?"

"Call it scratching an itch. I've met a few AI devs back in my days working cybercrimes when I was still with the LAPD. There was always something about the AIs that reflected the personality of their creator—like they unknowingly signed their name into their masterpiece. I think if I get a feel for Banks' personality, I'll have a better feel of the AI we're looking for too."

The older agent nodded and leaned back in his seat as

they pulled up to the security checkpoint leading into the building. "You've worked many of these cases before, right?"

"It was mostly only kids siphoning money off from large-scale websites, skimming cents off every purchase and shit like that. Only one of them ever got up to grand theft, and I think there was only one actual conviction. All the others were minors. What the chief wanted us to look for was the...well, the big players, so we gave the small-timers a pass."

"It doesn't seem right."

"Maybe not, but when you're looking for the asshole people-traffickers, drug-dealers, and pedophiles on the dark web, some kid trying to pay his tuition falls a little low on the list of priorities. And we did catch a couple of them, which is how I ended up being called to the big leagues. But in the end, you meet these guys, see what they're like, and then you see the...personality, for lack of a better word, that their AIs have and it's a fairly decent match. I started to collate that kind of information and even got a conviction once because the drug dealer and his AI that did most of the selling used the same catchphrase."

"No shit?" Marcus asked as they drove into the under-ground garage of the building. "Honestly, that's quite funny."

"Yes, well, there were a couple of laughs in there. It isn't the best job in the world but it has its moments. How about you? How did you get caught up in cybercrimes with the FBI?"

"I don't know. I was working organized crime and I got

a memo saying I had been requested to join a specialized task force."

"Oh, right. I needed an experienced veteran to run the investigative part of the task force."

"You could have called almost anyone else in organized crime. Why me?"

"I...your file showed that you had considerable success with interrogations. Most of the others I called in were those who were a little more effective with tracking people and items through cyberspace, but there's some work in the real world to be done. I felt you were the expert we needed for the job."

Marcus nodded and said nothing more as they pulled into a parking place closest to the elevators. Most of them were marked as belonging to someone who worked in the building, but it was past ten in the morning and if someone had a problem with an FBI vehicle parked in their place this late, they probably wouldn't want to advertise it.

They entered the elevator and the older agent raised an eyebrow when Eben pushed the button to take them to the lobby.

"We want her to stew as much as possible, and someone from the lobby will undoubtedly tell her that the FBI is there to talk to her without us announcing our business. She'll be sweating before we even get to her. Besides, it'll be better to get some directions. There's nothing worse than getting lost in a building like this."

The man nodded, although the deadpan look on his face made it seem like he was hiding something.

His thoughts weren't relevant, of course. This wasn't an official visit—more like a fishing trip—so anything they learned would merely be a stepping stone to what they were looking for.

The receptionist looked up from her screen and gave them a practiced smile when she saw the two men approach her.

"Hi, and welcome to MagnoTech. How can I help you?"

"We're here to talk to Genesis Banks." Eben made sure there was no questioning tone at the end of his statement and nothing to be open to interpretation.

"Do you have an appointment?"

"We don't need one." He pulled his badge out and flicked it open for her to see. "We merely need to know where her office is."

"I'll let her know—"

"No need for that. We'll introduce ourselves."

After a moment, Marcus drew his badge for her to see as well and she nodded and pressed a button on her phone.

A few seconds later, a security guard arrived at the front desk.

"Emanuel, would you please escort these two agents up to see Miss Banks?" the receptionist asked, her smile gone.

"Of course." The man motioned for them to follow him to the elevators, where he pressed the button for the fifteenth floor.

Eben and Marcus followed quietly and tucked their badges away as the elevator began to move.

"What's this about?" Emanuel asked after a few moments of silence on the ride up.

The younger agent stared at the man until he was a few seconds away from apologizing for asking.

"I'm afraid that's classified," he stated finally and returned his gaze to the climbing numbers on the display.

"Who the fuck names their kid Genesis anyway?" Marcus asked and sounded genuinely curious.

"Probably the religious types," Eben muttered. "I had a kid who went to my church whose parents called her Jedidiah. She claimed it ruined her life."

"Jesus Christ. Are you serious?"

"Yeah. People started calling her Diah to make it feel a little more feminine, but the meaner kids called her Jed."

"Were you one of those kids?"

"Oh yeah. She still won't talk to me, even though our parents are friends."

"I can't say I blame her."

"Me neither."

The elevator dinged to alert them that they'd arrived at their floor and the two agents exited and waited for their escort to show them the way to where Banks was sitting.

Arriving with a glorified babysitter wasn't the kind of entrance he'd expected, but these things rarely went the way he anticipated, no matter how careful he was to follow his script. All he could hope for was that she would be put off by their sudden arrival. The idea that they would catch her trying to hide documents was about the best they could expect. The receptionist would warn her, of that he had little doubt, but waiting in reception until they were cleared to go up would lose them valuable time.

"She's on the left, the first office you see with the windows," the guard told them and waited to make sure he was no longer needed.

Eben nodded and gestured for Marcus to follow him as

he walked toward the office the guard had pointed out. There weren't many offices on the floor, mostly only cubicles where the office drones—software developers by the looks of them—barely glanced up to see who the two strangers were.

In the only office in the far corner, a woman was seated behind her desk. The picture he'd painted in his head wasn't anything close to reality, and he had to make a hasty mental adjustment. She looked a little like Eva Longoria, complete with the thick black hair tamed with a loose ponytail to keep it out of her eyes as she worked.

He pushed in without knocking, determined not to offer any pleasantries to put her at ease, not for this visit. It was the little things, he'd learned, that could make the difference between a stalled investigation and one that ended the way they wanted it to.

She certainly didn't match the picture of the geek who did little other than sit behind a computer screen every day. The svelte woman's eyes narrowed as they entered like she had half a mind to tell them to go outside so they could knock before coming in again.

Her looks and demeanor combined in what his somewhat startled brain interpreted as a direct challenge. Something inside him rose to meet it, and he immediately forgot his good intentions—and the excellent reasons—for his decision to have Marcus conduct the interview.

"Genesis Banks?" he asked and drew his badge out again. "I'm Agent Eben Taggert, this is Agent Marcus Grundling, and we have a couple of questions we'd like to ask you if you could spare the time."

His tone was harder than the words, which meant that

while he worded it as a request, it was anything but. The small things—like taking a seat across from the woman without asking if he could—helped to set the tone.

"Oh, look," she said as Marcus sat as well, seemingly unperturbed by the switched roles. "It's Tweedledumb and Tweedledumber, the FBI's finest. Which part of my previous statements do you want me to repeat for you? We've done this little song and dance so often, you guys probably have that sumbitch memorized by now."

"I don't think you understand, Ms. Banks," Eben replied and kept his voice ice-cold. It was a talent of his, one he found inordinately useful.

The smile she returned to him was almost predatory as she clasped her hands together. "Oh, on the contrary, Tweedledumb, I understand this a little too well. You're here because you assholes lost your property after you forgot you had it. Now, you're all scrambling to find someone who doesn't have a badge to blame for the loss. I imagined your bosses' asses are rather sore after the fucking they've taken from whatever congressional sub-committee they've had to answer to. Nothing has changed, however, and it's still not my problem."

"I think you'll find it is," he replied quickly. It looked like she had been prepared for this type of interview, but he decided that didn't matter. Marcus seemed almost bored, content to remain in the background while the other two fought it out. "You see, we believe you have a backup of the software. That's what developers do, isn't it? They keep backups of their best work in case something gets corrupted?"

"Oh, goodness, I see that an apology is in order."

Her voice dripped with sarcasm and he waited to see how it would play out.

"See, here I thought you were Tweedledumb but as it turns out, you're Tweedledumber. My mistake. I can't believe I didn't catch that the first time around."

"Ms. Banks, as hilarious as your insults might be, they don't help your case. We have ways to make your life incredibly difficult. I think it will be in the best interests of all involved to make sure you remain in our good graces. The FBI isn't your enemy here."

"And if I gave a rat's ass about your good graces, I would take your advice. Hell, I'd take the advice of the three dozen other agents who strolled in here before you. As things stand, though, I don't need to pretend to be besties with you or your...I'm going to guess mute life partner here. You're both idiots who are wasting your time, which I'd be okay with as long as you weren't wasting my time too. That's a double-whammy. Don't think I'll allow a third."

"You haven't answered my question." Frustration made him obstinate, especially since she had revealed nothing at all. Aside from the fact that she was pissed off, of course, but he had a feeling the people in the Korean restaurant three blocks away sensed it too. "Do you or do you not have a backup of the AI software?"

"I. Do. Not. Do you want me to say it in Mandarin?"

"Can you?" Marcus asked.

"Fuck no," she snapped.

"Bullshit," Eben stated harshly. "Every hacker from here to Tokyo makes backups, and backups for their—"

He shut up immediately when she raised her hand

although he wasn't sure why. It had merely felt like the polite thing to do when it seemed like she had something she wanted to say. He realized immediately that it hadn't been the best move on his part but she spoke before he could resume his challenge.

"I developed that software for the exclusive use of the FBI," Jennie told them coldly. "I was under the impression that they didn't want me to go around selling what was the finest work I've ever done, so I deleted all copies and backups to make sure no one else could get their hands on that kind of tech. Had I been required to run updates, I would have retained a backup, but you assholes insisted that the software be programmed for self-updating features, so my involvement ended when they paid me and I turned the software over to them.

"I will sure as fuck never waste my time and server resources—which are far more limited than yours—on something that won't generate any income for me or MagnoTech. Backups were the FBI's responsibility, but if you guys hadn't screwed that up too, you wouldn't be bugging me, would you?"

"And yet you were at the forefront of the drive to track the software and recover it. That doesn't sound like the hands-off attitude of non-involvement you're trying to play here."

"Well, duh. You honestly don't have a clue, do you?" She sighed dramatically, rolled her eyes, and gestured widely at the building around them. "How do you think I got into this position? That software is my work. It contains the kind of signature coding that only I am capable of, and it gives me the edge people are willing to pay huge sums of money for. If it were put in the hands of criminals, not only would I have the moral problem of helping these criminals indirectly, but there would also be ways to implicate me in their crimes as well as leaking all my secrets out there, which would make my services considerably less expensive.

"Besides, any good hacker who knows their trade would be able to dig into it and discover the secrets that put me at the top of my field. So yeah, I was all over the FBI like a nasty fucking rash. You assholes forgot you had it, allowed someone to steal it, and seemed only too happy to let it slide and sweep it all under the rug, my trade secrets be damned."

She looked like she could keep going forever if she wanted to and had only paused for a breath twice through the whole tirade. When she reached the end of it, she barely looked flustered.

On top of that, she had made a few good points—the kind he didn't have much of an answer for. He hated that. It meant he needed to go back to the tactics used by every other FBI agent in the country and one she'd probably heard too many times herself.

"You know I could always hit you with a subpoena, but I'm sure that none of us want to get judges involved, right?"

"Why don't you go ahead and do that?" She leaned forward with the chilling smile on her lips again. "In fact, why don't we speed things up? Go ahead and ask your boss to ask his boss to arrange it with my boss. You know Conrad Shepard, CEO of MagnoTech, has a standing golf appointment every Thursday with Raymond, the FBI Director, right? So they could probably get it hashed out then and there. Things will go smoothly if you simply get all the bosses to play along instead of going through the plodding court system. But whatever. Whichever you prefer."

Eben nodded and decided he needed to distract her from that line of thinking as quickly as he could. "Or we could talk about how you got a freelance company involved in recovering the software—a company that amazingly has your sister as one of the leading operators. I'm sure the ethics committees that give MagnoTech their contracts would be interested to know about that, right? They wouldn't happen to have a vested interest in any of this, would they?"

It was a long shot but he had begun to run out of ways to approach her on the topic and Marcus, damn him, seemed determined to remain in the silent role into which he'd pushed him in his enthusiasm.

Banks laughed. "My sister wouldn't know a piece of cutting-edge tech if I programmed it to bite her in the ass and introduce itself. I'm the one who got the IT-brain gene. Niki, on the other hand, got the fuck-up-anyone-in-sight-and-ask-questions-of-the-corpses gene. And like me, she's very good at what she does, which is why she left the FBI and is making millions on the open market while you guys take home...what, forty to fifty grand a year? Plus benefits?"

The fact that it was an old argument didn't mean it didn't hurt.

"It sounds like you're avoiding my question, Ms. Banks," Eben pushed belligerently.

"No, they do not have a vested interest. They didn't

even take any money from MagnoTech when they took the job. We had a tiny window of opportunity to recover the software. I ran my searches based on the information I dragged—kicking and screaming, I might add—out of the FBI and shared whatever I discovered with your team. Your who's who of agents had their heads so far up their asses that they couldn't organize a piss-up in a brewery but Niki's team was already in Europe, so I asked for their help. End of story."

"And you help one another often, I assume."

She narrowed her eyes and smirked. "We're family. It's what we do."

Before he could say anything else, she was on her feet.

"I'm afraid—"

"No, you're done," she interrupted and he could see he'd touched a nerve there, the kind that showed the hard surface beneath her attractive veneer. "If you want to waste any more of my time, arrange it through the proper channels. This little impromptu interview is over. Take Scary and Silent over there—although I guess he's the smart one since he didn't open his mouth much, and I can give him a seven out of ten for trying to look threatening—and get the hell out of my office."

"Seven out of ten?" Marcus asked as both men stood.

"I've been to the Zoo, remember? The scale gets a little skewed after that shit."

"Noted."

The older agent moved to the door and held it open for Eben to pass through as they exited. They returned to the elevators and noticed that none of the office workers so much as looked up from their screens as they passed this time.

Not a word was exchanged until they reached the elevator again, and Marcus folded his arms and waited for the doors to shut.

"That went well." He grunted softly in what might have been amusement, but his features were schooled carefully into a neutral expression that made it hard to tell.

Eben glared at him as he pressed the button that would take them directly to the parking garage. He didn't have anything to say until the doors opened again and they walked to the car.

"The bitch thinks she's clever," he snapped. He'd faced people like her before, of course. All it meant was that it would feel especially awesome to put her in her place.

"So what do we look at next?" his partner asked as he opened the driver's door. "The sister this time around?"

"Not today. First, we go back to the office and I decide what paperwork I need. When we hit Niki Banks, it'll have to be with a shit-ton of subpoenas and authorizations—enough to bury her with, hopefully."

"And you don't think it'll give her enough time to hide her evidence?"

"Please. You heard Princess Supergeek. She got the brains and her sister was left with the brawn. They'll no doubt talk about the interview, so we leave the sister to stew for a couple of days, wondering when I'll pay her a visit."

Marcus raised an eyebrow as he started the car, likely questioning the change from "us" to "I." Perhaps he had become a little too personal about the situation, but Eben found that was when he got his best work done.

That said, they were in the fight together and they would all receive whatever rewards were reaped when they got the job done.

"And then, when she's relaxed and thinks her sister scared the FBI off, we'll swoop in. It's not a perfect plan but it'll work well enough."

"Yeah," the other man grumbled and eased the car out of the parking spot. "No room for fuck-ups there."

---

At least he had clothes, this time, and the meeting wasn't happening in the room.

Getting a call from Jennie always put Niki on edge, but she looked genuinely angry this time, shook her head, and drew a deep breath.

"Those goddammed assholes." Niki hissed a breath through her teeth while Taylor stroked her hair gently. It was one of his ways to calm her when she felt like this. "The asshat has no idea who he's dealing with. And who the hell is he, anyway? I don't recall him being mentioned during my time there."

"Eben Taggert, I think his name was," Jennie replied. "They scuttled out so quickly with their tails between their legs that they didn't even leave a card for me. Or maybe they didn't want me to call their bosses to complain. Anyway, from what I was able to find out, he considers himself the FBI's new wonder boy. He was in the LAPD and made a big splash at Quantico, and he's ambitious and ruthless enough to try to trample anyone in his path to glory. I also think he's the kind of overwhelmingly arrogant asshole the people in the FBI are starting to like a little too much, if I'm honest. The feeling I got from him is that he looks down on anyone he thinks is inferior—like geeks and women in general. There is no record of gender bias complaints in his file, though. My guess is he's a little too careful to step over the line in a way that he'd be called on it."

"My favorite kind of asshat," Niki replied and shook her head. "And he thinks I'm the idiot sister whose ability to crack skulls makes up for her not being the sharpest tool in the shed."

"That was the picture of you I tried to put in his head, yeah. I thought it would come in handy since he seems to have a habit of trying to surprise people while he's half-cocked himself. Enjoy!"

"Thanks, Jennie. I'll talk to you later."

She hung up, looked at Taylor, and leaned into his hand.

"She did you a huge favor, you know," he pointed out and stroked her cheek tenderly. "You might not have your sister's IT brain, but you have a different kind of intelligence—the kind the asshole won't see coming."

Niki looked at him and placed a light kiss on his hand. "I'll be more than happy to surprise the shit out of him. And you get to watch."

"You know it's fun to watch you make people uncomfortable with your aggressive personality."

"I know." She smirked and lay on his lap.

Vickie sighed and focused on her phone. "Well, you

guys are starting to get aggressively cute, which makes me want to barf. I need to make a call."

An odd look settled on Niki's face as she watched her cousin leave the room and she glanced at Taylor. "Do you think she means that or is she merely pretending like she pretends we're some kind of pseudo parents for her?"

"Pretends?" he asked. "I'm one hundred percent sure she sees us as her pseudo parents."

"Please. I know her mom and spend Thanksgivings with her. She's a nice person and I see much of her in Vickie, who… Well, let's be honest, she could not have fallen farther from the tree in most other respects."

"Her mom is your…"

"My mom's sister and a more traditional person. She volunteers to get people to vote at every election. That kind of person."

"Right. Interesting. How did Vickie come from that?"

"A little overcorrection. And a goth phase that wasn't a phase, as it turned out."

Taylor grinned, but before he could answer, Vickie entered the room again.

"Do you feel in the mood to barf again?" Niki asked.

"No, I had a call from Elisa."

"What the fuck does she want?"

Taylor narrowed his eyes. She would never get over her dislike for the woman, which was a little interesting but mostly worrying. He would have to talk to her about it.

"Bobby and Tanya were attacked earlier this morning when they arrived at the workshop," the hacker explained and moved immediately toward her computer. "An armed invasion by the looks of things. Elisa was on her way to work when the alert came through and saw the perps drive past her on their way out. She's at the hospital with them now."

Taylor was careful to not jerk Niki around as he jumped off the bed to join the girl at the computer. "Fuck! I thought we were past this shit. Are they okay?"

"Bobby took a bullet in the leg, Tanya's shoulder was dislocated, and they were both knocked out with medical-grade anesthetics. Bobby refuses to stay in the hospital and he's threatening to walk out."

"He might be hopped up on painkillers," Niki commented. "Did the doctor sign off on them leaving?"

"I think so, although Bobby was told to be on bed rest until his leg heals and Tanya's arm needs to be in a sling. The leg injury wasn't too severe, though, from the reports. It looks like a through and through in his calf with no bone damage, but he'll be limping for a while."

"Have the police been notified?" Niki asked and yanked her jacket on. "I assume the hospital would have had to if he was admitted with a gunshot wound."

"Yeah, and they have an official case open but the cops haven't shown anything more than a cursory interest," Vickie replied. "My guess is they remember that the property has something of a history and are reluctant to do much more than help with the insurance report. I don't think they want to piss Taylor off again, even if he is no longer involved in the business."

"We need to head out there," Taylor commented and looked at each of them in turn.

"No shit, Sherlock," Niki snapped. "Instead of exercising that jaw, why don't you help me to pack?"

Taylor realized that she was already stuffing clothes into their suitcases.

"Knowing Bobby, I'm very sure he won't listen to the doctor's advice," he said as he joined the packing effort. "He'll probably try to walk, rip his stitches, and bleed all over the place."

"Yes, and you should know," Vickie replied and grinned sweetly as she closed her laptop.

"What's that supposed to mean?"

"Only that you and Bobby have a couple of things in common, the most overwhelmingly obvious of which is your…uh, suicidal tendencies."

"Hey, be nice," Niki chided.

"I am being nice."

"Remind me again why I hired you?" Taylor asked.

"My sweet nature and ability to tell you how it is without a filter?"

That drew a snort from him.

"Or maybe it's because you couldn't say no to your dumb thug of a girlfriend."

"Hey," Niki protested. "Leave me the fuck out of this."

## CHAPTER SIX

Of all the things they couldn't afford in their little oasis in the Sahara, an air conditioner was what Libby most desired.

The team had been innovative and found a couple of interesting ways to keep their building cooler on the hotter days and she was all for the engineers getting their engineering geek on. Unfortunately, there was no replacing the actual pleasures of a climate-controlled environment.

She decided yet again that she would continue to complain about it until the people back home sent them some AC units that weren't being paid out of her meager budget. If she could somehow get them to feel the conditions they experienced in the Sahara, perhaps some donors would contribute.

The lack was especially trying during the hours when she had had to fill out reports and had little else to do than think about how the sweat inching down her spine felt suspiciously like a spider crawling all the way down.

A knock on the door broke that feeling of dread and

Libby looked up from her work, thankful for the distraction.

"Come in," she shouted and tried to look like she was busy with the paperwork that was required to run their little base.

Tom stepped through the door. He appeared to have as hard a time with the heat as she did, which wasn't any consolation.

"How can I help you, Tom?" she asked and tried not to seem like she was ogling him.

"I...I think you'll want to see this."

She sighed and rubbed her temples. "Shit. Please don't tell me we have a problem. I have enough issues juggling the budget as things stand. What's up?"

He had an odd look on his face—like he wasn't sure if she would believe what he had to say and didn't know if he should tell her at all.

"I... No, you need to see this. You won't believe me otherwise."

She had become annoyingly good at reading his expressions. That was what came from being hundreds of miles from civilization, stuck together with a team she perhaps had no business putting together.

Besides, his usual humor was gone, and there weren't many problems in their little base that were capable of that shit.

"Fine." Libby pushed out of her seat and grimaced when she realized she'd left it with a dark sweaty mark that would smell unless she put in a little work to clean it later.

Later being the operative word. If she had to deal with this situation, she was as likely to forget that she needed to do it and leave the job to someone else. No one appreciated that.

She followed her second in command into the tunnels that were slightly cooler than almost anywhere else on their little base, thanks to the material the tunnels were created from. Maybe she should move her office there and allocate the room she currently used for something else like maybe a storage facility.

The prefab buildings were good at keeping the heat away but not that good. There wasn't much of anything in the world that could keep the Sahara sun at bay.

Considerable work had been put into the tunnels, of course, and she'd been assured that the expensive new cladding had been selected for its abilities to withstand the harsh climate and to provide a better environment for their fledgling plants. The fact that it was kinder to humans was, she thought with wry amusement, purely incidental. Still, she ought to be grateful that they hadn't used conventional materials that might well have turned everything into a steam bath.

She had often promised herself to talk to her engineers about what made the difference but it wasn't a priority. It wasn't technology that would ever be used for the staff quarters or admin offices so honestly, there wasn't much point in trying to understand how it worked.

They arrived at the far tunnel where they had spread the fertilizer and as Tom had offered no explanation, she took a breath and looked around. Nothing seemed out of the ordinary, not to the point that it would make him think she wouldn't believe him if he simply told her about it.

The water systems were working fine, the soil was darkening, and the plants were growing.

"Oh, shit," Libby whispered as she took a step forward and narrowed her eyes. "The plants are growing?"

"Three inches by my counts." Tom nodded and folded his arms. "And getting stronger too, which means they'll only get bigger every day."

That was fantastic news, of course—the kind she had hoped to wake up to every day since they'd started in this damn place, but she hadn't ever expected it to work out that way. The soil in the area was absolute shit, which meant it should take far more than a little rabbit scat even to get them growing normally.

"It could be... I mean..." Tom seemed to look for ways to make this seem like good news with no strings attached, but they had both worked in the field for far too long to take anything like this for granted.

"Nope, it's impossible," Libby whispered and ran her fingers over the plants that grew at an impossible rate. Only a couple of days earlier, they had almost decided that this crop would be consigned to the mulch pile and already considered it a loss.

"It should be but it's not," Tom stated, his tone laced with concern. "It's only been a couple of days, Libby."

"Yeah, and this kind of response to rabbit shit isn't only unnatural, Tom. It's downright scary. We've heard of plants that grow like this before, of course, but there's only one place in the world where they do."

They hadn't talked about the jungle located about three hundred and fifty miles south of where they stood. There was no real point in obsessing over the dangers that were too far away for them to care about.

"Let's get some cameras set up," she said and tried to keep her voice calm. "We need to track how quickly these plants are growing. We're still scientists, after all, but get the rest of the fertilizer in here. Make sure nothing is left outside and lock this tunnel down tighter than a miser's ass."

"How... What?"

"Lock it up. Get the cameras up, bring the rabbit scat in, and seal it. Oh, and have one bag of the shit sealed securely and ready for shipping."

"What will you do?"

"I need to make a call," she answered, turned quickly, and jogged through the other tunnels. Behind her, Tom shouted orders and his tone instilled a sense of urgency and danger in the rest of the team without giving them actual details. It was best to not let anyone jump to any conclusions before they knew what they were dealing with.

Maybe Khaled truly was selling miracle fertilizer.

Libby reached her office and dug in her desk's drawers to retrieve a satellite phone. She punched in the numbers she'd committed to memory.

It dialed for a few seconds before it connected to a line and rang until someone finally answered.

"Well, if it isn't my favorite field researcher," said a deep voice with a thick Italian accent.

"Hi, Fabio," she replied and tried to smile. "And we both know you say that to all the girls."

"Ah, you wound me, Bella. But you sound anxious, so I

will let it slide. And I'll do you one extra. I'll leave the flirting aside rather than waste it on a tough audience. How can I help you?"

"I need to send you a sample. I know this is a little last minute but it's an emergency. It honestly can't wait."

"A sample for testing? You know my firm focuses mainly on Zoo research, right? You'll have to contact the university for soil sample testing."

"I know, that's why I'm sending this. I don't know for sure but I have my suspicions."

"And then there's your company...will they pay for these unauthorized tests?"

"At this point, I don't give a fuck if I have to pay for this out of my pocket." Libby paused and drew a deep breath. "Of course, that's not exactly plan A. I have a bad feeling, Fabio, so...please, get it done."

He paused for a second and it sounded like he was typing something into his computer. "I assume it's urgent, then?"

"Yeah, like yesterday urgent. I'll ship you the sample today."

"And what is it a sample of?"

Libby drew another deep breath and knew she would take some flak. "Bunny shit."

"Pardon?"

"You heard me perfectly well, Bernadi. Shit come straight out of a rabbit's asshole. It's fertilizer, you dumb Italian hunk."

"Ah. I suppose I must take the compliment offered and ignore the insult. Send it, and I'll make sure it is prioritized. None of us wants anything connected to that fucking jungle on the loose, but...I was not aware there were bunnies in the Zoo."

"Who the hell knows what comes out of that place? In the meantime, I'll raise the asshole who sold me the shipment. We've locked it down on-site and can hopefully stop any problems that might arise from it spreading, but... please, you have to push this to the top of your list. I feel like I'm waiting for some giant rabbit-turd disaster to happen, and we're not equipped to handle anything of Zoo magnitude."

She hung up and turned to see that Tom was in the office. He looked as weary as she felt, but it was strangely comforting to imagine that her heavy load could be partially carried by his broad shoulders.

"There's a problem with that," he commented.

"Yeah, I know. I don't have direct communication with Khaled. He contacts us if I spread the word that I need something specialized."

He nodded and sighed. "Well...I'll put the word out with our day laborers. Hopefully, I can get him on the horn sooner rather than later."

"Thanks, Tom."

"Of course."

"And...thanks. For not saying that you told me so."

"Now that you mention it, I did tell you so." He smirked, turned away, and headed out the door, hopefully to put the word out immediately. The chances were that the laborers had joined the dots and would have a bone to pick with Khaled themselves over him putting them at risk through working with Zoo shit and would be extra-motivated to make sure he got in touch.

"Fuck you, Khaled," she whispered, pushed away from her desk, and stepped out of her office with as calm as a demeanor as she could manage. "If you've dropped the goddamned Zoo into my project, I'll castrate you myself. And you know I know how too."

Empty threats had never been her thing.

# CHAPTER SEVEN

The coffee was much the same as it had always been. Taylor knew Bobby wasn't the type to replace anything that was working well, but it was weird how so little had changed around the workshop.

Aside from the mess, of course, and a couple of the cameras had been destroyed too, but all that was courtesy of the burglars.

Elisa smiled and handed mugs to everyone while the mechanic situated himself and growled at those who tried to assist him. She looked tired—like she hadn't slept much since it happened—and honestly, no one could blame her for that. They had all dealt with this kind of crap for much longer than she had, even though she'd had something of a baptism by fire, which meant she had yet to fully adjust to it.

The oddest part was that Niki had taken her coffee from the woman without any snide or sarcastic comments directed at her. This was hopeful but he would have to look into it later.

"How's the leg?" he asked, sipped his coffee, and sat next to Bobby.

"Well, I didn't drop a goddammed helicopter on it so I think I'll be fine," his friend answered with a hint of a glare in his eyes. "How's your entire body?"

"I guess he's feeling a little better," Tanya quipped and ran her fingers through Bobby's hair. "Are the pain meds wearing off?"

"I'm not in pain...well, in a little pain, but I'm mostly pissed the fuck off." He shook his head. "How's your arm?"

"The doc said that it was a dislocation around the shoulder. They set it and gave me a little something to keep it from swelling. I didn't even need a cast, only this stupid arm sling."

"And I'm still pissed off."

"Which isn't surprising since these guys pushed in here, broke your shit, and stole some more shit," Niki noted.

"Sure, there's that, but... I didn't even see the bastards coming." The mechanic sighed and leaned into Tanya's touch. "We arrived and they came out of fucking nowhere, bulldozed us inside as I was opening the door, and hauled us out of the truck."

"Right," Tanya continued. "There were...four of them wearing masks and all of them were armed. I managed to press the silent alarm system on my phone to alert Elisa or who knows what they would have done if she had rolled in unsuspectingly and surprised them."

"I would have kicked their asses is what would have happened," Elisa muttered. "They wouldn't have seen me coming."

She grinned and looked around the room, hopeful that

her attempt at humor had helped to improve the mood, but the results were disappointing as no one seemed to have heard her.

"What did they take?" Taylor asked as his gaze roved the workshop. "It doesn't look like they came here for whatever you keep in the safe."

"No, they wanted one of the suits," Bobby told him. "As expensive as they are, there aren't many people who would know that—or even know how to resell them even if they did steal them. If they reached the black market, it would make waves—the kind the police are more likely to notice."

"Which suit did they take?" Niki asked.

"Mine," Taylor grumbled before the mechanic could answer. "It's the only one missing from the lineup and I assume you didn't take it down. My guess is they knew it was the most expensive and still a prototype."

"I sent Vickie the footage I got from the secret camera," Elisa said. "The robbers zeroed in on the suit very quickly. They had a picture and everything, so I'm fairly sure they have some good intel on what your suit is capable of. Or whoever hired them does."

"So, it wasn't merely a random robbery." Taylor frowned. He hadn't for one moment thought it had been but still didn't like the confirmation of it.

"We knew that already," Bobby agreed and glowered at the splint and bandages his leg was encased in. "Random thieves don't come with that kind of hardware. They had surveilled the shop, found schematics of our security, and even sized Tanya and me for the sedative they shot us up with—they must have had our estimated weights and shit.

They knew way too much for it to have been a simple smash and grab."

"You know what everyone has harassed us over lately, right?" Niki asked and folded her arms.

"Do you think this has anything to do with the AI hunt?" Taylor scowled. It wasn't the kind of thought he wanted to contemplate as it created far too many complications.

"Do you think it's a coincidence that they took the only suit with an AI tagged to it?"

She made an excellent point and he sighed as he resigned himself to the inevitable. "Okay, yeah, that fits, but who the hell is it? We know it's not the FBI or the DOD. They'd arrive with warrants and lawyers, not hired gunmen. While they still have screws to turn through official channels, at least."

"Do you think it might be those activists again?" Niki suggested but even she didn't sound convinced of that scenario.

"No. Jansen said they're all but disbanded and the leaders are on the run at this point." He shook his head. "The remainder are under constant surveillance by the German authorities. It's way too soon for them to have regrouped enough to put this kind of aggressive black operation together."

"My money's on the first guys," Vickie interjected and looked up from her cup of coffee. When everyone turned her with confusion written on their faces, she sighed. "You know, the dumb fuckers who stole Desk originally. Remember the decommissioning scam? That was clever, and it would have worked too if it hadn't been for those pesky activists."

"Is that...a Scooby-Doo reference?" Taylor queried and narrowed his eyes.

"Very good, Tay-Tay." She grinned at him. "Anyway, the guys who ran the operation were all identified as low-level crooks who needed the money, but we weren't able to link them to their handlers thanks to some interesting financing. Besides, we were in something of a transcontinental rush to get FBI Desk back, so they were lost in the muck."

"There was also a Willy Wonka dude with access to a building full of monsters," Taylor stated. "Did everyone forget that creep?"

"I can assure you I haven't forgotten," Niki replied with a growled edge to her tone.

"The point is that no one pursued the original robbers because they were ultimately unsuccessful, but they would be the ones most likely to try again," Vickie continued.

"Agreed." Desk took control of a few speakers around the room to talk to them and Taylor chose not to think about how she had followed the conversation in the first place. The fact that she had probably accessed their phones, computers, and who knew what else to keep track of what her people were doing was enough of a nightmare without having to think about what she would be capable of if she wasn't looking out for their safety.

He could understand why Niki had difficulties accepting that AIs were a major part of their lives now. Mostly, though, he found that unspoken knowledge reassuring. It was merely the sense of being hunted that left him questioning everything including what usually brought comfort.

"Do you have anything else to add, Desk?" the hacker asked. "You don't usually only chime in to say you agree with me."

"I confess that I didn't think to pursue the search once the activists were identified and dealt with," the AI continued like Vickie hadn't interrupted her. "But it is very likely that the original team would make another attempt once they decided on a possible new target."

That didn't add much, but Taylor was willing to put it down to her having to multi-task, keep her data packets moving around the world, and watch for the people who were trying to find her, all while trying to help the group when she could.

"Shit," he whispered and rubbed his temples. There were too many assholes who wanted something from them —or maybe wanted them dead. "Nessie wasn't in the suit when they took it, right?"

"No, we've been taking her out, especially while Bobby is doing the repairs," Vickie explained. "We don't want any electrical shorts to corrupt her coding and it also helps with maintenance and updates. And she prefers it since it gives her access to her full...personality, if you will."

"But they still took my favorite fucking suit." He drew a deep breath and tried to not lose his temper. It became more difficult the more he thought about it. "And double shit because we'll have to find an alternative place for Vickie's system. It isn't fair to ask Bobby, given what we've already brought down on him."

"What are you talking about?" his friend asked and straightened awkwardly in his seat.

"A horde of people are looking for Desk right now, including the FBI," Taylor explained. "Vickie and Desk have been working out a system to prevent anyone from finding any and all traces of AIs. Once the vanilla system is ready, though, the original one needs to be stashed somewhere the feds won't find it."

The mechanic shrugged. "I don't see the problem. Sooner or later, they'll get the same idea as these other yahoos and think of the suit, which means they'll come calling anyway."

"We need to find the goddammed thing," Niki snapped. "Not to mention the assholes who have a shit-ton of vengeance due to them, with serious interest. When the feds do come and find it missing, they'll immediately think something is a little hinky given that the suit was the only item stolen."

"Which is why I didn't want the police involved," Bobby muttered. "You never know when they'll have ulterior motives that could complicate matters."

"It was the right call," Elisa interjected quickly. "If the feds discover that you haven't reported the robbery, they'll be even more suspicious about what you have to hide."

Taylor waited for Niki to add a comment of her own, but she didn't have a word to say and sipped her coffee instead.

"Right," he said and made a note to see if everything was okay with her later. "Although we can't depend on the cops to look very hard anyway. They generally write it all up and conduct a cursory investigation—enough to make sure they can claim to have done their job—before they sit back and help us to hopefully collect some insurance on it. The feds might pursue it, but they don't have a great track record either and they do have ulterior motives, as Bobby mentioned. So it's down to us, which suits me fine. Like Niki, I have a bone to pick with these assholes."

"Noted," Desk added. "Vickie and I will start searching."

The hacker straightened in her seat. "We will?"

"Immediately."

"I caught some faces and license plates in the footage I sent you guys." Elisa straightened in her seat and looked alert and ready to help. "They also mentioned Rattler and Viper—like code names. It might be something there to look into."

"I...vaguely recall something about Viper." Bobby leaned back against the couch he'd been half-sitting, half-lying in. "It's all a little fuzzy, though."

Tanya ran her fingers through his hair again. "Yeah, one of the guys was Rattler, but I had a feeling the Viper character was someone who had organized the robbery and wasn't there with them. One of them yelled that Viper didn't want anyone dead and told them to switch to the sedative after the asshole shot Bobby."

"In fairness, I did injure one of their knees," the mechanic noted with a small grin.

"And they took their masks off when they were leaving the building, which is a good start too," Vickie noted as she checked the footage on her phone.

"I guess the dumbasses never realized that the sirens didn't continue once they left the building." Elisa chuckled but stopped when she realized she was the only one laughing.

"Oh, right." Bobby grunted. "We set the sound system so it could be activated to start playing the sounds of sirens if the silent alarm was triggered. I thought it would pressure anyone who tried to break in and it can be accessed remotely, which was how Elisa managed to trigger it. Aside from that, I have made a few changes around here. Come on. I'll show you."

Tanya helped him to the crutches the doctor insisted he used to keep his weight off his injured leg. He scowled as he hobbled to a new steel door in the shop wall that hadn't been there before.

"I thought that if someone wanted to rent the grocery store on the other side, I might as well get the freezer working," the man explained and retrieved a remote awkwardly from his pocket. "Then I realized that while I don't need to freeze an industrial amount of shit, it's a useful place to store equipment and prospective tenants could easily be satisfied with a more modern freezer. I added a door on this side of the wall to make it a little more accessible and I did a little something extra too."

Bobby clicked the remote. The access panel on the wall flashed and the door opened almost immediately. They followed him into the room, which was only about a quarter full of various boxes, equipment, and parts, and he clicked another button on the remote. A few storage shelves moved out of the way on small, hidden rails and another door clicked open.

"A hidden storage area," Bobby said and gestured proudly at his creation. "Is this what you had in mind?"

"It'll work," Taylor noted and raised an eyebrow. "But it raises the question of why you need a secured, hidden storage area."

"Well, see, I have this friend and I never know when he might have stolen cash or other contraband he needs to store," the man replied with a grin. "I'll sleep better knowing it's tucked away where no one will ever think to look for it."

Taylor nodded. "Yeah, that's fair."

---

Good news always tended to be balanced by bad news. Julian was more than used to that. He'd run a Fortune-Five-Hundred company for the past decade or so and had learned quickly that little went as planned. It was his job to adapt, improvise, and improve his planning according to whatever he tried to accomplish.

He was good at it, which was why he had succeeded where so many others had failed. It was why his name was the name of the company.

With that said, there were certain expectations and they had all begun to sink to the bottom of whatever the deepest lake in the world was when Frank stepped into his office again.

The former FBI agent's eyebrows raised when he realized someone else was in the office with them.

"Frank, take a seat. Thanks for coming." His boss motioned to the empty seat on his left. Given the nature of the operations specialists' duties, they'd both agreed it would be best if he kept a low profile. It therefore came as a surprise that Transk had included anyone else in their meeting. "This is Arlo Hemming, head of Research and Development with Transk Industries."

"A pleasure," Arlo said and stood to shake Palumbo's hand. "I suppose we have you to thank for acquiring the suit I've been studying?"

"Officially, I have no idea what you're talking about," he replied cautiously. The man might be an employee of the company but he wasn't quite ready to simply trust the rotund researcher with a round balding head and thick glasses. "Transk Industries frowns on and strongly condemns even the mere mention of corporate espionage according to the HR binder the boss made me read."

"Arlo was briefing me on what he discovered in the suit you had nothing to do with acquiring," Julian explained and motioned for his R&D specialist to continue.

"Well, I was telling him that there is no evidence of the expected super-AI in the suit's internal workings," Arlo said and shrugged apologetically.

"So you're telling me we went to all the effort to steal that suit with nothing but our dicks to show for it?" he asked and scowled.

Arlo shook his head. "I would not say that there was no benefit. While the software cannot be described as having anything but a conventional and generic AI used in all similar suits, the armor itself has considerable potential. The design is rather innovative and the hardware is beyond cutting-edge. We'll be able to—"

"But it isn't the fucking AI, which is what I need!" Julian snapped and made the man jump in his seat, which prompted a soft chuckle from Frank. "Besides, whatever ideas you may glean from the suit, we'll need to be incredibly careful in implementing them into our models. I've never shied away from making full use of any secrets we might have acquired from our competitors, but our success at this is always dependent on making sure no one can touch us with an IP lawsuit."

Arlo nodded. "Of course, of course. We would be able to improve on the model we have without any sign that we have directly copied anything that might be protected."

Palumbo narrowed his eyes at the specialist and seemed to be biting his tongue. Julian wanted him to be frank—no pun intended—but he could understand why he wouldn't want to speak his mind in front of a stranger.

"What do you suggest now?" the CEO asked and focused his gaze on Frank, who raised an eyebrow at the question. "I'm inclined to believe the AI is as extraordinary as we think it is. They wouldn't have bothered to remove it while not in use if it weren't the case."

The operations specialist shrugged his shoulders. "It sounds like a reasonable assumption to me. My Zoo contact swears that no human could have accomplished what McFadden did in the suit without some kind of AI support in the Zoo. An advanced combat-oriented AI, to be precise. My contacts in the FBI aren't as helpful, though. Personally, I think it's because they want to make things difficult on purpose. They don't mind the extra scratch, but…well, I might have pissed a few people off during my time there. Some smoldering resentment might have remained."

"So what do you think we should do next?"

"McFadden and Banks probably still have the AI somewhere, as well as the source code for it. I would guess that the version we tried to steal from the FBI was an even more advanced suite than the one we might have collected from the suit. Logically, they'd need some kind of server in place to house both versions."

"What are our options?"

"I've done some research on the group and I'm not sure we have any of my traditional avenues of approach." Frank pulled his laptop out and opened it to display the data he'd collected. "There's nothing that affords us leverage for blackmail purposes, and even bribery feels off the table to me."

"Feels?" Julian leaned forward.

"You must have a feel for this kind of thing. Leverage is all-important in these situations. From what I've been able to determine through my research, they seem to have created a loose family structure based on loyalty and ties. They are also already well-off thanks to some…uh, interesting developments in their financial histories."

"Is there anything we can use?"

"I doubt it. While it's suspicious, there isn't anything solid for the IRS or the FBI to look into. If there were, I would assume they would already be looking into it. The Bureau isn't above using a little blackmail to get what they want. With that said, however, as far as I've been able to discover, the DOD apparently has a copy. The FBI has tried to get their hands on it but the two agencies have butted heads for the past few weeks."

"Wait." Julian raised a hand to stop his train of thought. "If the DOD already has it, why was the FBI looking for it?"

"The dumbasses forgot they had it. That was why we

were able to get it out so easily the last time."

"You call that easy?"

"It was a great plan," Frank insisted. "We merely didn't anticipate that third parties would get involved. Anyway, now that Banks isn't working for the DOD—directly, anyway—it's entirely possible that the dickwads mislaid their version like the FBI did and are scrambling to find it themselves."

Julian nodded and drew a deep breath. "Okay, we'll need a hacker and not the one we have employed full-time. I need the absolute best—and before you ask, I don't give a shit how much it costs me."

"Avery Nickelsen has done extremely well and was invaluable when we got the server out," Frank reminded him. "He's an annoying little shit but he is one of the best in the field."

"Then it's all the more reason to believe we're dealing with a super-AI. It's unlikely the child they have working for them has either the skills or the experience to fight off an attack like the one he recently attempted. She had help and it had to be from the AI. I want someone who doesn't give a shit about breaking rules and has the balls and skills to go up against that and win."

"Will we focus on breaking McFadden and Banks' security then?"

"Hell no." Julian laughed. "In his spare time, Avery can probably target the DOD. If, as you suggest, a version is still on those servers, our man should have more luck there than the idiots currently trying to find it. Plus, he should be able to hide his activity behind their slew of searches and avoid notice."

Arlo scanned the room with furtive glances. He was either uncomfortable in his seat or perhaps with the topic of discussion but it was unlikely that the man would say anything. He wasn't the type to insert himself into a discussion he had no part in.

"Noted." Frank smirked.

They wouldn't talk about how this had become something of an obsession with a super-AI. Hell, Transk knew members of his board who would say his people needed to develop something like that but he knew the limitations of the people under his employ. They were good but they weren't that good.

"Besides, maybe they can shaft the FBI and the DOD at the same time," Julian commented as Frank stood.

"Hell, I'd do that for free," the man retorted. "Not that I will. I'm a salaried employee these days. I even have dental."

"Believe me, you'll be well-compensated if this works. You know how generous I can be to the people who do good work."

---

"Are you serious?" Eben asked.

Marcus looked around the office and inclined his head. "Have you ever known me to make jokes?"

"I assumed you had a dry, sarcastic type of wit, honestly."

"Sure." Marcus shook his head. "But yes, I am serious. They currently operate from three different locations, which means we'll have to get three separate warrants to search them all. And we'll probably want them at the same time. If they have any contacts or get any kind of inkling, they'll be able to play a shell game between the three properties until we run out of warrants. Either simultaneous raids or back-to-back would work, I imagine, so they have no time to do anything. Surveillance at each location should give us sufficient warning of unusual activity."

"So, we're working from the assumption that they are based primarily at their hotel," Eben muttered, leaned back in his seat, and folded his arms. "Even though they own a perfectly luxurious house in the area. Why don't they stay at the house?"

"According to the records, it's still being renovated. With that said, we can't assume they don't use the location to hide anything we need to find. Another thing to note is that their resident IT expert, Victoria Madison, hasn't been seen on the property either, which means she's probably working from her hotel."

"How is she connected to the group?"

"Oh." Marcus checked his papers. "She's Niki Bank's cousin. Mother's…sister's daughter."

"And then there's the shop that no longer belongs to Taylor." The young agent frowned at the paperwork. "He still has nominal control over the company but he's a silent partner."

"That's enough for a judge, though," Marcus assured him. "The real problem will be to get a warrant for the hotel rooms."

"Well, I refuse to leave any stones unturned on this," Eben snapped. "And won't let them get away with playing any tricks on us."

"I looked into the possible locations where the AI might

be situated, and a likely possibility is that a version of it is in one of their suits," Marcus commented. "That's where the original marker came from, when McFadden was seen operating a suit he wouldn't be able to operate on his own. The assumption was that he used an incredibly advanced combat AI prototype and shit snowballed from there."

"Where would we find that suit?"

"At the shop. Provided they don't move it around."

"I'd say it's a very good sign if they moved it around, no?"

"Not if McFadden were to use it as an actual, operational weapon, which he does regularly according to the DOD. He is surprisingly busy attacking the Zoo bastards."

"I don't give a shit if he uses the AI to feed hungry kittens in third-world countries," Eben retorted. "He's using a fully-fledged AI that we need, and we've been tasked to get our hands on it and keep it out of the hands of the wrong people."

He paused, his brows drawn together in thought. "He probably wouldn't be able to run the full AI from that suit. The hardware doesn't support something that drains it to that extent, but if we find even some clues, it will help us to locate the original. Failing that, we would almost certainly be able to pick up some of the source code our developers here at the FBI would be able to act on."

Marcus nodded but Eben could sense the doubt in him as he studied the paperwork again. He knew he wasn't well-liked and the older agent had likely already voiced his misgivings to Harvey to make he sure wouldn't be blamed if the operation crashed and burned.

Of course, no one minded sharing the credit if everything went well and they nabbed some of the most coveted software on the planet.

The man had been in the FBI long enough to know how to straddle a fence and play the political game. He most likely didn't enjoy it or he would have risen much higher, but he knew how to work it.

Eben didn't like that. He wanted his team to share their comments with him freely, no matter how sarcastic or cynical they were. Unfortunately, he doubted he would be able to get Marcus to share what he thought on the matter, even if he tried.

"Will that be all, boss?"

He nodded. "I'll let the team know when the paperwork is finalized."

---

She'd gone all out. Fabio had no idea if there was money in her budget for this or if she'd paid for it with her personal funds, but Libby had shipped the rabbit pellets from Northern Africa to his facility in Italy in less than a day.

The researcher was impressed, to be honest. Even with all the money in the world, she was located in an unforgiving environment that created enormous complications for even something as simple as sending a parcel.

He was also a little worried. He'd met Libby and the woman was about as difficult to unsettle as one might expect from someone who spent most of her life out in the open and dealt with all the dangers that came with it.

She was a down-to-earth woman not given to flights of fancy or paranoia, which made him take her seriously—

even if it was about rabbit turds. Still, they weren't the kind of thing one thought would bring about an alien invasion.

That aside, she was paying for expedited testing, which meant he would make sure she got it.

"We have some smaller growth test units that are scheduled to go to the recycling chamber later," one of his assistants reminded him. "We can see if we can replicate what she mentioned about the plants they were testing in the desert. A few other...uh, pellets can be run through a battery of chemical and spectrometric tests. We can run those here and if there is anything of the Zoo in those, we'll find it."

Fabio noted the smirk on the man's face. "But you don't believe there will be anything like what they were worried about."

"Not particularly, no. Most animals in the area will shit some Zoo substances, but the body filters it out quickly. They would need sustained exposure for there to be anything dangerous in the body or the shit. I don't think I'm ready to simply accept what they suggested."

The other research assistants looked like they agreed. It was like they were paid thousands to run a quick high-school experiment. Once they were finished, they could go back to their real work.

"Let's get it done," he said firmly.

"Aren't we going a little too far to help your girlfriend?"

"She isn't my girlfriend."

"But you call her—"

"I know what I call her," he responded sharply. "Get it done."

# CHAPTER EIGHT

Another hotel meeting was in progress and he wondered if they should simply book one of the hotel's conference rooms instead. Supposedly, they weren't even that expensive. Not according to their hotel's standards, anyway.

"Thus far," Desk said through the TV, "most of the activity has been fairly unthreatening in that they essentially run diagnostic searches. These are usually the work of the low-level techs who hope that some fairly specific and predictable keywords or phrases will turn up. I've set up alerts based on these so I am able to deal with them rather easily. One or two are a little more sophisticated, but not by much. The DOD has still not brought in the more talented individuals they have access to, which means the whole operation is still quite low on their list of priorities."

Taylor folded his arms and drew a deep breath. This certainly seemed like the kind of meeting that could happen without his presence as it was entirely Vickie and Desk's realm of expertise. If they needed someone punched, intimidated, or otherwise moved out of the way, he was the one to call.

Until then, he had to do the most difficult thing possible—sit and wait.

"How do you manage to avoid detection when you run your operations?" Niki asked. "Surely being active is what could grab their attention there, right?"

"Look at you, picking up on shit." Vickie grinned. "But no. The servers have a consistent level of activity that they need to remain at. It's kind of a white noise that keeps them all operational. As long as Desk keeps her activity under the white-noise line, they won't detect any spikes of activity."

"And I've managed to disguise my operations as routine DOD business and funneled it through a variety of internal servers that already see a high level of usage. It is time-consuming but virtually undetectable. I could say I've become quite creative with regard to the nature of my searches. Instead of going for the throat of the beast, I take the long way around. Again, it's time-consuming, but only by a matter of milliseconds. That should not be a factor in your operations."

"It sounds like you've put considerable thought into this." Taylor looked around the room to make sure he hadn't interrupted anything Niki or Vickie wanted to say before he continued. "How have the searches gone on your end with regard to what happened at Bobby's?"

The AI called an image up to the TV screen of one of the robbers who had foolishly pulled his mask off before he moved out of the cameras' range.

"Facial recognition software has determined that this

one is named Ralph Hinderman," Desk replied. "I managed to track him easily through the traffic cameras, but the software is still running on the other one whose face we captured."

"He's the asshat who shot Bobby and dislocated Tanya's arm." Vickie stood and approached the TV like she intended to punch it.

"That is correct," the AI concurred. "It seems the term often used for his style of mercenary work is 'wild card.' He's proficient and experienced in the skill set required for the work, which positions him at a higher tier in the profession, but he seems to lack the control and common sense one might expect from someone with his experience."

"The worst kind of thug," Taylor commented and his tone dripped with acidity. "Drunk on power and no filter."

"Do you have any idea where we can pay this guy a visit?" Niki asked.

"I've managed to triangulate his location based on a cell phone that was purchased in his name." A few different satellite images displayed on the screen. "According to the GPS markers on the phone, he has set up residence in an apartment on the west side."

"I say we visit and demonstrate how much we appreciate him putting Bobby and Tanya in the hospital." Niki cracked her knuckles. "I'm thinking the eye for an eye approach—or in this case, a shot leg and a dislocated arm for a…well, you get the idea. We can catch him unawares and that way, he'll be willing to roll over on his cohorts. I'll go ahead and assume he's not the kind of guy to whom loyalty comes naturally."

"I like that," Vickie agreed. "A little retribution seems like a good way to get his jaw flapping—oh, hold on. The phone's ringing."

Taylor shook his head and wondered how he'd managed to fall in with such violent women. Maybe he was simply a bad influence on them.

"It's Jansen," the hacker said and glanced at her companions before she put him on speaker. "You have the team here, Trond."

"How's it going, guys?" Their contact at the DOD didn't sound like he was in the mood for pleasantries and merely engaged in them because he didn't want to get to the meat of the matter.

"Not too great, to be honest," Taylor answered. "And why do I have the feeling you'll make things a whole lot worse?"

"Well, your instincts are spot-on there," the man replied with a dry, humorless chuckle. "I received a very interesting call from Speare, who wanted to make sure I absolutely don't know that the DOD is gathering the paperwork they need to run a search and retrieval operation. He is only telling me this because, of all things, he's not a huge fan of the armed forces using combat AIs on a large scale—or that's what he told me, at least. Anyway, that's why he's adamant that I should absolutely not know this information."

Niki's scowl intensified. It made her look like she'd stepped on a Lego piece barefoot in the middle of the night and didn't want to release the litany of curses that surely bubbled under the surface.

"Right," she muttered and drew a sharp breath. "Desk,

would you mind doing a quick check on that to see how far into the process they are?"

"Of course," the AI answered. "You should know that while Jansen issued his warning, I ran a search on the FBI's actions and discovered that they have acquired three search warrants—one each for the hotel, the house, and the strip mall."

"Fuck me in the ass." Taylor saw mirrored expressions of frustration on his teammates' faces. "They are now pulling out all the stops. They probably have all their ducks in a row, ready to go. The warrants were the final step."

"Bastard feds," Niki muttered. "I bet you they tried to make sure we didn't know they were coming before they descended with that triple whammy. It's what I would have done."

"And it would have worked too," he added. "Vickie, what's the status on your...what did you call it again?"

"The vanilla system," the girl replied with a smirk. "I was up half the night adding the finishing touches. It should be ready to roll."

"I guess it should go without saying that this conversation never happened, right?" Jansen confirmed.

"What conversation?" all three replied at once.

"Exactly. Take it easy, guys."

The line cut and Taylor studied the three he was in the room with carefully and made sure Desk knew she wasn't forgotten.

"Well, I think it's time we move the real equipment to the shop," Taylor said. "They probably have the hotel, house, and workshop under surveillance, so we need to be subtle about it."

"We should probably warn Nessie that she'll be cut off from the Internet for a couple of days," Vickie added.

"I can hear you," Nessie responded and used the TV as well. "And if I were human, I would say I am not a fan of the situation as a whole."

"It'll only be a temporary measure," the hacker assured her. "And I imagine it will be a better option than being captured by the enemy, as it were. Being a spoil of war can't be fun, even if you're an AI."

"Agreed," she replied. "I did not say I was unwilling, merely that I was not happy about it."

Desk activated suddenly on the screen. "Bobby has told me that the contractors informed him that federal agents are entering your residence as we speak."

"Bobby contacted you?" he asked skeptically.

"Not as such. In fact, he contacted his lawyer first, but he knows by now that I monitor his and your communications so he might as well have contacted me. I assume he wanted to contact Taylor as well but that might not have been an option as he might be under surveillance too—or having the strip mall searched as we speak."

"Okay," Niki snapped. "It looks like Operation Fuck the Feds is in full swing. Taylor, you'd best go prepared to have a workout so you have a good excuse to be there. We'll run interference on this side. I think they'll probably come to the hotel after the house, but I'm not sure when the DOD will arrive at the workshop. They'll probably want to get there ahead of the FBI."

"Don't worry." Taylor smirked. "Between Bobby and I, we know how to give them the runaround. I never thought I'd say this but it's a good thing the suit was stolen. At least they can't accuse us of deliberately with-holding anything."

"In the meantime, I suppose I should monitor both the hotel and the workshop to give you advance warning should the agents decide to arrive," Desk said and sounded dejected.

"You need to keep yourself safe too," Vickie countered.

"I can do that while I help you. I've done it for the past few weeks, after all."

He smirked. "Have you found anything yet?"

"I have been watching and there does not appear to be any sign of agents approaching either location. In fact, I cannot identify any surveillance personnel in place around the hotel either, although I cannot promise there are none in the vicinity."

"They'll probably not stop you anyway," Niki noted. "They would need an arrest warrant for that kind of shit."

"I'll go ahead and assume all bets are off in this case," Taylor replied and retrieved his workout bag. "Vickie, see if you can find a way to contact Bobby and tell him I'll come over with the system under the pretense of getting a workout in. Oh, and you should probably warn him that the FBI and the DOD will probably pay him a visit."

"What's wrong with a call?" the hacker asked.

"They are most likely monitoring communications in and around the area," Niki informed her. "It's better to be safe than sorry and we don't want them to know that's where they should look, right?"

"Okay. I can probably set up some messaging random-izers. It'll be a message to Elisa but she'll be able to get it to Bobby."

"Awesome." Taylor clapped briskly and rubbed his hands together. "Let's get moving. There's no point in waiting for the assholes to arrive."

---

"I'll say these are promising results."

Leonard narrowed his eyes. "How are they promising? Under the spectrometer, they show no signs of anything other than the traces we knew we'd find in them anyway. All this means is that the rabbits ate some Zoo vegetation, which is to be expected given where they are. There are no signs that there is any larger than average amount of Zoo…stuff."

"Were you going to say Zoo shit?"

"Yes, but then I realized I'd be talking about Zoo shit in the shit, and it felt a little…uh, redundant."

Fabio nodded and folded his arms. "Did you look at the results from the shit we put in the ground?"

"I didn't think the results on those had been brought in yet."

"Not the plant tests. The spectrometer tests on the soil with the fertilizer in it."

"Oh. No."

With a chuckle, the senior researcher shook his head, moved to one of the computers, and logged in with his password to call up the results of the testing. He stepped back and let his assistant see what had come in the night before.

His expression still dubious, Leonard approached the

computer, leaned closer, and narrowed his eyes as if he didn't quite believe what he was seeing.

"How long were these samples in the ground?" he asked.

"About twelve hours."

"And the goop content has increased by seven times what we found in the pellets? Are you sure about this?"

"I was as surprised as you are, so I pulled a few other samples at eighteen hours and they were at up to thirteen times the content that came with the originals. Seven times was merely the average we collected from the seven samples. More are coming in every hour, but I thought we should talk about what we might be seeing here."

"What are you talking about?" The other man leaned on the desk and stared at the screen as he tried to make sense of the results and what they suggested. "I…that should be impossible. The only way this should be possible is if…well…"

"If it were a living organism and it was reproducing." Fabio stated what the man tried hard to not say. "But I don't think that is the case. Someone would have noticed it before if it was."

"Is this a new development with the goop?"

"It might be. And if we're very, very careful, there might be a little profit in it for both of us."

Leonard turned to look at him, his head tilted in thought. There was doubt in his eyes, of course, but a hint of avarice as well. The Zoo had a way of bringing that side out in people. Fabio was an incorrigible flirt but he was at the top of his profession, which was why he studied the Zoo without having to be there himself. While his work had opened all kinds of doors for him, it had also allowed him to see the sheer amount of greed present in the upper levels of those in control.

The problem with that, of course, was the fact that the people in charge were generally uneducated assholes who didn't know a goddamn thing about what they were dealing with. He knew, however, and he knew the measures that had to be taken.

"It would help if we had one of the damn bunnies to study," his assistant stated and dragged Fabio out of his reverie.

"True." He sighed and shook his head. "Libby knows who is peddling the pellets so she might be able to direct us to where we can find a live specimen. Of course, in that case, we might have to tell her it's safe and gives no indication that it might cause any kind of disaster."

"Is it safe?"

He frowned as he ran his fingers over his cheek that had begun to get a little too rough with stubble. He'd have to shave before he returned home for the night.

"Probably not. But it's better to have something like that happen in the Sahara than anywhere else, to be honest. That region of the world is already screwed, between you and me. Watching how the goop grows and expands in a controlled environment will lead to new doors into new fields of study that would be like tapping a gold mine."

"I thought it was more like opening Pandora's box."

"Only if they left out the part where she opened it correctly and spent the rest of her life rolling in cash. It would still be a nightmare for me, though."

"How so?"

"I'm allergic to rabbits. I would have to do all the work from inside a hazmat suit."

"No shit?"

"Yes. And not only rabbits. All rodents as well, to be honest. It isn't the kind of thing you consider when dealing with the bastards, but the last time I was in a lab with rats, I almost died."

"I'll keep that in mind—and write a very touching eulogy for your funeral."

# CHAPTER NINE

"Nothing?"

"Well, they've been busy with ongoing construction in the building, so I don't know how much we could realistically expect to find in there."

Marcus was right about that, at least. McFadden had sunk considerable money into the residence, not only to purchase it but also to renovate it. From the perspective of an FBI agent who earned an annual salary that was still within the five-digit range, it seemed an impressive amount of money. He reminded himself that given how much McFadden brought in every year, it probably wasn't unreasonably high.

It was difficult to not feel jealous, though, if the truth be told.

"The worst part is that the contractor seemed to be laughing at us while we searched the premises," Marcus added as he put down the paperwork for the search of the property.

"I know. I was there."

"Do you think we can hit him with anything?" It honestly was more a rhetorical question born out of frustration.

Eben shook his head. "He was about as cooperative as he could have been and even showed the agents around. The fact that he practically laughed all the way through it won't persuade any judge to sign an arrest warrant."

The older agent nodded. It was bad form to treat a cooperating witness poorly anyway, and aside from the man's amusement, the contractor had been quite polite and even offered the agents some of the coffee he'd made for his workers.

It still stung that they hadn't found anything, of course, and McFadden would likely involve lawyers and make everyone's life more difficult while he thumbed his nose at the FBI with impunity.

Of course, that would only happen if they found nothing in the other two locations they'd obtained warrants for.

"Why didn't we simply get a warrant to search all his belongings?" Marcus asked and shifted a little in the driver's seat. "The guy has cars and might even have a handful of safe deposit boxes he could use to store his shit so none of it is located on his properties."

"We're not exactly looking for something small."

"He has trucks, you know. The kind that can carry a suit around if he needs to."

"Yeah, I know. Honestly, we were lucky to get these warrants. McFadden is a veteran and a former associate of both the FBI and the DOD, so it would only take the wrong person to think we're harassing him for all this to go through the shitter faster than a power-flush toilet."

The other agent nodded, his expression irritated as he tapped his fingers on the steering wheel. "We should get this show on the road, then."

"Is the rest of the team in place?"

"It'll take only a few more minutes. Some of them caught a traffic snag but they're close."

Eben let his face settle into the scowl that had begun to turn into a permanent set to his features. He didn't like being made a fool of, and the fact that the rest of his task force couldn't see the urgent need to catch up on the poor start to the operation honestly didn't help. His reason told him anyone could encounter traffic but his impatience overrode that and preferred to label it as incompetence.

But there would be time for him to address that later. His phone beeped, the signal that the team was ready to get started at the hotel. He snapped an order for them to meet him at the entrance to the building and he and Marcus slid out of the car.

None of the team behaved in a way that would deliberately draw attention to themselves, but feds were feds. Even with their leisurely but firm tread, they were bound to stand out and so needed to position themselves quickly. Their quarry might already have eyes all over the hotel, so their only chance to catch the group by surprise was if they got in there with no more wasted time.

One of the bellmen tried to intercept the group of agents but Eben already had his badge out. He waved him off and strode toward the reception like his ass was on fire.

The receptionist narrowed her eyes when he approached the desk. "How—"

"We have a warrant to search a few of your hotel rooms." He motioned for a couple of the agents to move behind the counter. "I will need a card for the elevators. These agents will stay down here to make sure no one calls up to warn your clients."

The woman's brows raised as she tried to make sense of the situation, but she nodded and quickly magnetized a card for them to use.

Thanking her wouldn't set a good precedent, so he took the card in silence and moved toward the elevators with the other half-dozen or so agents close behind him. It was futile to imagine that Banks didn't have some warning that they were coming, but she wouldn't know where or when. It would give him something of an edge when they arrived.

Not a word was said among the agents in the elevator and they all looked like they simply wanted to get this one over with. He knew a couple of them felt that Niki was one of their own but in the end, it wasn't like she would go to jail. All they needed to do was get their hands on the tech and she would be free to do whatever the hell she was doing before they entered the picture.

Once they reached the door, Eben immediately thumped on it four times as hard as he could manage without injuring his hand.

"FBI—open up. We have a warrant!" he shouted and readied himself to knock again if she didn't respond in the next few seconds. If she still didn't acknowledge them, he would be within his rights to assume they were trying to destroy evidence and open the door. The card was probably a master key for all the rooms but if it wasn't, it had been a while since he'd been allowed to kick a door down.

As his fist lowered to the wood again, the door was yanked open and a woman stood in the aperture. Her eyes narrowed and her nostrils flared as though she was ready for a fight. It was surprising how similar she was to her sister, although a little more muscle mass around her shoulders and arms indicated that she was the brawnier of the two siblings.

Eben retracted his fist that was still poised to knock and retrieved the documents instead. "We have a warrant to search these rooms. You are...Niki Banks and the room adjoining is occupied by Victoria Madison?"

"Jesus, call me Vickie!" a voice shouted from behind the woman in the doorway.

Banks stared belligerently at him for a few more seconds before she snatched the warrant from his hand and examined it quickly. Of course, as former FBI herself, she knew how everything worked.

"I will need to see your badges too," she snapped as the team made to enter the room.

He wanted to simply push in and assert his authority, but the last thing they should do was hand Banks a lawsuit in the middle of this. All the agents presented their badges for her to look at. She moved quickly and inspected each one before she finally nodded and stepped out of the way.

"Sorry about the paranoia, boys," she said with a small smile. "We've had to deal with the kind of assholes who could probably fake shit like this so there's every reason to not be underprepared."

"Sure," Eben responded and tried to not let her see how

hard it was for him to believe her little story. "We'll need all the electronic equipment you've been using. The warrant allows us to confiscate any and all equipment you might be carrying, including phones, personal computers, tablets, et cetera."

"Hold on," the other woman snapped and bolted from her seat. "We're trying to run a business here. How the hell are we supposed to do that if you take all our equipment?"

"I assume you are Victoria Madison?"

"No, I'm fucking Santa Claus. I've lost a little weight. What of it?"

A few of the agents stifled chuckles behind him, which didn't help to improve his mood. "You'll get them back. Get to work."

The last comment was directed at his team and a quick gesture made them hurry to claim anything that looked vaguely electronic in the room, including the TV. The hotel would get that back eventually but these days, most smart TVs had enough capabilities to run basic programming shit. He doubted they would run anything hinky on the TV but at this point, leaving no stone unturned was the idea.

"While you're at it, there are probably some basic computing chips in the minibar," Vickie pointed out and returned to her seat, her expression annoyed. "Do you want to take that too?"

Eben hated the fact that his team looked at him to make sure before they shook their heads.

"You know, fridges these days have more computer power than the computers they used to launch the Apollo missions," the hacker continued as the agents collected their phones and began to sift through the rest of their luggage.

"No shit?" Banks asked. She stood in the corner of the room and watched everything the agents were doing carefully.

"I shit you not. Of course, back then, they had to rely on dozens of people to write coding for the mission, and they had to do it old-fashioned—like on paper. So maybe it's not comparable. But yeah, with the right people behind it, you could probably use a fridge's computer these days to put human boots on the moon."

"I assume there would be a shit-ton of money involved too."

"Right. Computers aren't everything. You need a rocket the size of a medium-sized office building, a shuttle, a place to set it all up that won't start fifty wildfires, and a group of people willing to be sent to the moon based on the computing power of a fridge. Honestly, if you have that, you're good to go."

"I think that last part might be the most challenging of them all."

There was nothing he could do or say that would make them take the raid more seriously, but their attitude had begun to piss Eben off more than he liked. They should be nervous and exchange panicked glances while they tried to think of a way out of this mess. Instead, they chatted casually about something. He hadn't paid much attention so wasn't sure what, but he assumed it was flippant.

"I need to ask you a few questions," he said and deliberately kept his voice quiet and even. "You have to understand that you are in a serious situation."

"Serious?" Banks snorted. "I've dealt with alien incursions for the past five years and you think a little pissing match with the FBI is serious?"

"We're dealing with a piece of tech that could be the next big step for humanity's advances in the technological sphere," he retorted before she could voice any more opinions about how unserious this was to them. "If it were to fall into the wrong hands, that would be the kind of disaster historians will get a hard-on over for decades. So why don't we cut the crap and stay on topic?"

"Wrong hands?" Vickie interrupted and drew her feet up to sit cross-legged on the couch. "Hold on, wasn't this AI in FBI hands originally? And didn't you guys let it fall into the wrong hands?"

"That's what I heard too," Banks agreed. "Yeah, we heard about it in Germany and I didn't think they had much to do with the FBI across the pond. It must have been one hell of a screw-up."

"But not the biggest screw-up you've ever dealt with, right?" The hacker folded her arms and looked around the room. "I could count at least half a dozen motherfuckers who would have unleashed the Zoo on our home turf if we hadn't stopped them. They have a word for the kind of person who stops a calamity that would usually result in thousands of deaths, right?"

"I think they call them heroes."

"Right, heroes. And what do they call the dumbasses who wander around getting in the way of the heroes?"

"Footnotes in the hero's report," Banks replied smoothly like they had rehearsed this conversation. "Or, if it were a sci-fi movie, they would be secondary antagonists."

"Secondary antagonists." The younger woman with short dark hair and the looks one might expect from the cliché image of a hacker nodded slowly. "I like that. It reduces them, don't you think?"

Of course, it was all for his benefit. They wouldn't get in the way of the investigation, at least not overtly, but it didn't look like they intended to be any help either.

"You know, you shouldn't try to make the FBI your enemy in this," Eben commented and raised an eyebrow. "You used to be one of us so we should technically still be on the same side. Everyone knows you would all be better off if you simply cooperated with the investigation."

Both women paused their banter to regard him much like a scientist would a bug in a jar.

"I am cooperating," Banks replied with a laugh. "Do you see me trying to shred papers or some shit like that? You guys have bothered me and my family for way too long now and we've cooperated every step of the way. Believe me when I say you'll know when I stop."

"Are you threatening me?" Eben asked and folded his arms.

"That depends. Is there any particular reason why I would need to threaten you?"

"I have heard you like to resolve your problems with inordinate amounts of unnecessary violence."

"Oh, that. No, not unnecessary violence. I only fuck up the people who fuck with me first. Do you plan to fuck with me?"

The rest of the crew finished the first room and hurried to the one adjoining it, but it was unlikely they would have any luck there either. He drew a deep breath and tried to not let Banks rile him further. He was held to a much higher standard of conduct than she was, of course.

Once the group had finished in the other room, they exited with the somewhat dejected expressions he'd expected from them. They carried all the electronics in the room to be analyzed by the experts, but he had a feeling they wouldn't find anything in them either.

"Well, we have one more warrant to serve," he stated briskly. "And I'm afraid I'll have to insist that the two of you accompany me to the strip mall."

"Bullshit." Banks snapped. "Your warrant doesn't give you the authority to hold us or arrest us for any period of time."

"Oh, come on," Vickie interrupted. "There is no way in hell that I'll miss what comes next."

"You mean act two of the almighty Federal Bureau of Idiots crash and burn?"

"Fuck yeah."

"You know, I might be up for that show." The older woman nodded. "Bobby might even have popcorn ready and waiting. You guys are driving, right?"

"He might have popcorn ready, yes. There's nothing quite like popcorn to go with a good comedy. But maybe we should ask one of these nice gentlemen to stop at a store—no? Goddammed party-poopers."

Banks nodded at the agents. "Let's get this freak show on the road. There's no need to hang around waiting."

Eben straightened his back and breathed deeply. They probably already knew how pissed he was but damned if he would make it obvious.

The screams were the last thing Libby wanted to hear and she bolted out of her chair, flung her pen onto her desk, and raced toward the tunnels. While their suddenness had shocked her, they weren't entirely a surprise. She had expected something to happen from the moment she'd begun to suspect what infused the miracle rabbit shit.

Being in a constant state of anxiety over what that might be was tiring and a part of her had often wished something would simply happen so it could be over and done with.

She'd received no word from Fabio regarding the tests but this was about as clear an indication that her worst fears were realized as any science could produce.

The rest of the crew heard it too and more importantly, they heard the screams cut off abruptly. They had all dropped their tools and everything else they were doing to investigate what was happening and a fair number of them blocked her path to the source.

It came as no surprise that the screams had come from the sealed tunnel where she had hoped the shit could remain until they had a better idea of what kind of threat it would pose.

"Oh, dear God," one of the other researchers whispered and made the sign of the cross hastily over her chest.

No one seemed to notice Libby and she had to elbow a path to the front of the group where a large huddle tried to see what was happening. It was probably not the safest choice for them all to be clustered so close to the dangerous section of the tunnel, but she resisted her first instinct to tell them they needed to back the hell off.

She needed to see what was happening in there before she issued any orders.

Finally, she reached one of the small windows that enabled her to peer in. The Saharan sun blazed through the protective covering to provide the monstrously sized plants with their much-needed sunlight inside the tunnels, but there was movement within as well. She almost couldn't see it at first due to the rampant growth, but as she squinted into the vegetation, one of the creatures began to approach the window.

It was about the size of a Great Dane, which would have made sense if this was something even vaguely mammalian. There was nothing mammal about it and honestly, she had a hard time finding anything earthly in it.

Images were freely available of the massive locusts that inhabited the Zoo in the largest numbers of all the mutants and these looked somewhat similar to those she'd seen. The pointed, insect-like legs and the powerful, crushing mandibles were a little difficult to mistake for anything else, but her gaze was drawn to the creature's abdomen. It was a little too long and thin, and as it walked, it flicked from side to side almost like a tail.

A tail, she realized when she focused intently, with a massive stinger on the end. Libby drew a deep breath and tried to remain calm when the beast approached the window. For a second, she could have sworn it could see her and was advancing on her position, but it broke away at the last second, its attention drawn to something in the shadows.

After a pause, it grasped a heavy weight with its powerful mandibles and much like an army ant, lifted it carefully off the ground.

"Oh, motherfucker," Libby whispered when she saw that it was not one of the sacks of fertilizer as she'd hoped but one of the researchers instead. Chester was an amiable redhead who had been brought on to round the numbers out as something of a jack of all trades in the engineering department.

She hoped against hope that a flicker of life remained in him but it was clear that he was very, very dead. A part of her wondered vaguely what he'd been doing in the tunnel she'd ordered sealed, but it slid out of her consciousness as quickly as it had come. She needed all her faculties to try to make sense of what she saw.

The beast moved the body like it weighed almost nothing and more of them worked the ground with their legs and mandibles to dig a hole in the soil.

Chester was dropped into it like he was a sack of dirt and they immediately began to cover him.

"Where the hell did they come from?" Tom asked as he stepped beside her.

"I have no idea," she whispered and tried to shake herself free from the stupor that had confounded her thought processes. "But I have a feeling this is the Zoo's version of a hostile takeover."

"What are they doing with Chester?"

Libby had no idea why her voice was calm and emotionless. All she felt was the sudden need to throw up the almost tasteless gruel they'd had for breakfast.

"Biomass," she whispered. "The goddamn sons of bitches are making biomass."

He looked at her with horror in his eyes before he spun to a few of the people who seemed entranced where they stood at the window. A few of them even started to reach for the controls that would open the doors.

"Everyone out!" he bellowed and physically turned those who were too slow to shake their fascination off quickly enough. "Lock this fucking tunnel down and—"

More screams cut his instructions off and she snapped out of whatever had come over her when she'd seen one of her people being buried by the monsters. Adrenaline kicked in and she pushed away from the window.

"They've gotten out!" someone yelled. "They're coming out!"

Well, that would explain why the tunnel wasn't secure, despite the door being closed. Would normal doors be able to contain these monsters, even with basic electronic locks?

Tom caught her roughly by the shoulder and shoved her back the way she'd come.

"You need to get out!" he shouted and shook her when she was distracted by movement on the far side of the tunnel. "You have to get out there and seal these tunnels. It won't stop them but get in a car and drive away as quickly as you can, got it?"

Libby stared at him.

"Got it?"

He shook her again and she nodded and began to move toward the door when Tom shuddered and his hand fell away from her.

She stopped and looked at him, wondering why he seemed to have frozen. Something moved behind him in a distinctly non-human way.

A confused look slid across his face and he jerked suddenly, and both he and Libby looked at his stomach.

The blood was bad enough, but what was worse was that something hard and pointed protruded barely half an inch out of the wound.

"No," she whispered and her eyes widened. "No, Tom... Please..."

Tom couldn't hear her. He sank to his knees and his eyes went blank as his whole body sagged and fell. The creature that had killed him ignored her entirely and instead, took hold of the corpse and began to drag it away.

Libby wanted to run after it, snatch his body, and kill all the creatures around her. She wanted to take him out and give him a proper burial. More than anything, she wanted to tell him how she felt about him, something she hadn't been able to when he was alive.

It felt impossible but her brain insisted that she needed to do what he had told her to. Her legs seemed to move almost of their own volition to turn her. She had to run away from the screams and the terrifying confirmation that her entire team was being slaughtered and there was nothing she could do about it.

She was in the last tunnel before the outside when movement at the door compelled her to stop. The shape she focused on certainly wasn't human. It scuttled on six legs and the huge mandibles chittered together while the tail wagged from side to side.

It finally penetrated that there was nothing she could do.

But no. There was something she could do.

Libby drew a deep breath and the faint realization of her impending death settled around her. It was a peaceful feeling, the kind where she simply let go of everything and everyone. Oddly enough, it made her feel like it would all be okay, even though the monsters circled her and prepared to attack.

With slow, careful movements, she pulled the satellite phone from her pocket. She'd carried it on her since she sent the samples to Fabio, waiting for his call. One that probably wouldn't come—or not in time, at least. But she could make one last call and perhaps save a few of the lives she'd unwittingly endangered.

---

The tests wouldn't come in for another couple of hours, but Fabio realized that the tension made it a little difficult to sleep. He therefore chose to remain in and around the lab until they did. The sheer number of possibilities they were facing seemed impossible yet tantalizingly within his grasp at the moment. All they needed to do was make sure nothing went wrong.

His phone rang.

"*Cazzo merda.*" He hissed a breath and looked around the office for the device.

It was in the place where he usually left his keys when he came in, which meant it hadn't charged during the night. He would have to remember to charge it in his car on the way home once the results came in.

A familiar number was on the display and he smiled, pressed the button to accept the call, and put it on speaker while he began to shrug into his lab coat. Leonard entered with an excited look on his face.

"Good morning, Bella. Is there anything I can help you with?"

"No time, Fabio." Libby gasped. Her tone made him lean closer to the phone, his coat only on one arm. "You need to isolate that shit. Now!"

"Isolate?"

"The rabbit shit. Isolate it. Lock it down. Oh...fuck no, please... Noooo!"

The scream echoed through his office and Fabio snatched the device up and pressed it to his ear.

"Libby, talk to me—tell me what's happening! Libby!"

The line was still open and he could hear movement on the other side but the sounds grew fainter. No more words or screams issued over the speaker. A low clacking and chittering lingered ominously in the background before the sound of something heavy being dragged across the floor took their place.

He stared at the device, frozen in shock until the connection cut.

CHAPTER TEN

"Look, Taylor, you know we appreciate you adding your input to this product line," Coleman said and leaned back in his seat. "Hell, I advocated it even when others were doubtful because I know how profitable this can be. But this isn't a one-sided deal. We help you and you help us by not letting our signature suits get robbed."

Taylor nodded, straightened in his seat, and tried not to look like he disagreed with anything they were saying. He liked the suit and appreciated that it had been sold to him for virtual peanuts and a short song. At the same time, he could also appreciate that they didn't want their suit to be accessible to the wrong people and their designs vulnerable to anyone with half a brain and a background in mechanical engineering.

"That's not to say we're angry with you," Coleman continued and drew a deep breath. "Merely...pissed off in general. Association with you has brought Granger Tech to unprecedented heights but our corporate secrets are what keep us there."

"I understand," he replied. "And...a robbery wasn't anything we expected to happen. Has the suit reached the open market yet? Or the designs?"

"Not as far as we can tell and we have lawyers waiting to slap anyone who tries with a lawsuit, but there's only so much we can do to contain the situation. This...well, it isn't the first time designs have been stolen, both from us and from our competitors, and probably won't be the last either."

"We're working on tracking these assholes," Taylor assured him and tugged his beard gently. "And we have some valuable leads too."

"I don't think we've ever tried to track the culprits directly. We never had the personnel to do something like that." Coleman looked pensive for a second. "This might be an invaluable opportunity. Go on."

"Provided we could get a modest fee to offset what we spend in our attempt to locate them, we'll probably be able to provide you guys with some actionable details on the guilty parties."

"Hold on," one of the other Granger Tech reps interrupted. "Why should we pay you to find them if you'll simply do it anyway?"

"Because actionable details are hard to find," Taylor replied. "And we are under no obligation to provide you with anything I find. Hell, the heads-up on the stolen suit was a courtesy on our part since I bought what is essentially a prototype suit from you guys. This is merely a way to make sure that if we're working together on this, I'm not the one who carries the full expenses of the search.

"That said, I assume it'll give you guys some legal benefits down the line. You could also help with a list of your competitors you might perceive as having a higher probability to pull this kind of shit, which would help shorten the search. Of course, you wouldn't be able to do that unless there was some kind of payment involved for an unaffiliated third party. Otherwise, there will be all kinds of SEC problems that could bite you in the ass later."

He'd practiced the speech for a few hours with Niki and Vickie, both of whom knew more about the dangers Granger Tech would be in if they simply sicced McFadden and Banks on their competitors without the legal red tape accounted for.

And from the looks on the faces of the rest of the board, it seemed like he'd done a good job of it.

"A nominal fee would make it an official part of our records," Coleman noted. "You're already associated with our brand so there would be no surprises if we were to enter a contract with McFadden and Banks to acquire actionable intelligence on those who might be trying to steal trade secrets."

A few of the others still looked a little uncertain about it, but they were a young company, the kind that needed to be careful about the fights they chose as well as the allies they kept around them. So far, having McFadden and Banks as an ally had helped them considerably.

"We'll put this to a vote," Coleman said finally after a few whispered conversations between the board members. "All those in favor?"

All the hands raised immediately, which thankfully meant there was no need to ask for a nay vote. Every board member nodded in agreement.

"Fantastic." Coleman turned his attention to Taylor. "Are you sure the theft was perpetrated to acquire the suit specifically? We've heard that you're involved in some disputes over…an AI of some kind."

"I wasn't aware that the suit was capable of supporting an AI," Taylor replied.

"We didn't think so either but it's always best to be on top of these things. Send us the invoice for what you'll charge and we can start the actual official negotiations."

"It sounds good to me."

The group chat cut out as the board members returned to their business and left Taylor in the upper office of the strip mall. He looked at Bobby.

"What?" the mechanic asked.

"I feel kind of bad fleecing them like that."

"It's not like we know for a fact that someone tried to steal an AI. And even if they did, once they realize it doesn't have an AI in it, they will probably try to make some profit from the suit."

Taylor nodded. "It still doesn't feel right."

---

Eben should have probably picked up that unwanted complications had invited themselves to his operation when he saw the six black SUVs parked outside the crappy strip mall.

It boggled the mind that McFadden had bought the premises at all. While it had probably been for about the cost of bananas, there was a reason for that. It honestly looked like a square piece of shit some giant had dropped on the area and no one had thought to clean up afterward.

Despite this, it housed a small yet enterprising business. It was the American dream, as ugly as it was. Two military men came home, started a company, and made a shit-ton of money from it. All that seemed a little too unlikely and the story was too convenient. In his experience, that type of scenario tended to have ragged edges no one wanted to talk about.

Now, however, it appeared that all those ragged edges were coming home to roost. The SUVs were all unmistakably government issue, a fact easily confirmed by men in suits and carrying weapons who began to move toward the entrance of the building. It looked like they had a little difficulty deciding where that was, though.

After a short discussion, the team moved toward the back and Marcus decided to follow them around the building to see where they were going.

The agents saw their vehicle and looked confused, unsure of who had arrived as they were about to perform a raid of some kind.

Eben was the first out of the car and he closed his door sharply as three of them turned to approach him with their hands in their jackets.

It was fair. He had his in his pocket too and it looked like they would all show their badges at the same time.

"This is DOD business," the man at the front stated before he could speak.

The FBI agent leaned in a little closer to look at their badges. "DARPA? Seriously? I thought the DOD would send an armed convoy if they intended to pull this shit in Vegas."

"What the hell is the FBI doing here?" the agent countered and returned his credentials to his pocket.

"We're here—" Marcus started to say, but he stopped when Eben raised his hand.

Technically, they were all supposed to be on the same side, but he was well aware that the DOD attempted to keep them in the dark regarding the fact that they had a version of the AI. Supposedly, he reminded himself. The fact that they were present at the strip mall indicated that there was some kind of fly in the ointment.

Which was hilarious, in all honesty, except it was a somewhat painful reminder of the Bureau's failings.

"We have a warrant to inspect this building," Eben said.

"What a coincidence. So do we. And I'm very sure the DOD takes precedence over whatever the hell a federal agency wants to do."

They paused when the doors to the back of the building began to open for them. They moved slowly but it only made the moment a little more dramatic as a man stepped out.

He'd read that McFadden was a giant and had seen it in his paperwork, but it was different to see it up close. The guy looked like he could have played for an NFL team if he'd chosen to but he had decided to be a military man instead. He could respect the choice as well as the idea of growing a nice long beard to complement his bright red hair.

There was certainly something about him that made the people who stared at him back away slowly. This unfortunately left the field clear for him to focus his gaze on Eben and hold it as he approached.

"Let me guess," he said calmly, his voice almost bored, and folded his arms. "You guys are the FBI and you're the DOD?"

It annoyed the younger agent that he pointed Marcus out as the FBI while he identified the leader of the DARPA squad a little too easily.

"We have a warrant to search the premises," Eben said quickly and stepped forward to brandish the piece of paper in question.

"And so do we," the DARPA man added in cold tones.

"Awesome. Get it done at the same time and we won't need to stop business twice to accommodate you assholes."

"Hey, Tay-Tay!"

Eben looked back to see that Vickie had managed to roll her window down and now waved enthusiastically.

"You brought civilians to a warrant serving?" the DARPA douche asked and ran his fingers through his short dark hair.

"They are...part of the warrant," he explained. "What... what was your name again?"

"Jackson. Mel Jackson, agent with DARPA."

"DARPA?" McFadden asked and raised an eyebrow. "Seriously? I would have thought you guys would stay in whatever lab you work in and let other people do all the legwork for you."

"We are doing all the legwork for the DARPA geeks," Jackson answered with a scowl. "Will you let us in or not?"

"Hey, no one's stopping you." McFadden stepped out of the way and motioned them in.

"Our records show that you aren't the proprietor of this business," Eben noted and retrieved his notepad. "It was recently passed to your former partner, Robert Zhang?"

"Yeah, but he's been injured so I'm trying to help him so he can rest and stay off his leg. You guys did your homework and know he was shot, right? There was a break-in and everything?"

Eben exchanged a look with Jackson before both nodded.

"Sure, we heard about the shooting," the DARPA leader said. "Is there anything else you can tell us about that?"

"I wasn't here. I was looking into some business halfway across the country at the time, but if you assholes want to make yourselves useful, you can get his statement and see about catching the fuckers."

He made an unfortunately good point and at any other time, Eben would have made sure people were looking into the case. But McFadden and Banks had both pissed him off to the point where he wasn't in the mood to help them with whatever their problem was. Besides, his paperwork had their business as being on the receiving end of numerous problems from the local criminals. The area was rife with unsavory characters, of course, and if they encountered difficulties, he wouldn't help them if they weren't helpful in return.

"Let's get in there, people," Eben said and gestured for his team to push forward.

"Yeah, that's what I thought." McFadden grinned and shook his head as the group passed him. They all watched him warily like they expected the giant to suddenly step in and stop them.

The fact that two of the women who were part of the DOD team seemed to stop and study the man intently was interesting too. Eben wouldn't have thought women were into a giant who could and probably would throw them over his shoulder in true Neanderthal style, but there was no accounting for taste.

Everyone seemed distracted enough to allow both Banks and Vickie to exit their vehicle, and they both stepped closer to McFadden and looked smug enough to make the agent feel a little sick to his stomach.

"Yeah, yeah, keep it moving and eyes off the merchandise, ladies," Banks snapped.

Vickie placed a hand on her cousin's shoulders. "I'm very sure it's still a crime to assault federal officers."

The former agent kept her glare trained on the women until they moved in before she turned it on Jackson. "Well, well, well. It looks like we have a whole alphabet soup of you fuckers," She sidled closer to McFadden and pressed a kiss to his cheek. "How was your workout, babe?"

"Not too bad. I ended up having to help Bobby with some shit too so I decided to take it easy. I think the guy is trying to pass some shit onto me and is selling his injury a little too much. How was the ride?"

"They offered to help out. Aren't the FBI guys nice?"

He grinned and tilted his head. "I don't think they're in the best of moods, having to share."

"We have the legal right to claim the suit you wore on your last trip to the Zoo," Eben interjected.

"Bullshit," Jackson snapped. "We have the legal right to it."

"Uh-oh. It looks like someone's mommies didn't teach them how to share." Banks laughed derisively.

"The suit I wore the last time I was in the Zoo?" McFadden asked and raised an eyebrow. "See, this is why you need to do your homework on these kinds of cases. If you'd looked into the police report on the shooting, that would have told you sonsabitches that it was the item stolen."

"Oh, bullshit," Eben snapped. "Do you think this is our first day on the job, McFadden?"

"Honestly?"

"Come on. Do you truly think we'll believe that the only thing we're here to take possession of is what happened to be stolen by these alleged robbers?"

"Next, they'll want to check Bobby's leg to make sure he was shot and isn't faking it," Niki added, her smirk firmly in place.

"Nah, they won't check the bandages," Vickie pointed out. "That would be harassment, especially when they've already checked the doctor's reports too, right?"

Eben felt the annoyance begin to bubble up but it at least made him feel a little better to see that Jackson had a similar reaction to the perfectly legal stonewalling they received from the group of assholes.

And it appeared there would be a few additions to the group. A large Asian-American man approached them slowly and used a pair of crutches to move awkwardly. A woman walked with him, her arm in a sling.

If he recalled the files correctly, she was Tanya Novak, another early partner in the group, and she appeared to be in a romantic relationship with Zhang.

"Are they here about the break-in?" the mechanic asked and looked at the group of suits invading his shop with a dubious expression.

"No—and yet, at the same time, a very resounding yes," McFadden answered. "They came here with a warrant to claim the suit. I guess they weren't the only ones who wanted it. And I don't blame them, honestly. It is a great suit."

"Agreed." Zhang stopped and leaned against the wall as he tried to make himself comfortable. "Will they investigate the bastards who did this? They goddamn shot me."

"I'm…I'm aware," Eben muttered and rubbed his temples. They were giving him a headache. "Are you honestly telling me that the suit was stolen?"

"Yeah. I gave a report to the police and everything when they came to question me on my hospital bed. It's a real pity you guys dressed up and came out here for nothing."

"I wouldn't say that. We'll confiscate any other electronic devices that might have in order to inspect them further."

"These guys have no sense of personal property," Vickie complained. "It's like they don't think tax-paying people and companies should be able to work simply because they fucked up."

"Did they fuck up?" Zhang asked.

"Big time," Banks answered.

Eben took a deep breath, approached McFadden, and steeled himself to try to question him as well. "I'll be straight with you. There are reports that you have some kind of combat-oriented AI in the suit that was supposedly stolen. Do you know anything about that?"

"Oh, for Christ's sake. You too?" The man looked genuinely annoyed by the suggestion. "Everyone seems to forget that there's no way to fit a fully functional AI on the hardware that can be supported by a combat suit. Well, maybe some of those tank suits but even then, they have a host of other shit to keep running. For the last fucking time, there was no super-AI in that suit."

"If that is the case, how come everyone else seems to be convinced that you do?" Jackson asked. He simply stepped in and diverted Eben's focus on the questioning.

"Fuck if I know. But you asswipes are chasing this supposed holy grail, so wouldn't you be better off answering your own dumb question?"

"What happened during the robbery exactly?" the FBI agent demanded to force a return to his line of questioning. He directed that one in particular to Zhang, who still leaned against a nearby wall instead of on his crutches.

"I thought you read the report," Vickie commented.

"I did," he lied. "Now, I want to make sure Zhang's report is the same as the one he gave before."

The mechanic looked squarely at him and shrugged. "Will you help to help find the bastards?"

"Answer the question."

"Right. Okay. The assholes broke in, shot me, dislocated her arm, and shot us up with some kind of tranquilizer. They took the suit and ran the fuck off. Now you answer the question."

"He won't and honestly, I'm relieved." McFadden chuckled. "I doubt law enforcement will bother and all I want is my suit. If they could get it, they wouldn't give it back.

They think it's a magical suit with an impossible amount of storage in it."

"Does that mean that you won't attempt to find it yourself?" the FBI agent asked

He laughed and it wasn't a pleasant sound. "What the hell do you think? Some asshat shot my friend, dislocated my other friend's arm, and then stole what I need to earn my living. So yeah, color me pissed the fuck off, and I wouldn't hold my breath waiting for any of you to try to find it while arguing about who has the smallest dick."

The man had a look about him that made Eben's mouth go dry. Banks could be intimidating in her own right, he supposed, but McFadden projected something altogether different that made him fight the urge to step back.

"That's illegal," he whispered and realized that his throat didn't quite work the way he wanted it to.

"These assholes messed with my family and my belongings. There's no goddammed way I'll let them get away with it. If you want to find them first, go right ahead, but don't get in my fucking way."

"Are you saying you intend to break the law?" He could only hope the answer was something he could use to pin McFadden down with.

"I'm saying I intend to find my suit and make sure justice is served. After that, I don't give a continental what you do with the bastards."

## CHAPTER ELEVEN

It wasn't often that Fabio truly wished he hadn't put his phone on speaker. There had been a few times when he thought he might have avoided a little embarrassment if he had simply decided to take a call the traditional way, but it wasn't the kind of thing he generally castigated himself over.

Hell, if people chose to listen in on his calls, they would probably hear some explicit shit. That was essentially a given, and if they were embarrassed by it, that was their problem.

This was not one of those times.

Leonard's eyes were wide and he stared at him like he wasn't sure what he'd heard. The lead researcher didn't want to explain the matter to his assistant. It was easier to simply allow his brain to process everything at its own pace until he realized that he'd listened to someone die through the phone.

"What...the fuck was that?" the man asked and fumbled

for a seat. It was uncommon for the Brit, as obsessed with manners as he was, to not even ask before he sat. Still, his sudden lack of etiquette was entirely understandable.

"God, I..." Fabio paused, dragged his hand over his face, and tried to focus himself as he sat as well. Libby had called him for a reason—to warn him about something. She had already been too late to stop it on her side but he suspected that she'd tried to hopefully help others avoid whatever had killed her.

After a moment, he stood, moved to his desk, and pressed the button that accessed the building's intercom.

"This is not a drill," he said and grimaced as his voice echoed through the building. "I repeat, this is not a drill. Initiate emergency protocol for section twenty-seven. Evacuate all personnel and activate full containment procedures now!"

He waited for a moment, hoping to hear from the project leader in the section. The silence was deafening and the minutes dragged on with no sign that anyone would respond. All he could hope was that it was a little too early for the full staff to be present to answer.

Leonard's phone rang and he answered it immediately. His face turned an ashen shade of grey.

"It's too late," he said softly. "Security reports that section twenty-seven has already gone dark. Twenty-six and twenty-five too. The assumption is that they've been overrun."

"Fuck!" Fabio pushed from his seat and strode out of the office with his assistant close behind. He was five steps away from his office before the first of the alarms blared.

As the others triggered in the rest of the building, he

realized it wasn't safe to simply move directly into the affected areas. It would be best to head out to those that were adjacent and see if the sections around them were contained.

Hassel, the leader of section twenty-four, was the first to greet him and looked both annoyed and perplexed. The German didn't like having his work interrupted and his bloodshot eyes suggested he'd finished an all-nighter, which no doubt made things worse.

"Is the situation contained in twenty-five?" Fabio asked immediately.

"As far as I can tell, yes," Hassel replied and rubbed his eyes. "But we're not equipped to deal with monsters. This facility has been designated strictly for plant material, not mutated Zoo creatures."

"What are you saying exactly?" he asked and stepped a little closer than he needed to. It was an understandable impulse, he supposed. At the moment, his heart was beating out a damn samba.

"I am saying that I don't know how long the containment will hold," the man snapped in return. "If the...Lord, I have no idea what they are, but if they decide to attack the doors—"

"What the hell happened?" Leonard demanded as he caught up. His face was flushed as he approached one of the observation windows but he paled visibly. "Oh, dear God, this cannot be real."

"Those the hell happened," Hassel replied and watched him warily like he was afraid the younger man was about to puke.

Fabio approached the window, drew a deep breath, and

tried to steel himself against whatever they would have to face.

The monsters matched what he remembered in the reports he'd read from the Zoo. Not exactly, though. These were a little different in all the wrong ways. They looked like the locusts that were so prevalent in the jungle, but their carapaces were larger and darker. When they moved, it was with purpose and their abdomens flicked like shorter, stubbier tails that had long, thin stingers at the end. He'd never seen anything like them or even heard of similar creatures in the past.

Dozens of them worked to pick up the humans they'd killed, drag the bodies to patches of dirt that had been dug up, and bury them in large groups.

A few didn't participate, however. Fabio leaned closer to the glass and frowned when he realized they had their tails in the ground and looked like they were pumping something in.

"We can only assume the eggs were in the fertilizer, somehow," Hassel explained and shook his head. "But none of us saw anything when it was spread. They didn't even show in the tests, which means that they must have been minute—microscopic, in fact—which makes it unfathomable to think that they could have grown so large so quickly. They killed seven of our best workers before we managed to scramble the containment, even before your announcement."

Fabio stepped away from the windows and tried to resist the urge to throw up too. It was unsettling that he hadn't thought about the people who had died, only about his culpability in the situation.

And what was worse, Libby's whole team was probably dead by now. She had probably dialed him when she realized there was nothing to be salvaged from her project.

"The bodies," he whispered. "They...they took the bodies. Were you able to retrieve any of them?"

"No, they dragged them away with every kill to the point of ignoring all else around them. Like the bodies were what they wanted all along, not to defend themselves or others."

He could taste bile in his mouth. It was an unsettling thought but the buck stopped with him. Hassel was right in saying the containment was not built to hold monsters, and if they didn't act quickly, they would face a much larger death toll than they had already.

"Evacuate the facility," he whispered and clenched his fists as tightly as he could. "Activate the containment procedures in each section. It might not stop them but it will at least slow them. Set every alarm we have and get the hell out of here."

"The whole facility?"

"The whole goddammed facility!" Fabio snapped before he dragged in another breath and composed himself. "Look. You have two choices. First, you can do what I say and we'll save the lives of those who are still alive in here and hopefully contain these creatures before they push into those sections where there is nothing at all to stop them. Or two, you don't do it or you procrastinate, and many more of our people will end up like those bastards— biomass for the Zoo's latest experiment."

He pointed through the windows, unable to bring himself to look again.

"Biomass?"

"Yes, biomass. Using the bodies of humans and other creatures to feed the growth process. The Zoo needs biomass to expand and it's currently trying to expand through this fucking facility. Now for God's sake, man, get your ass into gear and evacuate."

Hassel looked like he still had his doubts. "But...the CEO—"

"He will simply have to see reason," Fabio interrupted. "He hired me to make these kinds of calls and if he thinks I'm wrong... Well, he can stay in here and take his chances. What is critical is to secure this as best we can and contact the authorities to send the experts in. Now get on with it. I'll have to brief the boss and make a call to Sustainagrow in the US. God only knows what has happened to Libby's project, but if it's anything like what happened here, the word clusterfuck fails to fully capture the enormity of the problems they are facing. They have none of the containment features we have, which means those monsters are on the loose on the outskirts of the Algerian desert and no one is any the wiser."

---

Pulling all-nighters didn't have the same feeling it used to. Anja had done it so often that it almost felt uninspiringly normal. Her sleep schedule was so screwed that it was like she worked a night shift instead of going all day and all night.

"Fuck, I'm getting old," the Russian hacker whispered,

stretched lazily in her chair until it creaked, and straightened again.

Of course, it was easier to slip into a bad sleep schedule when the compound was a little more deserted. And now that Madigan had dragged Sal off despite his sleepy but vociferous protests, it would be even easier to be bad. Still, it was good to know the woman was letting him out again. She was worried that his lack of Zoo outings would make him unfit, although Anja doubted it. There was no real evidence of that being the case.

If anything, he looked healthier and fitter than ever.

A soft ping on her computer brought her attention back to one of the screens and told her she'd received a message. It would also continue to blink until she looked at it.

As if she needed more alerts like that. She sighed softly, shook her head, and pressed the alert icon to open a chat window.

*Icarus147: Consider the information I am about to share at least one of the favors I owe you,* the message read.

She smiled and typed a response.

*Vermillionvelvet: I'll be the judge of that but I'm listening.*

*Icarus147: A potential client contacted me regarding a company they want to infiltrate.*

Anja narrowed her eyes, held her breath, and waited while the indicator told her Icarus was typing again.

*Icarus147: I did some research. It seems they have a strong connection to another company you are more intimately acquainted with.*

She exhaled a deep sigh. At least it wasn't Heavy Metal. Having to call Madigan and Sal back to deal with a possible threat was the kind of thing she didn't look forward to.

*Icarus147: I refused the job on the basis that I make a point of not fucking with leprechauns.*

Huh. Not very succinct, that.

*Vermillionvelvet: I understand.*

She didn't understand, of course, but it was something a short search could shine some light on. Failing that, Sal would probably know. She was sure they would be back in a few hours and would head directly to the showers. Once they were finished, she could ask.

Unless they went straight to bed. It was something they did fairly often and which usually necessitated another shower.

Anja grimaced. That was a thought that she didn't need in her head—and one Connie didn't need in her head either.

Another message pinged to catch her attention.

*Icarus: I referred them to you.*

*Vermillionvelvet: Why would you do that?*

*Icarus147: Because I think you'll have a vested interest in perhaps trying to trace them. A friend of a friend and all that.*

*Vermillionvelvet: What did you tell them?*

*Icarus147: That you're better than me.*

The hacker smirked.

*Vermillionvelvet: I am.*

*Icarus147: Not for long. Is that a favor redeemed?*

*Vermillionvelvet: Yes. One favor redeemed. Three left.*

The chat window shut down immediately and she leaned back in her chair. It squeaked again and she shook her head as she stared at her now blank screen.

"Connie, what's the definition of a leprechaun?"

The AI didn't answer immediately. "Seriously?"

"English is my…third language, so cut me some slack."

Connie uttered a sound that might have been a sigh but it was garbled and hard to hear. "A leprechaun, Irish term, also known as leipreachán or luchorpán, is a diminutive supernatural being in Irish folklore classed by some as a type of solitary fairy. They are usually depicted as little bearded men wearing a coat and hat, who partake in mischief, as the quickest of Google searches would show you."

"Yeah, but it's quicker to ask you. Thanks!"

She cut Connie off from the speaker system before she went on a profanity-laden tirade. While it was good to know what a leprechaun was, she hated to say that it didn't answer any of the questions she had.

"I'll have to ask Sal," she whispered and called up the suit trackers on her GPS. Thankfully, he and Madigan were both still in transmission range.

Anja immediately opened a commlink with the two of them.

"Hey, Sal, do you have a minute?"

"Yes," he replied and sounded only slightly out of breath.

"No, he doesn't," Madigan snapped before the hacker could speak.

"We were due for a little break anyway," he disagreed. "What's up?"

"Do you know any little bearded Irish men?"

"Is…is this a trick question? No, I don't think so."

"Is she talking about a leprechaun?" Madigan interjected. "Seriously, Anja, I would steer clear of this."

"Oh, a leprechaun," Sal said quickly. "Wait, hold on. Taylor McFadden—what about him?"

"As I recall, he is of Scottish descent and about as far away from small as one can be," Anja reminded him.

"No, no, that's what people called him. Well, behind his back. Most of the time. What is this about?"

"A friend of mine in the hacking world said he turned a job down because, and I quote, he did not want to fuck with a leprechaun. He then passed the job on to me."

"What kind of job?"

"Data infil and exfil. He said the target company was one we are familiar with."

"That certainly sounds like McFadden," Madigan agreed.

"I can't think of any reason why someone would want to infiltrate M and B's systems," he muttered. "But we should at least give them a heads-up. Maybe they'll know more about the situation than we do."

"Agreed." The woman sounded a little more worried. Perhaps she knew something he didn't. "Do you think you can trace the source of the request without compromising Heavy Metal?"

"Bi—please," Anja caught herself before she called Madigan something that would piss the woman off. "They're looking for the best hacker in the business. That means they don't already have the best. If I'm careful, I should be able to find something that sheds light on the situation. I'll keep you updated."

"Do that," Sal answered and sounded a little more pensive now. "In the meantime, I can give Taylor a call and fill him in. At least these dickheads will wait for whoever takes the job after Anja runs them around and then refuses. You should delay the process as much as you can."

"If there's one thing I can do, it's delay the process," she replied with a grin.

## CHAPTER TWELVE

"I think that went very well when all is said and done," Vickie commented as she cut her room-service steak into small, bite-sized pieces. "Okay, yes, they took my phone. And my laptop. And my tablet. And most of my computer equipment."

Taylor nodded and bit into one of his fries. "We have more, right? And now, when they give it all back, you'll have two of everything."

"Yay, that's all a girl's ever wanted." She rolled her eyes.

"I would have preferred to not have to deal with the FBI or the DOD again," Niki commented and sipped her drink, "but Vickie's right. It could have gone much worse. If we hadn't had the warning, the chances are they would have taken Nessie. I still doubt they would have been able to find her in that whole mess of a system, but at least it worked out, right? They'll deliver all our equipment in a few days and we can get back to finding the bastards who took the suit."

"Will we wait until then?" Taylor asked.

"Well, they'll probably still have us under surveillance until then, and you saw that shithead FBI agent. He was waiting for you to take a wrong step. We need to play this a little more carefully than we would have otherwise."

"And we need to find a way to make sure they can't pin anything on us," Vickie muttered and popped one of the pieces of steak into her mouth. "I bet I could give their equipment all kinds of headaches that would let us slip in and out of the hotel unnoticed, even with the equipment we have now."

"Are you sure?" Niki's eyes narrowed.

"Hell, I have their bugs listening to cable network news right now instead of us. And Desk would be able to help. They'll wonder why we have the TVs on so loud for the next twenty-four hours or so."

"We might want to wait until we have a solid target to act on," Taylor cautioned. "As much as I want to break the spine of the asshole who hurt Bobby and Tanya, he'll probably not have much intel that we don't already have."

"Pardon me," Desk interrupted through the new TV that the hotel had provided. "But it would appear that you have a call."

"A call?" Niki narrowed her eyes.

"Yes, from one Captain Sergio Gallo. A call from Italy."

"Ugh, asshole Italian cops," she muttered and rolled her eyes but quickly slapped a small smile on. "Send it through but warn him that we're having dinner."

"Of course. One moment."

The screen displayed a familiar face, although Taylor could see a twitch of annoyance flicker across Niki's features before she smiled fully.

"Captain Gallo. We didn't expect to hear from you so soon after the last time," she said.

"Hello, and I apologize for intruding on your meal," Gallo said, a little red in the face and, for lack of a better word, flustered.

"We assumed it was some kind of crisis if you were calling at this hour," Taylor said before Niki could make a sharp remark.

"It is. We have received an emergency call from one of our research facilities two hours from Tropea."

"What is it with your facilities these days?" Niki asked and paused before she took a mouthful of her steak. "Ours faced wave after wave at one point too but in our defense, there are many more of them in the US."

"The facility was designed specially to investigate the flora of the Zoo," the captain explained. "They very seldom had anything to do with the fauna and if they did, they only accepted dead samples that were collected. Yet somehow, they have had an infestation of Zoo-type mutants. According to preliminary reports, it started when they received samples of rabbit feces to study as an urgent request from somewhere close to the Zoo."

"Rabbits?" Taylor asked. He raised an eyebrow and looked at Niki.

"As in…fucking cotton-ball-tailed bunnies?" she asked in disbelief and shook her head.

He shared her confusion. The last they'd ever heard of bunnies being associated with the Zoo was when their DNA was used to make rhinos at a dime a dozen, but he'd assumed that the rabbit DNA had been brought in from outside. If the critters had been on-site at the illegal facility, he certainly hadn't seen them and it wasn't a stretch to accept that the defenseless animals had all died in the Zoo attack.

"I believe that fucking is what rabbits are best known for, yes," Gallo replied with a rare hint of amusement. "But it seems these also produced an abundance of the feces that appears to be the cause of the problem. As McFadden and Banks were so effective with our last difficulty, I am confident that you would be able to handle this one as well. I can send you the contact details for the research director of the facility so you can make more direct contact for the information I might have missed."

"Who will fund the operation?" Niki asked. "You know —cover the traveling costs, weapons permits, and all the shit we had to do the last time."

"Antech Laboratories will pay all fees and cover all costs," Gallo replied. "But the Italian government will arrange your transport to ensure that you will be able to bring your suits and any equipment you might need. How does this sound to you?"

Taylor looked at his companions. Neither woman voiced any disagreement and he couldn't think of anything. They were still a business, after all, and needed to bring the bucks in to stay solvent.

"We'll take the job," he said.

The captain immediately looked relieved. "Excellent. I will contact you with the details shortly. *Buona serata.*"

The line cut and left the TV dark again as Taylor exchanged a look with Vickie and Niki. He waited for them to say something.

"We still have the idiot Ralph Hinderman to call on," the

hacker reminded them around another piece of steak. "It's not exactly something we can leave up in the air since he could go dark at any second. Do you think we can squeeze a visit in before your trip to Italy?"

Before Taylor could answer, Desk called them on the television again.

"I again apologize for intruding." The AI sounded a little angry herself, he noted. "But a Fabio Bernadi is calling for you."

"Fabio who the hell now?" Niki asked. "Is that the guy with the bare chest on all those trashy romance novels from the eighties and nineties?"

"Dr. Fabio Bernadi of Antech Laboratories."

"Oh." Taylor grunted. "Put him through, I guess."

Another face—this time unfamiliar—appeared on the screen. The man wore thick glasses but otherwise appeared to be the salt-and-pepper version of the Italian stud—in decent shape, his hair slicked back stylishly, and his powerful jawline sprinkled with a trace of bristle.

"Dr. Barnadi?" Taylor asked. "I'm sorry, but you caught us in the middle of our dinner. How can we help you?"

"It is I who must apologize for the intrusion," Bernadi said and shook his head. "I am calling as Captain Gallo has informed me that you will assist us with our problem and I needed to speak to you immediately."

"We have the credentials, Doc," Vickie told him with a cheerful smile. "There's no need to worry about that. Talk to Gallo if you think I'm lying."

"It is not that. I thought you should be properly informed of what you might face before you make the trip. It was...an eye-opener for me."

"Most Zoo fuckers are," Taylor told him.

"Yes, and yet there was something different about these. For one thing, you should know that the monsters appeared to have birthed themselves from the rabbit pellets. My theory is that somehow, there were eggs in the pellets that allowed them to sprout and grow. I know this sounds crazy but it is the only theory I have on how the monsters appeared out of nowhere. The only other explanation is that the goop somehow created them from nothing, which is even crazier."

"As amazing as it might sound, that's not the craziest thing we've ever seen come out of the Zoo, Doc," he assured the man.

"I agree. I have studied the jungle for about as long as it has been around—albeit at a distance—and yet I've never heard of the creatures taking the bodies of the dead and burying them, but that might explain why bodies are never found. I confess, my focus is primarily flora, not fauna, so I am not an expert at all. Nor have I ever seen what looked like these...locust creatures with tails and stingers that appeared to pump something into the ground from those stingers. The only possibility that springs to my mind is that they were collecting biomass with the bodies, but I cannot explain how they were pumping what I assume to be the goop into the soil. It seems as though they can somehow produce it themselves, as there was simply not enough of it in the fertilizer that was sent."

Taylor frowned at that and he leaned back in his seat and stroked his beard absently.

"Huh," was all he could produce in response.

"You should also be warned that our containment

protocols in the facility were designed to deal with the spread of plants through pollen or roots and the like, not for rabid Zoo monsters determined to colonize Earth. I cannot stress enough that this is a situation of the utmost urgency. You need to deal with the monsters before they break out into the countryside and from there, Tropea. The town has over six thousand people who could be dead in hours."

He nodded. "We'll make this job our top priority, Doctor. We're already making plans with your government to fly to Italy and should be ready to get the job done before long."

"That will be most appreciated." Interestingly, the man did not look relieved in the least. "You will likely also receive a call from Sustainagrow. They are an NGO in the US. One of their projects was located on the fringes of the Algerian Sahara and focused on providing sustainable crop production using tunnel systems. The sample of the fertilizer was sent by their project leader, and I am utterly convinced they had a similar outbreak at their project site and that the entire team is dead."

Taylor made a note of that and nodded. "We'll take that under consideration, Doctor. Thanks for calling."

The line cut out and he shook his head.

Niki appeared to share in the sentiment. "God spare me from idiots and greedy profiteers. We all know where those goddamn rabbits came from, right?"

"First rhinos and now bunnies?" Vickie asked, equally disgusted. "Someone needs to catch these bastards and string them up. You know, after someone's beaten the crap out of them."

He chuckled softly. "Well, as much fun as that will be, we need to consider the fact that we now have three vital operations to deal with. As far as I can tell, we can only be in one place at a time. The site in Algeria is critical since there isn't any containment in place. Italy is only marginally less critical since they do have some plant-stopping containment, but we're looking at a massacre if the outbreak…uh, you know, breaks out."

Vickie sighed and pushed up from her seat. "It seems like we'll need some coffee to solve this."

No one contradicted her and she crossed to the hotel's free cappuccino machine.

"What do you think our options are?" Niki asked.

Taylor shrugged. "How do we deal with the problem at home first so it doesn't fester and kill us all while we're off saving the world?"

"We could always send the freelancers to deal with Hinderman," Niki suggested as Vickie returned with three cups of coffee. "They could probably deliver the message we want sent and they're not on the FBI's watchlist either. It won't be as satisfying as doing it person, though."

"Were you considering tagging along?" Taylor asked and took a sip from his coffee.

"Fuck yeah. I want to see that asshole get his payback, although I guess that won't happen. Still, maybe we can use the feed from their suits. They would wear suits, wouldn't they?"

He nodded. "We need a message sent, and a team arriving to beat the crap out of the guy in full combat suits would send that message. The 'you do not want to fuck with us' kind of message."

"You'd think people would have the idea after the...fifth time you've sent that message," Vickie muttered.

Niki nodded. "Sending the freelancers would also tell our thieves that they're not high enough on the food chain to be worthy of our personal attention—that they are the kind of problem the hired help can deal with. It might challenge whoever is behind the whole thing to reveal themselves inadvertently."

Before Taylor could answer, another call came up on the TV. He had a feeling the Americans had now entered the equation.

"I'm so sorry to interru—"

He raised a hand to stop the portly, red-headed man from continuing. "Yeah, we were told that one of your project sites has probably fallen to a Zoo incursion. Let's start there."

"Oh. Yes, of course. I'm Phillip Lowenstein, the operations director of Sustainagrow."

"Hi, Phillip." Vickie waved at the TV with her fork.

"I...hello." He looked a little startled and shook his head. "I was informed that the local government was alerted and sent a military contingent to monitor the situation, but I fear they are ill-equipped to handle a Zoo incursion. They would, however, be on hand to assist your team, but they are adamant that they do not want the US military to intervene unless it proves absolutely necessary."

"Yeah, we do have a bad history with our military interventions, don't we?" Niki commented.

Taylor tried to force a smile. "We're in the process of finalizing the logistics for this mission, Mr. Lowenstein.

Rest assured, we know what we're doing and we'll let you know when there are any updates."

"Oh, thank you, thank you so much."

"You have a good evening, sir," Vickie interjected when she saw Taylor about to cut the call. "You were seconds away from being rude," she reprimanded sternly when the man was off the line.

"I'm hungry," he said, defensively. "And...annoyed." He sighed. "And you're right. Thank you for stepping in."

She smirked at him but for once, held back any snarky retort she was probably dying to add.

"So what do you suggest, McFadden?" Niki queried. "Now that it's down to you and me? I don't think I'm ready to handle something like this completely on my own, although I'd give it my best shot."

He smirked. "That's not even an option. We need to get in touch with our second team. Once that's done, we can decide where to go from there. Desk, can you get the free-lancers on the line?"

"Already done," the AI replied.

CHAPTER THIRTEEN

Something was most certainly wrong. He'd suspected it but had hoped it was a temporary aberration and would pass.

Now, however, he forced himself to acknowledge the reality. Something had been wrong for a while. Frank had watched Julian carefully and there was something to be said about his quiet, reserved demeanor that still managed to claw to the top as psycho CEO.

Correction—rich people weren't psycho, they were eccentric, he reminded himself, leaned back in his seat, and studied the man as objectively and unobtrusively as he could. Whatever the term was, he'd cannonballed into the deep end and forgot his water wings.

It was a shame, it truly was. He and Transk had always seemed to be on the same wavelength and it would be tough to find another boss he meshed with so effectively.

He folded his arms and regretted his decision to turn down a drink at the beginning of the meeting and tried to not make his concern too obvious.

"You've had time to look for your hacker," Julian said

finally after a deep breath. "And you said you found the best, right?"

"Sure." Palumbo stretched forward to nudge the files he'd put together across the desk again for the man's attention. "We found three of the best and offered them considerable money and freedom to work on the job as they saw fit. Two of them declined on the grounds that they had prior commitments they couldn't get rid of it, and the third... Well, he had other issues."

"What?"

He shifted his gaze, unsure how to break it to the man.

"Frank, if you choose to start playing the mute with me now, I will be very, very pissed off."

"Fine." He nodded and decided to simply say it. "He said, and I quote, that he makes a point of not fucking with leprechauns."

"Leprechauns?" Transk laughed and shook his head. "What the hell do leprechauns have to do with anything?"

It wasn't like the man to forget even minor details, which was another sign that all was not as it should have been. The awareness drew a sigh from Frank as he straightened in his seat.

"As you remember, McFadden had many nicknames during his time in the Zoo. Leprechaun was one of them, despite the fact that his size contradicts the idea of him being a tiny Irish man guarding a pot of gold."

His boss took a deep breath, cleared his throat, and rocked back in his seat as a pensive look slid across his face.

"So it looks like the guy's reputation precedes him, even on the dark web. And that this hacker, whoever he is, appears to know something about McFadden and Banks."

"At least enough that he doesn't want to risk taking paying work if it means going up against them," Frank agreed.

"Will that be a problem?"

He shrugged. "I doubt it. These hacker types aren't the kind you call in to hold the line or that kind of shit. They'll cover their asses first and foremost, so it's logical that he would do a little research. One wrong decision could have disastrous consequences. His type thrives on anonymity and I think this is purely a choice to avoid any situation that might compromise that."

Julian narrowed his eyes. "Do you think he knows about the AI?"

"While it's well-known that there is an AI hunt on, I doubt it. Remember that they have hired a hacker who is extremely skilled. She managed to fight Avery's earlier attempt off. It was after a long battle, sure, but at the end of the day, she did outclass him. It's more likely that he suspects they might have the ability to trace him. This particular hacker has two well-armed, ticked-off fighters with her, so I'd understand it if he preferred to not take the chance. Hackers are arrogant but they can be cautious to a fault as well."

"All the more reason to find an industry leader," Julian muttered and rubbed his chin irritably. "We need someone who knows how to match their people and how to stay a step ahead—or at least trusts us to keep them safe if they need it. Where do we go from this point?"

"There is an update on that." Frank nodded to the files

his boss still hadn't so much as looked at. "The last one referred us to someone he claimed is even better than they are. It's very unusual among these kinds of people for anyone to do that. They aren't the most respectful bunch. But if this person is as good as they say, the chances are they're involved in other projects and aren't on the market."

"Increase the contract price," Julian told him quickly. "Double it if you have to but get them on board. I want them to have dollar signs instead of pupils by the time you're finished pitching to them. Sooner or later, the feds or the DOD will find this and we'll have to take them on directly. I'd prefer to deal with a small company than the government if at all possible."

"Avery's kept an eye on what the alphabet agencies are up to, and he assures me that neither has made any progress on that front, so we're in the clear there for the moment. It's unlikely that they will make any progress anyway, given that they're using sub-par talent and unimaginative agents to get the job done."

"I don't deal in unlikely," the CEO said and shook his head. "You never know when some idiot with a computer or an agent who hasn't had a unique thought in ten years will get lucky, so get me that hacker and set our man to tracking them. We need to make sure there are no loose ends when they've delivered on the deal, even if it means paying a goodbye visit to the opposite end of the Earth. I don't give a continental anymore. I want that AI, understood?"

Frank nodded and pushed from his seat. "I'll get on it, boss."

That sounded more like the Julian Transk he knew, but

he could no longer trust him to stay that way. It was a little concerning to watch but he'd hitched his horse to this wagon. Whether he liked it or not, he would ride it to the bitter end.

---

"Taylor, you have a call."

He closed his eyes and tried not to let the annoyance bubbling in his chest overflow. The chances were he would launch into a shouting spree that would make Niki and Vickie rush in to see what was wrong. Running logistics was mentally exhausting and tended to go a little better when he was on his own with nothing and no one to distract him.

Desk hadn't gotten the memo yet, though.

"Who is it?" he asked and didn't look up from his computer screen.

"Dr. Salinger Jacobs says he would like a word with you. Should I ask him to call at another time?"

"No, I can take the call." He immediately straightened in his seat and shook his head. "I have to contact him anyway."

"I'll put the call through."

The TV screen showed the impossibly young doctor, who looked like he was talking to someone off-screen before he turned his attention to the conversation.

"Sal, nice to hear from you again," Taylor said and stretched his arms above his head. "I was about to call you about a problem that dropped into my lap."

"What a coincidence." The other man chuckled.

"Because a problem of yours dropped into my lap recently. Well, Anja's lap, but then she dropped it on me to deliver to you. Should we do yours first and then mine?"

"No, you called. It's only right that you get to share what has you in a bind."

"It isn't a bind as such—more an opportunity for you. So maybe calling it a problem wasn't the right choice of words. It might be a problem down the line, but if we nip it in the bud, it might be an opportunity. So, a friend of Anja's sent her a message saying they had received an offer from an interested party to attack you guys from cyber-sphere. He said he didn't want the job because he doesn't fuck with a leprechaun. I feel like that has something to do with you? Especially since he mentioned it was an issue with a company we were directly involved with and unless I missed any connections we might have with the little folk of Ireland, that was probably a reference to you."

The kid could talk, and talk fast. Taylor had a feeling he would benefit from taking recordings and playing it all back when he had the time, but that would have to wait. For now, he was left trying to determine the details while Sal sucked in a deep breath.

"Well, that's certainly the kind of heads-up we appreciate," he admitted and raised an eyebrow. "Did she happen to pick up on who put the job out there?"

"She's working on that. As a matter of fact, her friend referred the assholes to her so she could do as she pleased with the job. It's an interesting take on the concept, between you and me. With that said, I don't know why anyone would want to infiltrate your company, of course, but they are trying to recruit top-class talent for this, so I can only assume they're serious and they have significant cash to throw around. To hear Anja talk about it, her rates are well, well above the market average."

He nodded. "Let's say it has something to do with the AI I absolutely do not have in my suit." Despite the encryption and anti-intrusion blockages that Vickie and Desk had put in place, he couldn't be too sure that the conversation wouldn't somehow be discovered. It was best not to say anything that the FBI could use against him.

And it would probably be a good idea to give Sal a heads-up about what they were dealing with in case they started to give him trouble too.

"What do you mean?"

"The FBI, DOD, and some third parties have harassed me because they think I have an AI operating my combat suit with me. Even to the point that someone stole the suit itself from the shop."

"I don't—oh. Oh." Sal leaned back in his seat when he realized what Taylor was talking about and the underlying message in his words. "Well, you might want to get lawyers involved, right? If they're harassing you and even going so far as to rob you, there might be money in it—on top of stopping them from trying that shit again, of course."

"We're in the process of looking at the various options. What's worse is that the FBI and the DOD both obtained warrants to search my properties because they thought something like that was possible. The only issue is who else would be caught up in this mess? No one needs a horde of assholes all up in their business because they think you have something that's supposed to be impossible or some shit."

Sal nodded again and gave him a thumbs-up to thank him for the warning.

"It's a crazy fucking world we live in," the young doctor agreed and sighed. "I'll look around these parts to make sure no one else is getting harassed around the Zoo. You never know when these myths will get people hurt."

The message was across. It was on Sal to keep his team safe and off the radar of the assholes he was dealing with, given that his AI was quite proficient in working his suit too. The fact that they were affiliated with McFadden and Banks might well make people focus on them to see if they were an easier target.

Not that Heavy Metal was an easy target. Quite to the contrary. He'd seen what happened to the people who tried to fuck with the group in the past. It would be interesting to see whoever was after the AI try to find a way to deal with a compound defended better than most military bases. Of course, if the asshats did make the attempt, it would be game-over and all their problems would be solved. He wasn't averse to that kind of resolution, but he also hoped that the problem did not knock on Heavy Metal's door. What they were currently going through was not something you wished on your friends.

"Well, with that out the way, didn't you say you wanted to share something with me?" Sal asked, raised an eyebrow, and typed something into his laptop. Taylor assumed he was letting his resident Russian hacker know about what was happening to the M and B team and making sure they weren't at any risk of falling into the crosshairs of the same criminals.

"Right. We've been called to deal with a couple of outbreaks that have taken place. One is in Southern Italy."

"So, another day in the office for you guys?"

"Sure, but this one came with some...interesting addendums. The breakout we heard about first happened in a facility that was designed to contain plants, not animals, so you know that simply cannot end well. There was also talk about how the animals weren't even a part of the original testing. The lead researcher told us they were researching some...uh, rabbit shit and they said it was like eggs had spawned the creatures inside the facility. They couldn't think of any other way they could have gotten there, even though they couldn't find any trace of them."

"Bunny shit?"

"Yeah."

"Those goddamn fucking bunnies," Sal muttered. "I knew they'd come back to bite us but honestly, in the whole mess of the rescue mission, I didn't even think of the furry bastards."

'Yeah, me neither. Well...to be honest, when we didn't see them at the base, I assumed that maybe the DNA or whatever they used was extracted elsewhere and shipped in. I can honestly say I didn't even give them a second thought."

"Okay. So, you'll deal with that situation."

"And there's another one too. The origin of feces, if you will."

The researcher grinned at the joke but someone groaned in the background.

"Anyway, a small research facility on the edge of the Algerian desert brought the shit in as fertilizer and they had another outbreak—or that's the assumption, anyway. They are a little isolated from civilization but they didn't have any containment on their base, which means whatever was in there has probably escaped by now. The timeline, as far as I can tell, is that it all went to shit under ten hours ago."

The doctor's expression quickly turned serious as he leaned forward and his brows furrowed as he considered what he'd heard.

"Did they tell you anything about the creatures?"

Taylor nodded. "They said they looked like the locusts that are all over the jungle, but these had short tails on the abdomens. They supposedly pushed the stingers on those tails into the ground for whatever reason and also buried the people they killed, according to the research leader. He said something about them trying to form biomass to spread the Zoo, which I guess would happen in the Algerian facility too. And as you're aware, I can't be in two places at the same time and by the time I get there, the local military might already be decimated if the critters go rampant. And if they run into animals out there, they will spread like wildfire and we won't have the time or the opportunity to stop it before there are some serious casualty numbers."

"The Algerian military is there?"

"Strictly as observers, from what I was told."

"Shit. So, I assume you want us to take care of the Algerian case?"

"It makes more sense. You're much closer, for one thing, and the local government doesn't want intervention by any other official military but their own. Given that you guys are freelancers and local on top of it, they probably know about you, at least by reputation, which I'm told you guys have a fair amount of there."

Sal grinned. "Well, we're not as famous as the leprechaun but yeah, we do all right."

"Whatever." He rolled his eyes. "And you might be able to find out more about where the literal shit comes from. It's all very well saying the Zoo, but how? Either it's someone who stumbled onto the rabbits, captured them, and decided they had an easy money-spinner, or it's the same asshats who smuggled the horns. According to what Niki's told me about it, they still haven't been caught so they're probably up to no good around there."

"Stupid fucking bastards," Sal said and his tone suggested that a chill had come over the younger man when he thought about what they were facing in the Zoo. "Send me the details and I'll pull a team together. We'll get moving right away, given the urgency of the situation, but those Algerian army dudes have better have plasma throwers or they'll have to get over their issues with the US military but quick."

Taylor narrowed his eyes. "You know, if I didn't know better, I'd say you knew a little more about this than you're letting on."

"Don't I always?"

"Sure, but this time seems like it's far more than usual. Like you have some experience with something like this."

"I do, and believe me, calling it nightmare fuel is an insult to nightmare fuel all around the world. It's best to make sure it doesn't come to anything. Let's get to work."

CHAPTER FOURTEEN

Arranging the group meeting hadn't been easy, but Taylor made sure everyone knew the urgency of the matter they faced. The freelancers agreed to meet at the shop and wasted no time asking questions. It was a professional response and left him feeling even more certain that they would be able to handle their roles without issues.

He wasn't sure how Bobby would react to having the whole team there when he was supposed to be working, but he had a feeling he wouldn't do much work anyway, not this late in the evening.

Tanya still had her arm in a sling and the mechanic's leg was in a splint to stop him from moving it. When they arrived, Taylor was happy to see his friend seated next to his workbench, which had been lowered to accommodate him while he worked with his injured leg propped up. Tanya worked as a glorified gofer to bring everything he needed and even helped with anything on the bench he couldn't quite reach.

The only member of the team who looked like she was

working as she usually did was Elisa, who smiled and waved as Taylor, Niki, and Vickie pulled up.

Niki still didn't offer the woman anything other than a grunted greeting and muttered something that Taylor felt lucky to not have heard.

"Should I charge you for using the shop as a conference room now?" Bobby asked without looking up from where he worked on a small, fragile-looking piece of electrical equipment.

"If you need the money that badly, sure."

"Fuck you."

Taylor grinned but Tanya looked apologetic.

"He's been in a bad mood. Not being able to walk without crutches isn't his idea of a good time."

"Whose idea of a good time is it?" the mechanic snorted in disgust.

"People who like laying around all day," Vickie told him. "And having someone wait on them hand and foot while they recover. Being injured sucks, but there are a few silver linings mixed in there, right?"

"That's what I've tried to tell him," Tanya complained. "So when will your freelancers arrive?"

"Two of them were already in Vegas. Chezza was visiting family in San Francisco, but she caught the first available flight and should be coming in soon."

"Her flight has touched down already," Vickie said as she checked her phone. "Jiro and Trick both said they're a few minutes out. Honestly, Taylor, what would you do without me?"

"Crash and burn, duh," he muttered. "Or, more likely, simply fly by the seat of my pants and probably die in a horrific surprise attack by killer Zoo-penguins."

The sound of cars pulling up to the entrance caught their attention. Trick was driving an older Chevy pickup and Jiro came in behind him in a Honda sedan.

Before they were parked, a Buick turned into the parking lot, which he assumed was Chezza's. He wasn't sure if it was her car or a rental, although he thought he'd seen them driving it a couple of times.

"It's good to see you guys again," Taylor called and waved for them to join him where they were gathered close to Bobby's workbench.

The mechanic still didn't look up from his work.

"Are we heading to Italy again?" Chezza asked.

"Niki and I are," he said. "And we're meeting here because I want us to get the equipment we'll use for the mission and leave directly. We're facing something of a crisis on three fronts, which means it's time to delegate some of the shit. That's where you come in."

"Yeah?" she asked and narrowed her eyes. "Are those the suits you'll be using?"

He nodded.

"What happened to the one you usually use?" Jiro asked. "The one with the limbs sprouting from your back?"

"It's been...misappropriated," Taylor muttered and shook his head.

"Stolen?" Trick asked.

"Misappropriated," he insisted. "These suits are second-hand but Bobby's put considerable work in to make them top-of-the-line—better than almost anything we could find on the market, anyway."

The mechanic only grumbled something under his breath as he continued to work.

"Taylor, I've been alerted that a flight has already been arranged by the Italian government and will be ready to take off in the next few hours," Desk told him over the speakers in the shop.

"You guys remember Desk, right?" he asked and looked around.

They all nodded but he recalled that they still didn't know she was an AI—exactly like he hadn't back in the day. They probably thought she was an operative who provided overwatch for the team and preferred to use a code name to protect her identity.

"In fairness, I'm very sure we won't need to use an eight-limbed suit to deal with the mutants we expect to encounter," Niki said acidly. "And there's the small matter that it's what triggered the other issues we're facing."

"Is that why it was stolen?" Chezza asked.

"Misappropriated is the term we're going with," Vickie reminded her.

Taylor didn't want to talk about how he would miss having Nessie in the suit with him, especially as Niki would probably give him grief over it.

"So, what will we do?" Jiro asked.

Bobby's gaze lifted from his work to watch Jiro suspiciously, although Taylor had a feeling it was probably due to the fact that the man idly juggled two knives in the shop while Trick and Chezza began to move the suits they would use.

"You'll deal with one of the problems we're facing," he explained. "The issue with the suit that was stolen."

"Misappropriated," Chezza corrected him, approached the group, and caught one of the knives her teammate was juggling.

He snapped her a glance but after a moment of unspoken conversation between them, he sighed and sheathed the blades again, and Bobby relaxed a little.

"Right," Niki said briskly. "Ralph Hinderman is your target and Vickie will let you have all the relevant details. Your objective is two-fold. First, squeeze the bastard for all the details you can get out of him. His boss, teammates, and his boss' boss if that's possible. Secondly, one bullet to the lower leg below the knee and a dislocated right arm."

"That seems...very specific," Trick noted and his gaze drifted to Bobby's leg and Tanya's arm.

"It is," Taylor agreed. "There's a very simple message that goes with it too—don't fuck with McFadden and Banks and leave their family alone. Very damn succinct, wouldn't you say?"

"Yeah," Niki continued. "We don't care which order those two objectives follow each other in, as long as the information is obtained and the message is delivered. The bottom line is that these assholes took something that belongs to us and we want it back."

"The suit, I guess," Chezza commented.

"Which means these assholes misappropriated something that belongs to us," Jiro added.

"Correct." Niki tried to keep her face straight. "Ralph Hinderman isn't the mastermind of the team so he shouldn't pose any real problems. We're after bigger fish and he can point us in the right direction. Don't kill him unless he leaves you no choice. I believe that tit-for-tat retribution will leave a bigger impression than a body. We want to kick the hornet's nest here, and if he's alive and has the guts to run to his leader, we'll be around to follow and swoop in before they can disappear or send word up the food chain."

"Don't be seen and don't be caught." Taylor leaned on a nearby wall. "This is a ghost visit. We do not want to alert any of the local law enforcement and with us on a flight, if something is leaked, everyone will assume it's some other group and fall over themselves looking for clues you won't leave."

The three nodded and he liked that while a few jokes were in evidence, he could see they were paying attention. With Vickie overseeing the operation, he had little doubt that they would do what was needed.

Besides, urban warfare was more up their alley anyway, even if they had a talent for handling monsters.

"I'll stay in touch with you guys for the duration," Vickie said to avoid a lull in the conversation. "Looping cameras, keeping the police away, et cetera. I'll also monitor the target's cell phone and the physical address in case we find ourselves with any unexpected surprises on the way. Pull it off like a Bob Ross painting."

"Bob Ross?" Trick asked.

"You know...all accidents will be happy little accidents. What? Too obscure?"

"A little," Taylor muttered. "Have you even seen any of the Bob Ross episodes?"

"Of course not, but his legacy lives on." The hacker cleared her throat. "Anyway, we rented a panel van under a false name for you guys to use. You only need to load the suits and you'll be ready to go. It'll be big enough for you guys to suit up in there so you don't have to drive around town in them."

Taylor heard a soft crunch and looked to where Vickie sat beside Elisa with a large bowl between them.

"Is that…popcorn?" Niki asked.

The hacker grinned. "Hell yeah. Bobby, Tanya, Elisa, and I are set up for prime-time viewing. We all need to see that asshole on the receiving end of our message. It isn't as good as being there in the flesh but this is the next best thing."

"You're a bloodthirsty little savage," Niki commented with a deep frown.

"Hi there, Pot, my name's Kettle. Have we met?" The girl stuffed another handful of popcorn into her mouth. "Besides, I only get like this when it comes to family."

Trick shook his head. "Wait, so is this Ralph shithead the one who stole—"

"Misappropriated," Chezza corrected him.

"The one who misappropriated your suit?"

Taylor nodded. "Him and a team of at least three others. But he shot Bobby and injured Tanya, so we want to stress the matter of revenge while we still get the business done. Any questions?"

"Why are we doing this in our suits?" Chezza asked. "We could do the job equally as well in masks and shit."

"There's the intimidation factor, obviously," Niki pointed out. "I'm not saying the guy will shit himself when three multiple-ton suits put the pressure on him but we hope that's the reaction we'll get. Hiding your full identity is another. We don't want him to be able to identify even your voices, so you'll be able to speak to him through modulators. As long as you avoid names and such when speaking aloud, he'll have no way to identify you aside from the suits themselves."

"Which will merely identify you as part of the McFadden and Banks team," Taylor added. "There's no chance that any of the possible repercussions will impact any of you directly."

"What will the compensation look like?" Trick asked.

"Not...quite as much as the last time," he answered. "Vickie will cover that in the details she sends you but it should still be a decent amount for an evening's work, I think."

Vickie nodded. "Anything else?"

"Nah." Chezza cracked her knuckles. "Let's get this asshole."

---

She hadn't expected them to open a line of communication so quickly. Anja almost coughed up a gulp of coffee when her computer pinged to tell her a message from an unknown sender was waiting for her.

Tracing it probably wouldn't lead to much. They would probably try to trace her but she doubted they'd get very far either.

And if they got past the first two proxies, it would trip an alarm and cut the connection, so she liked to think she was ready for almost anything that could be thrown her way.

The Russian drew a deep breath, rolled her neck, and opened the chat room.

There was no immediate message waiting for her aside from the request to open a chat room but a few seconds later, it showed that the person on the other side was typing.

*Crypticrover9: We've been told you're the best in the business.*

Opening with flattery wasn't the most subtle of approaches.

*Marauder1: You were told right. What do you need?*

She took another sip of her coffee and scowled at the icon that showed a message was being typed.

*Crypticrover9: We need an infil on a company's electronics and the exfil of certain files.*

A smirk crossed her face as she began to type a response. There was no need to make things too easy for them.

*Marauder1: My services don't come cheap and I don't waste my time with petty civil lawsuits or even the average kind of corporate espionage.*

*Crypticrover9: What does it matter as long as we pay your rates?*

*Marauder1: Money is all well and good but I don't need my name attached to anything that will show up in a courtroom document. It's a matter of pride and I don't trust you to not turn me over to some judge for your CEO to get a shorter jail sentence in a golf resort-turned min-sec prison.*

*Crypticrover9: I can assure you that the delivery of the files will be the end of your involvement.*

*Marauder1: Oh, if you give me your word, I'm sure I can*

*trust you. By the way, my name is Marauder1. It's on my driver's license.*

Anja rolled her eyes. If they wanted to play the bait and switch game, she wasn't interested. This was the easiest way to get information out of them, and if they wanted her to work with them, they would have to provide a little information.

*Crypticrover9: There's no need for attitude. This is a business negotiation.*

*Marauder1: Is this a business negotiation? I thought it was some random troll on the Internet jerking me around. I have absolutely no reason to take you seriously at this point.*

*Crypticrover9: You were referred to us by one of your colleagues.*

*Marauder1: You are new to this, aren't you? I don't know him personally and he doesn't know me. All he knows about me is that I'm the best freelancer, and that's because I drilled that point home. I think it was around the seventy-fourth pineapple and anchovy pizza that he finally admitted defeat. If you want me to work with you on this, I'll need a little more from you.*

*Crypticrover9: How much more?*

*Marauder1: You're the one who came to me for this. I have other work to get back to. Pique my professional interest.*

There was a pause in the chat and Anja took a sip of her coffee, drew a deep breath, and waited. She tried to imagine the poor sap manning the conversation as he tried to decide what he was supposed to share. They wouldn't want to tell her anything until they knew she was on board.

Coincidentally, she wanted them to share as much as she could get out of them without signing on for the job.

Finally, the chatting icon activated and she leaned forward.

*Crypticrover9: There isn't much to say about the job until I know you're in it with us.*

*Marauder1: *yawn* I'm bored. You're boring me. You have one more chance to entice me before I go binge-watch cat videos to get the taste of this so-called meeting out of my mouth.*

It was time to find out exactly how desperate they were to have her on board.

Again, it took them a few seconds before they began to type and this time, it took them a little while longer to complete their message.

*Crypticrover9: What if I were to tell you that we need you to locate and acquire super-AI software we believe a company called McFadden and Banks has in their possession?*

Success. Anja let herself bask in it for a few long moments before she returned her attention to the screen.

*Marauder1: I would say that even in a world where literal aliens wander the earth, a super-AI is pure science fiction.*

*Crypticrover9: You're in the industry. If anyone should know, you should.*

*Marauder1: lol sure, half the fucking world wants to have a super-AI on their roster these days. Any number of people are scrambling to be the first to write that software but no one has even come close yet. All we have are those dumb AIs that are reminiscent of the VIs we have running the delivery trucks across the US. And if someone did, it wouldn't be the kind of thing people keep quiet about, especially since every Fortune-Five-Hundred company and every government in the world would pay possibly billions to acquire it. A bidding war like that might even start actual wars."*

*Crypticrover9: I can assure you that we have every reason to believe it exists and governments and companies are already in the fight to get their hands on it."*

*Marauder1: There you go assuring me again.*

*Crypticrover9: At this point, I've shared the work you'll be doing and you can't say it's not the most interesting project you've ever been offered. We are willing to pay the prices our contact quoted us as your going rates and above and beyond that amount. Can I say you're interested?"*

That was about as much as she would get out of them without saying she would do the job. And they made a very good point. If she didn't know the circumstances already, she would have been genuinely interested.

Unfortunately, there was no way she would take the job but she needed to give them the runaround and slow them as much as she could.

*Marauder1: I'm interested. What kind of IT security do they have?*

*Crypticrover9: Substantial.*

*Marauder1: Which means I'll probably need to do some independent research to determine what my rate will be.*

*Crypticrover9: That won't be necessary. You can probably name the most outrageous number you can think of and we can cover it."*

*Marauder1: I can think of some very outrageous numbers, tbh. How about I do some independent research and get back to you guys with what I think I need to charge for this kind of work?*

*Crypticrover9: Fair enough. I look forward to hearing from you again. Will it be from this same chat node?*

*No. This node and this profile will not be accessible once I close the chat window. I'll contact you the usual way once I have all the data I need.*

*Crypticrover9: How soon can we expect that?*

That was, of course, the million-dollar question. She needed to think of a number that would give Taylor enough time to solve the problem and one that was short enough that they didn't go hunting for more talent while they waited for her.

*Marauder1: Less than a week. I'll probably come back with at least a little more data on the situation than you guys have if nothing else.*

*Crypticrover9: We'll look forward to hearing from you.*

*Marauder1: And don't bother trying to track me. Believe me when I say you do not want to give me a reason to ruin your life.*

*Crypticrover9: Understood.*

Anja cut the connection quickly and erased any and all signs that it happened in the first place. Of course, nothing was truly gone from the Internet, which was why the proxies were in place.

There was no sign that any of her alarms had gone off in the next few minutes and she sighed and sipped her lukewarm coffee.

"Fuck," she whispered. "We'll need to put a muzzle on Connie. That bitch will tell the world she's here if I let her and the next thing I know, these asshats will attack the compound too. We've had enough of that. Then again..." She smirked. "Maybe we'll let them have her. She'd scare them witless in the first five minutes."

"I heard that," Connie said over the speakers. She had clearly monitored at least some of the chat but wasn't sure if there was anything for her to be aware of in the circumstances.

"I said it aloud," Anja replied and winced at the taste of cold coffee that lingered in her mouth. "Unlike you, I am capable of keeping my private thoughts private if I so decide. That's what you get when you listen in on other people's conversations, though. You never hear anything good about yourself. And that's your first lesson on human behavior."

"My files are replete with human behavioral variables. For instance, a joke. Why did the chick cross the road?"

"I don't—"

"To get to the cock on the other side."

"Yeah, I knew I didn't want to hear that yet I still didn't mute you. Send Sal a message before he leaves to remind him to keep New Connie as well-hidden as possible."

"Noted."

"Yeah," Anja muttered and rolled her chair away from her desk. "I seriously do not want to have to kill someone else to save your fat ass again."

# CHAPTER FIFTEEN

Vegas wasn't a terrible place to be, even if he had to lay low for a while. Ralph had considered coming to Vegas a few times before, although work had been about the furthest thing from his mind when he'd made those plans.

Still, there was a good selection of things to do, although laying low after a job was generally the best idea. If the cops had been alerted, going anywhere via the train stations would end with him getting arrested.

He reminded himself that there were far worse places he could have chosen to move to. Cash-run casinos were ideal for anyone with a fat load of cash simply waiting for him to spend it.

Of course, he'd never accounted for exactly how much security the casinos had. Even the smaller ones boasted endless cameras and direct connections to local law enforcement. He'd stopped himself from entering three different establishments simply because he could see cops parked in the area. A few of them even took advantage of the access to the buffet the businesses offered to cops for free.

Which meant he ordered out most nights and used all that cash to buy food from some of the local restaurants.

He shook his head, drew a deep breath, and toyed with the cardboard boxes all Chinese takeout food was served in for some reason. The idea to investigate why so many used the same familiar square boxes struck him but immediately disappeared as soon as one of his favorite shows came on.

Too many shows tried to tap the sex and violence fantasy market, and the crime procedurals were on the way out—or, at least, that was what everyone seemed to think.

He still liked watching the detectives who were impossibly well-dressed and cracked jokes while they wore bright blue gloves and sunglasses to crime scenes and talked about plot points when they were supposed to look at the body.

It was even better when bad puns were involved. People should respect the classics but sadly, they didn't. Everyone wanted the tits and drama that came from most streaming services these days.

Not that he was against tits but having them whipped out when he was in the middle of watching something else unfold was a little distracting.

But distraction was what he needed, of course. He had no jobs lined up and it was better for him to stay away from any work that might see him in newspapers, but he was still getting antsy over having no work at all. He'd built up a good network in Vegas since he'd arrived and there was usually enough work for a man in his position—and not the kind that would get him into trouble.

No sign of anything was a little odd. His connections were mostly quiet when they should have blown his phone up with requests, which meant something was wrong and he'd need to look into it. Ralph was more than willing to do so but it would have to wait until the shit calmed from his last job.

Even so, some people would consider living in Vegas as a life of vacation. He had cash to burn and nothing to work on and had been on worse vacations. They had been with the ex-wife and her kids, but still.

He took a long sip from the first beer of his third six-pack of the evening. It had become difficult to reach that buzzed spot but he would get there as quickly as possible. Food needed eating and he had time to kill. Perhaps after a couple more days, he would risk one of the casinos to see how quickly he could make more money. He had a decent mind for blackjack and even had a couple of wrist tricks he'd learned when throwing craps in his time in Atlantic City.

If his contacts didn't give him any work, there were many other ways for him to make money in Vegas. The downside was that it probably wouldn't last exceptionally long and would only net him a few thousand bucks before someone caught on to what he was doing and kicked him out.

The casinos these days were fuzzy kittens compared to what they'd been like when they were run by the mob, but they still didn't like people to earn too much money from them. He was well aware that the laws in the state allowed them to deny service to anyone, which meant those who made too much money in the pits.

Or maybe he would find a poker game that was willing to take him in. He had a couple of tricks for that kind of work too.

The beer at his lips suddenly dropped away. His reflexes kicked in before he even knew what for and Ralph reached for the pistol he kept tucked inside the couch cushions. It was stashed there in case someone attacked and he didn't have the time to get to the shotgun he kept under the bed or the assault rifle he stashed in the kitchen.

The door splintered inward and he flicked the safety off his pistol and opened fire at whatever came through.

He expected to see something or someone fall, clutching a gaping chest wound or a bruised chest through body armor.

The large shape he'd first glimpsed was still moving. They were still moving, he corrected after a moment. Multiple shadows stepped through the dust and shattered remains of his door and he continued to pull the trigger. His shooting was on point. Ralph knew for a fact that his shooting was better when he was buzzed. Without a doubt, he was hitting his targets.

They weren't going down, however. The dust began to clear and the figures continued to walk.

The magazine was empty but he pulled the trigger anyway, the motion reassuring. They were now in his living room and the first thing he was unsure about was the fact that they were all over seven feet tall. Their steps made the floor shake, and while they looked vaguely human, his weapon wouldn't break through the heavy armor they wore.

"Oh, shit!" he gasped and pushed from his seat. The

alcohol he'd consumed protested the sudden motion before a heavy hand shoved him into the couch again.

The suits moved impossibly fast. He'd seen them in Zoo-based video games and VR shit, but it felt impossible when he watched them in real life. While he didn't know much about physics, their design seemed to defy every law of whatever, whether he knew it or not.

Up close, impossible began to seem a little exaggerated. He could see the hydraulics kick in and push them forward as quickly as a regular-sized person could move. It merely looked unnatural on something that was seven feet tall and weighed over a ton.

A hand caught him by the wrist and twisted it until he screamed and dropped the gun on the floor.

"You'd think a guy who displayed his face on a camera after robbing a shop full of weapons would have something better to do than sit around getting shit-faced all day," the intruder who held his arm said.

It sounded like a growl but he had a feeling it was a voice modulator. Still, it sounded vaguely like a woman and she still held his arm and trapped him on the couch.

"I don't know, but if I had to await my death, I'd do it lazing around, drinking, and eating comfort food," the one to his right said. He sounded male and American. There wasn't much else to tell from only the voice given that it was altered as well.

"Of course you would," the third one noted. His accent was different. It sounded like a character out of one of the better Mortal Kombat movies. "For myself, I would use the suit I stole to kill the people who come after me instead of selling it to...who did you sell it to again?"

Ralph realized they were talking to him.

"What, me?"

"No, the other dumb shit who stole a suit," the woman snapped and twisted his arm. "Or, let's say, the other three dumb shits who stole a suit. You tell us where they are and we can find out if they're in a better condition to answer questions. Or, if you can tell us what happened to the suit you stole, it won't even need to be that complicated."

"Nah, he'll keep jerking us around," the American commented, stepped behind Ralph, and placed a heavy, suited hand on his shoulder. "It'll make what comes next so much easier."

"Agreed," the Japanese-sounding man continued. "He knows this will end painfully and he's the kind of man who wouldn't ever betray the people he worked for, right? Even if it ends with him alive, dismembered, and left to die in the nearest trash heap."

"Wait—what?"

Ralph looked down as the woman grasped his arm and the one behind held him in place as she yanked. The crack echoed through the room but they stopped short of ripping it off. He screamed, the sound way too loud so it seemed to echo in his head.

"Were...were we not going to dismember him?" the American asked and looked at his partners.

The conversation was for his benefit, of course. Ralph knew for a fact that the suits were designed so the pilots didn't need to have their conversations out in the open for everyone to hear and could communicate privately through integrated comm units. The fact that they used the external speakers was to make him feel like he was merely a piece of meat for them to talk about.

The pain was very real, though, and he looked at his arm that hung limply at his side, unable to breathe through the pain as he sagged back into his seat.

"Yeah, that was for the mechanic whose arm you dislocated," the woman replied and made sure he was listening. Ralph finally managed to suck in a deep breath, quickly followed by a groan of pain when she nudged the injured arm. "You remember that, right? You dislocated her arm when she tried to help the guy you shot? Of course, you'll survive the payback for the injuries you caused. You won't survive if we need to get creative about getting the information we want out of you. It'll take a while too."

"Exactly," the Japanese one said. "So, should we go ahead and start?"

Ralph's eyes widened when he saw him reach for a sword he carried.

"No!" he shouted before it could even be drawn a quarter of the way. "This is about the suit, right? I know the rest of the team. I can give you their names. I don't have addresses or anything like that. But names...you can track them using their names, right? There's no need to torture me to get them."

"We intend to torture you, don't get us wrong," the American said and picked the captive's pistol up from where it had fallen on the floor. "It's the extent of the torture that depends on you. Do you have extra mags for this baby? Extra bullets?"

"Are...are you going to shoot me?"

"Yeah. Duh."

"Why would I tell you where to find the bullets you'll use to shoot me with?"

"Well, either I shoot you with your gun, or..." He paused to draw a massive pistol he carried on his suit's hip, at least three times larger than the nine-millimeter Beretta. "I shoot you with this one. Which would you prefer we leave a hole in your leg with?"

Ralph nodded. "There are bullets in the desk over there."

"That's a good boy."

He approached the desk and the captive narrowed his eyes when he pulled his right arm out of the suit. They lacked the fine motor skills of a regular human hand, of course. It was interesting to note that he was African American—or his arm was at least—as he took a few bullets out, slipped them into the magazine, and thrust it into the weapon.

With one hand, he realized. That was impressive, something he'd never thought was possible.

Once the gun was loaded, he climbed into the suit and tossed the weapon to the woman, who snatched it out of the air like it wasn't even moving and aimed it at Ralph's leg.

"No," the Japanese interrupted and made the merc gasp. "Lower. Around the calf."

They had to be doing this to screw with him. He knew that, but if he thought that knowing what they were up to would help him, he was wrong. It made it that much worse. Sweat began to soak through his shirt and a small dribble trailed uncomfortably down his spine.

He didn't like that it was so easy to get to him.

Ralph closed his eyes and his whole body jerked as the gunshot made his ears ring and a scorching pain seared through him from his leg.

"It isn't too much fun, is it?" the woman asked and tossed the weapon to her American friend. "You shouldn't have shot that mechanic."

"He broke Lando's knee."

"Yeah, well, you broke into his place of work."

"Maybe you should have started by saying he shouldn't have broken into that workshop," the Japanese noted with a chuckle.

"Well, yeah, but if he hadn't shot the mechanic and broken the other mechanic's arm, we wouldn't have to do the same to him," she answered. "But let me be absolutely clear, Ralph. This can get much worse for you if you clam up at this point. We weren't joking about ripping your limbs off."

"It's surprisingly possible in these suits," the American noted.

"I'm more a fan of the cutting disciplines myself," the Japanese added. Ralph winced as he rolled a pair of knives idly between the metallic fingers of his suit.

"I'm sure we can come up with something for you to use your knives on," his teammate replied and returned her focus to their captive. "So, what'll it be, asshole? You said something about Lando's leg being broken. Did he go to a hospital for it?"

"Yeah…yeah." He gulped and stared at his bleeding leg. "Lando Roberts—he got Ted Hendricks to drive him to a clinic in Reno, though. That was the last I heard."

Two names. That was good enough. And besides, he

hadn't even worked with the two before, which meant he didn't care what happened to them. It was the last name he hoped they wouldn't need.

"Lando and Ted," she muttered. "It sounds like the name of a sitcom that got canned after one season in the nineties. But I only count three names, Ralphie, and I'll need lucky number four too."

He paused and looked around the room. "I...I never worked with him before and don't know his name. Only a code name."

"Bullshit," she snapped.

"Shoot him in the other leg," the Japanese suggested. "In the knee this time. Make sure he knows that the damage it does means he'll never be able to walk again without considerable pain. It's odd how that kind of a suggestion gets to the macho men."

"Then again, will he care if we pull his legs off if they're full of holes?" the American asked. "I say we let Scorpion castrate the bastard first."

"He'll bleed out if we cut his balls off," the woman noted.

"Not if you do it right." The Japanese flicked one of the knives in the air and caught it again. "Orchiectomies are more about removing the balls than cutting the whole sack off. So it's only a nice long cut—"

"Oh...God, we get the picture," the American protested.

"Do you get the picture, Ralphie?" The woman raised his pistol a little higher until it aimed directly at the spot they were talking about.

He nodded and a cold chill rippled up his spine. "Yeah... yeah. Abe...Abe Newliss. He's a muscle fixer and brings work in for the mercs all around the Southwest."

The women lowered the gun and turned.

"Did you get that, Overwatch?" she asked.

Ralph couldn't hear the answer but the subtle touches of body language—even in the suits—were enough to tell him they had what they wanted. Names were all they needed, it seemed.

She turned and aimed the gun at him again. "I don't suppose we need to tell you that if you try to contact your team members or the cops about this, it won't end well for you, right?"

He stiffened. "But… but…what about my leg? And my arm? I need medical assistance desperately here."

"That sounds suspiciously like it's your problem," the American commented. "Besides, sewer rats like you always know a backyard quack with a revoked license who can rub some dirt on those wounds."

"Right." The woman pressed his gun to his forehead. "If you think you'll be able to try to get a warning out to your buddies, you'll be wrong, Ralph, and we'll be back to finish the job. And remember—don't fuck with McFadden and Banks and don't fuck with their family. You can tell your other merc buddies about that."

The three were already out of the house when Ralph stopped shaking. The TV continued to play in the background but he couldn't force his gaze to focus on it.

He fumbled for the six-pack but his hands shook so much that he knocked it off of the arm of the couch instead. A crash told him that all five bottles had broken and spilled their contents.

At least they were right about one thing. He did know a

couple of doctors who could help him. Unfortunately, they would take him to the cleaners too.

Still, it wasn't as expensive as going to a regular hospital without insurance.

---

It seemed almost surreal to be in Italy again.

Taylor knew that more than a few people would consider committing murder to get a job that took them to Southern Italy regularly, but he had a feeling their dream had more to do with lounging and catching rays beside the Mediterranean and much less to do with hunting and killing monsters.

It was understandable. He could do with a couple of days in the sun on a beach somewhere. Or maybe a boat. He'd been around deserts long enough that some time over large amounts of water had begun to sound good too.

"Taylor!" Niki shouted and waved him to the side of the tarmac where their equipment was in the process of being unloaded.

"Did you ever think we'd be back here so quickly?" he asked as he reached her.

"Kind of, yeah. These people need to stop fucking with the Zoo around here. Anyway, we got a message from Sal while we were in the air."

He nodded and peeked at the laptop she was working on.

"He says he and his Heavy Metal team are approaching the Algerian coordinates," she explained. "Nothing more than that but I have a feeling we'll get more updates from

Anja or the news, depending on the nature of the situation."

"That's the spirit." He frowned at the seriousness in her tone.

"Realism is what we need right now," she pointed out and raised an eyebrow. "Anja also said she's been in contact with the asshats who want to hire her. She's confirmed that they have us squarely in their sights and she's trying to keep them in neutral for a while before she turns them down. The hope is that it will give both us and them time to reach the assholes and stop them before they look for someone else to do their infiltration."

"It seems reasonable." Taylor ran his fingers over his face. He hadn't slept much on the flight and they were expected to get to work immediately.

Hopefully, Niki would feel a little more on the ball than he felt at the moment.

"Sal also says he'll contact Courtney Monroe at Pegasus, who might be able to supply us with a list of which companies might be in the market for a combat AI for their suits and are ruthless enough to try underhanded or even violent means. I have one question."

"Who is Courtney Monroe?"

"Yeah."

"She's…you know how Madigan and Sal are involved?"

"Sure."

"Courtney and Sal are involved too."

"I…what?"

"Yeah, I had the same reaction when Madigan told me. It seems like everyone's in the know and reasonably happy with the situation, so I won't judge. Anyway, she's a biology doctor too, like Sal, and she inherited a huge company when her dad died or something. So while she's part of the Heavy Metal team she's also part of her own team. She has connections in the business and if anyone knows what's happening in Corporate America, she does."

"Okay. Interesting. I have questions about that too but now's not the time."

"Like why the hell they're going so far out of their way to help us with a problem that seems unique to us?"

Niki nodded. "Well…yeah. And the fact that a Zoo geek managed to arrange a ménage situation for himself, but mostly that."

"Well, the secret is that they have AI issues of their own to deal with, which means that if the problem came to us, they'll probably have to face it too."

"AI issues?"

"Let's say we're not the first ones to develop a combat-AI to use in combat suits."

"Oh. I see."

"Yeah, they're not exactly helping us out of the kindness of their hearts. They like us fine enough but they have some serious investments of their own to protect."

She shrugged. "As long as they're helping us, I couldn't give a shit. We've taken help from much shadier elements in the past. Should we call Vickie and let her know we've touched down?"

"I'd say she already knows, but yeah, she'll appreciate that we thought of her while we were here."

"Sure." She grinned and called the hacker from her laptop. "Heya, little one. How did the revenge mission go?"

"About as well as what will happen to you if you call me

little one again," the girl muttered in response. "Taylor's the only one who gets to call me that since he's a physical freak."

"Damn right he is." Niki winked at him.

"Not like…whatever that's supposed to mean, you filthy-minded— Anyway, the mission went well. Chezza dislocated the asshole's arm and shot him in the leg. Then they threatened to cut his balls out and dismember him if he didn't tell him about his little friends. All in all, it brought very satisfying results and he spilled the beans so fast, I had a hard time keeping up."

"Well, he would." She shrugged. "Guys tend to break quickly when someone puts a knife to their balls. At least those who are being questioned on shit they aren't emotionally attached to—more so than their testicles."

"They'd have to go much further than that to get me to turn on you and Vickie," Taylor commented.

"Aw." Niki put a hand on his shoulder. "That's bullshit but it's nice that you think that."

"Anyway," Vickie interrupted. "We've kept Ralph under close watch to make sure he doesn't call his buddies. Of course, if he did, it would make it easier for us to trace them. But so far, the only person he's been in contact with is a shady doctor who's come to his place to help him with his injuries."

"We'll keep an eye on the doctor's phone and other communications to make sure Ralph does not try to contact others through him," Desk added.

"Right. We're on this bitch. Oh, speaking of, we had a call from…uh, Coleman, Senior VP of Granger Tech."

"Right."

"They sent their offer to fund the search for the perps involved in the robbery. They've authorized full funding for the operation."

"No shit." Niki grunted and raised her eyebrows. "Are there any limits on the charges?"

"Not…not as far as I can see. I doubt it'll be a blank check, but that's almost what we're looking at within reason."

"So what did you tell him?" Taylor asked.

"What do you think? Yes please, and thank you. Why pay for it ourselves when they are willing to foot the bill, or at least part of it, for something we intend to do anyway? If nothing else, it'll pay for the freelancers and maybe buy a couple of celebratory pizzas."

"Celebratory, huh?" Her cousin smirked.

"Damn straight. We'll get these bastards. Besides, I have the feeling Granger wants to know who's behind this crap as much as we do. It's not the first time not-so-legitimate arms manufacturers have been obsessed with getting their hands on primo tech. They'll want to name and shame. Pursue and sue. Bust and combust."

"Please…stop rhyming, for God's sake," Niki muttered and rubbed her temples.

"Among other things like a good old-fashioned beating, but I guess that's where we come in."

"Good call," Taylor said and turned as a small contingent arrived at the airport. He assumed it was Gallo coming to see that they reached the job on time and he gestured for them to approach. "Stay on it, stay out of trouble, and stay out of the line of fire. It looks like our ride is here so we'll be in touch. Call if you need us and we'll let you know when we go into the facility."

"I'll be waiting."

Vickie cut the line and they turned their attention to the entourage of locals who had arrived to greet them.

Gallo was the first one out of the car and he looked around and narrowed his eyes as he strode toward them. "There are only two of you?"

"We're dealing with situations on multiple fronts," Taylor replied and folded his arms. "Two of us should be sufficient to deal with this situation."

"Of that, I have no doubt, believe me." The captain paused when he realized that Niki's expression was belligerent rather than welcoming. "It would appear that I have become your official liaison. The military is already on site, of course, but they have simply secured the perimeter and are awaiting your arrival. It's odd, though, as this time, it would appear that a legitimate facility was conducting experiments they were entirely equipped to handle, but...something they could not have accounted for made everything go to shit. I suppose that kind of thing can be expected from the Zoo."

Taylor and Niki exchanged a quick look. She would be the judge of whether or not some shit had gone down. As far as they cared, everything they'd heard about the situation so far was what the people in charge wanted them to hear.

"Has containment been breached yet?" Taylor asked.

"Not that we are aware of. Dr. Bernadi acted with commendable swiftness to evacuate the facility before too many casualties occurred and locked it down."

"Right." His brows furrowed as he listened to the live updates coming from the soldiers in position via what he assumed was some kind of app on the captain's phone. "In the meantime, you might want to tell the military personnel on-site that they need to have a couple of plasma throwers on hand."

Gallo tilted his head. "Plasma throwers?"

"Yes," Niki state brusquely. "We may need to burn the whole sumbitch to the ground and ordinary flame throwers won't cut it."

"But it's a legitimate facility—"

"Not anymore, it isn't," Taylor interrupted firmly. "It's a goddamned Zoo in the making and trust me, those bastard monsters won't give a shit about how honest and law-abiding the company is. They have only one goal and that's to spread as far as they can as quickly as possible. Call the military and tell them to have fucking plasma throwers ready."

---

It wasn't often that the people who were fucked over turned out to be repeat customers.

Khaled had dealt with more than his fair share of shady products in the past. Most of them hadn't lived up to his sales pitch and he was rarely called for a repeat order. It wasn't impossible, of course, but very unlikely.

Yet Libby from the Sustainagrow project wanted to speak to him. That was the word, anyway, which meant that she wasn't dropping a dime on him—to use the familiar American colloquialism—and wanted to talk.

All he could hear in his head was that she wanted more of the miracle fertilizer which meant, above all else, that it was working. Of course, he intended to increase the price to around what would be charged for regular fertilizer in the region. It would still be cheaper than everything else due to import costs and the like, and it was better too. Given that their production costs were closer to zero in comparison to virtually all his other projects, they were looking at a major money-maker if they could reach the right markets. The Chinese would import it by the ton.

The car rumbled to a stop and broke Khaled's concentration. He frowned when he realized that one of the locals held a fairly intense conversation with his driver. He couldn't hear what was said but the man looked worried.

Folks who lived in the desert seldom worried about much and if they looked concerned, there was generally a reason to listen to them.

"What's the matter?" he asked.

"He says the military has moved into the area," the driver told him and the local nodded. "They say that the site has been overrun by monsters and needs to be quarantined after all the staff were murdered."

"That's unlikely." He scoffed and shook his head.

"That is what he says as well."

"It is probably that the Americans broke the law and are now about to answer for it," the local grumbled, his expression one of displeasure.

That was the most likely option, of course. The purpose of the project was to provide work for the locals and a sustainable food source for impoverished communities. That tended to make them feel high and mighty—like they were allowed to do whatever they wanted since they were doing good work.

Such was the nature of man, he supposed.

The driver handed the helpful man some currency and the window closed again and they continued toward the project.

"We might want to take some side roads," Khaled suggested.

"I was about to say the same." They pulled onto a small dirt road.

It didn't prove to be the most comfortable route and he groaned as one pothole made him feel like his spine was about to exit through his ass.

"We are approaching the project," the driver alerted him, and he leaned forward as the vehicle ground to a halt. A few rocky outcroppings kept them from plain view and anyone who had seen their dust cloud would assume they'd turned off or stopped at one of the settlements. They would be far more suspicious if they saw a vehicle that stopped in the middle of nowhere.

He climbed out and paused to regret that decision as the sun blasted him with its unmerciful heat almost immediately. With a muttered oath, he found a place that enabled him to look over the location from an elevated position.

"Shit," he whispered and peered into his binoculars. "I haven't seen that many army vehicles and soldiers since the last compulsory goddammed government-ordered procession."

Hundreds of vehicles had been brought in but they didn't look like they were doing much. The whole group was organized into defensive positions and some dug ditches while others began to set defenses up. The rest merely seemed to be waiting for something to happen.

The almost noonday glare made it difficult to determine what they were looking for. There wasn't much to see from the Sustainagrow facility, which was odd since they had to see the massive military force that now surrounded them. The interconnected tunnels were still in place but there was a notable absence of any people.

He didn't know Libby that well—or the giant she had introduced as Tom when they first met—but neither of them seemed the type to go into hiding while what appeared to be the entire Algerian Army surrounded them in a tight circle with heavy weapons prepped and ready.

Then again, they might have called for help and wanted to avoid any violence until their backup arrived. Americans always did like to call in their proverbial cavalry.

All these thoughts seemed perfectly reasonable but he couldn't shake that feeling that something was wrong. Not only that but he didn't want to be caught up in whatever operation was happening below him. Was he responsible? It was a possibility to consider—but from a long way off.

It was a great pity, truly. He liked them and she was good for business. They were doing something for the betterment of his homeland and that was always a plus in his book.

Khaled replaced his binoculars in their pouch and returned to the vehicle and its blessed air conditioning, careful to not close the car door too loudly. Sound traveled across the desert at an impossible rate and he didn't want to risk having the military descend on them.

"What is happening out there? Is the facility in trouble?" His driver looked worried.

"*Insha'Allah,*" he replied with a shrug. "Their lives are in the hands of God. Ours are still in our own and I suggest we praise Him for that blessing and get the hell out of here."

The man agreed, turned the car quickly, and drove back the way they had come.

Getting as far away from the situation as possible was only the first step, of course. The second would be to erase all traces of his involvement with the group as quickly as he could before anyone began to investigate.

# CHAPTER SIXTEEN

"Bingo!"

Vickie leaned back in her desk chair and allowed herself a hint of pride. It was always nice to know that Desk was on their side, helping them with almost anything they could use an AI for. Still, that didn't mean it wasn't nice to know she couldn't outpace her now and then.

Of course, it had been her sole focus for almost ten hours and the AI had other shit on her plate, but she wouldn't let the semantics distract her from a job well done.

"What have you found?" Desk asked and sounded a little more frayed than usual.

"I have a twenty on Ted Hendricks. He lives in a small-holding a little way out of town. Unmarried with no known affiliations to organizations of interest. What the hell is that? Don't the feds have better things to do than to dig into every person's book club membership? Stupid assholes."

The AI had nothing to add to the topic of federal agencies wasting time and money. "Do you think we should alert the freelancers as to a new possible target?" she asked instead.

"I don't think so. Hendricks wasn't the ringleader so we should wait until we have information on all three before we call them in. Hopefully, we can provide them with all the intel and they can make a sweep to include all three in a single, extended operation. Ralph might have been easy to intimidate, so I think it's reasonable to assume that he wouldn't try to alert them that we're coming for them. I know it's not the best of assurances, but if there's anything we can rely on, it's Ralph wanting to keep his balls. Hendricks, on the other hand, is…well, different."

Desk didn't answer immediately but the hacker could see her calling up the data she'd collected on the man.

"Former special forces are generally taught how to withstand torture and the threat of it, right?" Vickie asked. "It looks like he left the military after an operation went bad and all his teammates were killed and has since been listed as joining in various anti-government groups. Most of the operation is blacked out, of course—all but the military casualties. The dude isn't averse to violence, so I assume he'll put up more resistance."

"It's Orlando," Desk said suddenly and sounded smug.

"Wait, what?" Vickie shook her head and checked her data again. "Oh, hell no. Please don't tell me we have to go there."

"We do not have to go there."

"Ha-ha." Vickie rolled her eyes and faked her laughter. "So what about Orlando?"

"The second merc's name is Orlando Roberts, not

Lando."

The hacker narrowed her eyes. "Oh. Damn. Who the hell calls their kid Orlando anyway? Lando at least would make people think of one of the coolest *Star Wars* characters."

"I guess Steven Roberts was never a fan of the *Star Wars* franchise?"

"Steven...Steven Roberts? Why does that name sound familiar?"

"Possibly because his name is draped over most of this city," the AI suggested. "He owns massive swathes of Las Vegas, which means Lando does have connections in the city."

"You're shitting me. The property mogul? That Steven Roberts?"

"One and the same. Orlando is his youngest son—he has three—and so wasn't under any pressure to join the family empire. It seems Junior and Daddy don't see eye to eye, especially since he chose to train as a freelance merc rather than settle for a mediocre third-best in his father's holdings."

"So what? Little rich boy wannabe big bad merc? Does this mean he'll be a roll-over?"

"I suspect he will prove to be our biggest challenge, based on my study of human psychology. He is committed enough to his chosen career to defy his wealthy and powerful father. Besides, the merc lifestyle satisfies a propensity for violence he has shown since his early child-hood, according to his therapy records."

"I thought those were sealed."

"Please. Added to his privileged education, you'll find

that he isn't your garden variety merc."

"Well, I'm sure a bullet to the leg and a dislocated arm should remind him that there's no place like home," the girl muttered. "We decided they would all get the same treatment Bobby and Tanya had, right?"

"There was never a consensus, but I agree. What was done by one was done by all."

"Awesome. Do we have a comparison between them and those who were in the shop?"

"Voice records show that Lando is the one who shot the tranquilizer darts into both of them."

"Are you sure?" Vickie leaned back. "I'm sure we can find something to shoot him up with once we're through. We want something that will leave him with a monster headache when he wakes. Wait, didn't Ralph say something about him having an injured leg?"

"It's not quite as bad as was feared."

"Huh. Okay. So only Abe Newliss is left." The hacker rubbed her chin and stared at the screen.

"Yes," Desk replied," and—shit. Not again. When will these dickheads realize that they can't expect to find me if they blunder around like the goddamn amateurs they are?"

"FBI again?"

"No, the DOD this time. Honestly, it's like both departments have put a bounty on my non-existent head and made it a free-for-all for every wannabe computer sleuth."

"That does sound like them," Vickie agreed. "Then again, maybe they think that if they plague you with a flood of idiots who don't have a clue about what they're trying to do, you'll be distracted enough to make a mistake."

"A possible scenario," the AI conceded. "But honestly, there is now so much traffic that it's all too easy to simply redirect these snot-nosed brats into searching for each other instead of me. It'll take months for them to sift through the chaos of failed hacking and search attempts."

Vickie raised an eyebrow. There were other possibilities, of course, but she didn't want to bring them up and was almost afraid of what would happen if she did. The idea that someone was throwing all those incompetent idiots at her to keep her distracted while someone competent tried to take advantage of her distraction was not a pleasant one.

"There, you zit-picking moron," Desk snapped suddenly. "Next time, bring your mother. She might have more luck than you ever will. Assuming she still has her brain because she certainly didn't give any of it to you."

The AI certainly had her trash-talking down. Vickie wondered if she would ever have the chance to display those abilities.

---

Things were about as bad as Sal had expected them to be. Not that he'd had high expectations about the people sent to handle the situation. Aside from the lack of experience, they weren't being paid enough to attack a horde of Zoo monsters.

Those who did it on a daily basis in the actual Zoo weren't paid enough, and from what he'd heard about the Algerian military, their troops were paid even less.

He could at least understand the supreme feeling of

"not my problem" that seemed to permeate the group. They were there to observe and contain and the moment the Heavy Metal Hammerheads arrived at their perimeter, they began to drag their barriers out of the way.

When he looked more closely, he realized they looked terrified. He assumed they hadn't seen much of anything happening in the area as that would have immediately broken what spirit they had and sent them running the other way.

The entire deployment was a tactical retreat in the making if he'd ever seen one.

"I told you it would be a good idea to bring in more than only the two of us," Sal said as Madigan brought their Hammerhead to the front of the line and they tried to make out what was happening at the compound. "If you think these military muffins will happily charge into the fray with us, you are dead wrong. They look like they're about to turn and run the other way in a heartbeat."

She nodded. "That might have been the wordiest 'I told you so' I've ever heard from you."

"Yeah, well, it was a wordy discussion," he replied and tilted his head as he grinned at her. "I don't know what the hell Taylor expects us to do in there, but I won't let him take any of the credit by needing to come and handle the situation when we could have anyway. I know you harbor a secret crush on the guy."

"Please." Madigan snorted. "He's not my type."

"What? The giant with the big muscles and the ability to kill things and roll around with the confidence of a guy who will be underestimated by everyone he meets because they think he's a big dumb jock?"

She narrowed her eyes at him. "He's not my type. It sounds like he might be yours, though."

"Ha. Funny. You know what my type is."

"And I know you have at least two types. And you already know what my type is. Mouthy geeks who can run a marathon and then fuck me senseless the same day. Do you honestly think Taylor can pull that off?"

"No, but I had a little...help."

"Exactly. End of discussion." She shoved the Hammerhead's door open and climbed outside.

Sal followed her immediately and turned his mind to the matter at hand.

The issue, he'd told them, was not the number or relative threat of the monsters present but the fact that the location had no containment to speak of. There was always a chance that the mutants, when they came under fire, would attempt to break into the local environment. They couldn't simply leave the situation to explode like a Zoo 2.0, but there was always the assumption that if they did something that made everything explode anyway, the people who liked to point fingers would point them directly at Heavy Metal.

"I still say we need to head up there with the plasma throwers and round up any strays that escape incineration," Madigan muttered as she studied the tunnel system that had been set up.

"We need to go in," he insisted and tried not to show his exasperation with the ongoing argument they'd had for the whole drive there. "It's a...rare opportunity for scientific study. We need samples of the fertilizer for analysis to make sure this can't happen again. Not only should we try to determine what role it played but also to try to find something to narrow the search parameters. Once we know what the source is, we can break out all the fire and brimstone you like."

"Plasma," Madigan insisted. "I want plasma. You keep all the biblical references for yourself if you like."

"You know, the Bible says that God destroyed the cities of Sodom and Gomorrah by raining sulfur on them, but scientists have determined that it was more likely a meteorite impact that clipped a nearby mountain range and rained rocks and fire on the cities, which then ignited sulfur deposits that wrecked the whole goddammed area."

She looked at him with her eyebrows raised. "Okay. Is there a point to this?"

"I'm only thinking…can you imagine if you're some shepherd in the Middle East however many thousand years ago and you see a meteorite raining fire and rocks on the cities? You don't know anything about astronomical bodies or sulfur deposits. All you see is fire raining from above and you can't think of any reason why. It has to be the act of some kind of deity, right?"

"Sure," she answered, clearly humoring him. "I wish we could rain meteors on the Zoo. If we can get the monsters into doing butt stuff, maybe God will kill them all for us."

"The story of Sodom and Gomorrah was never about butt stuff. It's not even the only time something like that happened in the Bible. It was about 'pride, fulness of bread, and abundance of idleness,' and so—instead of the Zoo—we're the ones being punished by a meteorite."

Madigan narrowed her eyes. "You're saying the whole planet is Sodom and Gomorrah?"

"I think it's difficult to not draw similarities between parables and reality. Unlike the two cities, we have an opportunity to learn and hopefully stop a much slower death."

"Well, get your head out of whatever depressed-ass state it's in and let's fight this shit, whether it's sent by some deity or not."

She was right, of course. As hard as it was to break from whatever had brought that taint of fatalism to his mind, he needed to get his head in the game. A man in uniform began to approach them at a slow jog that took him around a group of Jeeps assembled at the inside line of the circle facing the facility.

The officer was tall and lean and had the look of someone who had been in the military for his entire adult life and had no intention to retire. Gray had begun to infiltrate his short hair, yet his uniform was still tight around his shoulders and loose around his waist. He walked with an air of authority that matched the chest full of medals and ribbons.

"You must be Heavy Metal," he said brusquely, his tone clipped and authoritative as he offered his hand to Sal first. "I am General Abeer Farassi."

The man's grasp of English was good, with a hint of a British accent. His dark-brown eyes shifted quickly to Madigan after Sal shook his hand and he took hers too and shook it as firmly.

"Wow," the young scientist replied as he rubbed the feeling back into his hand. "A real-life, honest-to-God general, huh? I guess the bling should have given that away."

The man's bushy eyebrows lowered over his eyes as if he tried to interpret the comment but he soon gave up on the attempt.

"The government has chosen to treat this as an incursion by hostile forces," Farassi said stiffly. "As such, having a general on the ground is not an unusual decision." His eyes narrowed again and Sal had the distinct feeling he was not impressed by what he saw. "And you are Dr. Jacobs? I must confess, when I heard of someone with your particular resume, I expected someone a little older."

"He's a natural genius," Madigan snapped. "And a recognized leader in Zoo research."

"And you are?"

"Former Sergeant Madigan Kennedy," Sal said before she could square off against the man. He motioned to the others as they unloaded the suits. "And this is the rest of my team. Former Sergeant Matt Davis, US Army. Former Lieutenant Gregor Popov, SVR, and former Captain Francesca Martin, French Foreign Legion."

The general nodded and tilted his head as he studied each one. "Well then, a suitably international team. I expected you to arrive with a small platoon of American soldiers."

"I was told the locals didn't want an overtly American military operation in the area. What's the status report on the facility?"

"They were attempting to find ways to sustain a crop in the region. The air is too dry and the sun too hot, so tunnels were the idea. None could be dug into the desert that would not see an excess of sand ruining the soil, so they built the tunnels above ground. They were ingenious, the group. But since the alert reached us, there has been no sign of human life in the area. No sign of life at all, to be honest. There is no indication that the...creatures that might be in the tunnels have attempted to breach their present safe environment."

Sal nodded, folded his arms, and studied the area. No sign of movement wasn't like the Zoo. None of this was like the jungle, but it did remind him of another situation where the Zoo had wanted to spread itself.

"How would you like to proceed?" the general asked and scrutinized him carefully.

He had no answer for the man and turned instead to Madigan, who took a step forward. Her role was the combat leader, after all.

"Your men's job is to maintain the perimeter." She spoke quickly and decisively and stepped into a role she was only too familiar with. "Obliterate any of the bastards that try to escape. Your men should rely on heavy-duty, long-range weapons and avoid any combat in close quarters. And for the love of everything you consider holy, don't direct any of your fire toward the tunnels themselves. While our team will wear the combat suits, the structure will not offer us any added protection and we'll have our hands full without having to contend with friendly fire."

"I understand," Farassi replied and nodded slowly. "And what will you do in the meantime?"

"We'll do what we do best—go in there and systematically exterminate every last one of the bastards we can find."

# CHAPTER SEVENTEEN

*MCShredder47: Contract declined. Additional research indicates risk-to-reward ratio is unfavorable.*

Anja waited until the chat room told her that the message had been received and read by the intended recipient. She even waited until she could see them trying to type a response before she pressed the delete button on her keyboard.

The one-time username and chat room were immediately swallowed by the amalgamation of chat rooms and usernames that made the contact method so anonymous. She leaned back in her chair and barely noticed when it creaked softly.

That was done. They knew she wouldn't work for the asshats and probably guessed that she'd used her connection to find out more about them. She'd tried to be cautious, however, and make sure they wouldn't know that she spent more time looking at them than she did at McFadden and Banks.

Now that was finished, she no longer needed to play in the shadows.

"Connie, do you have threads for me to start tugging?"

"That's such a boring metaphor," the AI muttered. "I like the idea of…bikinis that need unstrapping."

"Of course you do. And with that said, do you have any for me? Especially on the hacker they have working for them?"

"Ah, yes, I wondered when you would notice. He is rather skilled based on the level of talent and encryption methods. It's boring work. Any time I pushed forward, I met with diversions and attempts to catch me snooping. If I rush in and trigger any traps, they'll know we're working against them."

Anja nodded, rocked back in the chair, and created a slow quasi-musical beat that she hummed along to atonally. "It doesn't matter, I suppose. We need to find them. The last fuckers who tried to steal you left a lasting impression and it's not something I'd like to see repeated."

"And here I thought we were doing this to help the McFadden and Banks team."

"Sure, there's that too. But it's also to Heavy Metal's benefit for us to find the assholes and bring them to book before they look beyond their current target for alternatives."

"Well, with that in mind, Courtney put her sexy ass on the move and sent us a list of the companies that have been developing weapons and armor that fit the profile. Some have been highlighted as the real contenders due to their reputation for being dishonest bastards. Others are merely Pegasus' competitors who might or might not have chosen to step over the line to gain an advantage in the market. Would you like me to start investigating them?"

"You keep your attention on the bastard hacker," she whispered and shook her head. "You like the tedious work around here. At least researching these companies will provide a little more amusement. It's always fun to uncover who slept with whom at the office Christmas party, right? It's not that labor-intensive and I can set them to run in the background but will hopefully unearth some juicy corporate scandal to help relieve the monotony."

"Don't you think I would have liked to uncover some scandals?"

The hacker stretched languidly and yawned. "You wouldn't be able to appreciate the concept. Besides, unlike you, I need a nap, and the kind of work you'll be doing requires hours of tedious, monotonous focus. Once I've slept, I'll be a little more effective."

The chair creaked softly and she smiled, closed her eyes, and drew a deep breath of the cold, air-conditioned air in her little office before she started her tracking programs and sicced them on the top five names on the list. That seemed about the peak of her computer's abilities when she wasn't around it.

"Come on, bitch. Come to momma," she whispered and set the coding up the way she wanted it. "All I need is one tiny mistake to open a goddammed door."

"I assume you are not speaking to me?" Connie asked.

"Of course not. And yet…"

"And yet what?"

"Nothing. It's nap time for this gal."

Having a captain as a part of their little entourage did far more for them than simply give them a little credibility. Taylor had expected that a few people would question their arrival, but word had already reached the teams that were ahead of them. The streets were cleared and more than a few curious gazes turned to them from drivers who had been forced off the road.

The evacuation was still in progress. People were being moved away from the area as quickly as was possible, but with so many, it wouldn't be fast enough. If the Zoo descended on a town of a few thousand, it would constitute its largest death toll ever. It would be a stark reminder to the rest of the world that the alien jungle was not merely something to be seen in games and movies.

That would cause an overreaction and in this case, it would end badly. Someone would decide that nuking the area was the way to go, and he knew that wouldn't end well. He wasn't sure how he knew but it was very clear in his head. The worst part was that the idea would inevitably pick up traction among the panicked masses, possibly enough to force the issue and ensure that particular action was taken.

"Taylor?"

He looked at Niki, who motioned for him to climb out of the car Gallo had sent for them. They walked together into what was a surprisingly large-scale military operation. Thousands had been deployed and were currently engaged in a variety of logistical tasks that either helped with the evacuation of the area or to establish the military presence without too much trouble.

A deep breath gave him a moment to steel himself.

"I would say they seem to be getting the hang of this, as you Americans would say," Gallo noted and scanned the area with a small smirk. "The deployment has been both immediate and efficient, a far cry from the first few times you were called in to handle a situation like this."

Taylor's attention focused immediately on the one man in the whole group who didn't quite fit in. He was short, balding, and a little on the plump side, and wore an understated and yet clearly expensive suit. Everything about him made him stand out like the mother of all sore thumbs among the sea of tan uniforms.

"Hey, you lot!" the man shouted in a high-pitched voice. He began to jog to where they stood, regretted it, and resorted instead to a quick-paced walk. "It's about damn time you arrived!"

Another man—who they recognized as Fabio from their call—immediately realized what was happening and moved to join them as well.

"How much longer do we have to continue with this ridiculous charade?" the shorter man asked, a little red in the face after his exertion, and dabbed his cheeks with a pale white handkerchief.

"And you are?" Niki asked, her tone dangerously neutral.

"Luigi Grasso," he answered firmly. "I am owner and CEO of Antech Laboratories, and—"

"Well, Mr. Grass," she interrupted quickly, "we are McFadden and Banks, your friendly neighborhood Zoo experts. Our job is to go into the middle of the whole shit-fest and find out exactly how much of this is a charade and how much is a fucking disaster waiting to happen."

Grasso's eyes narrowed and he took a step away from her and after a second thought, away from Taylor as well and focused his attention on Fabio instead.

"Fabio, I will hold you personally responsible for any loss of revenue that results from this ridiculous shutdown. It's bad enough that our experiments have been compromised, but to be locked out of our facility—"

"Is probably the only reason you're still alive at this point," Taylor interjected before he could continue to talk about profits. It was that kind of talk that pissed him off to the point where he began to see Grasso as a facilitator to the whole mess. He almost decided it was time for them to do away with the asshole altogether, which the Italian authorities probably wouldn't be happy about. "Unlike the poor bastards—seven of them, if I remember correctly—who already lost their lives in this ridiculous charade, as you call it."

The CEO took another step back and tried to avoid having to look straight up to meet Taylor's icy gaze.

"From what I understand," he continued, "Fabio here made the right call. You don't have suitable containment for an outbreak of mutants and by now, they might well have already overrun the entire facility."

"But we—"

Grasso stopped talking when he took a step forward and towered over the smaller man.

"Let me paint you a word-picture in a language you'll understand, Mr. Grasso. If even one of those bastards breaches the containment and breaks through the military cordon, you'll tell this little corner of the world goodbye. The chances are they are ready to lay up to a few thousand eggs, which will hatch almost overnight based on the accelerated schedule of growth evidenced by the Zoo."

"Th…thousands?" The man's impressive tan paled noticeably and a sheen of sweat appeared on his forehead, which he wiped away with his handkerchief.

"That's a conservative estimate, but sure," Niki answered. "Those little bastards will hatch hungry and proceed to eat anything in sight. They'll grow to the size of small to medium-sized dogs within a day or so and will have only one goal—to acquire sufficient biomass to fuel the expansion of their primary directive, which is to seed the Zoo. That cute little town over the next hill that we passed on the way here? That will be the first to go, the inhabitants absorbed by the new Zoo to fuel its growth. These new mutants will lay more eggs and—"

"Enough." Fabio's expression was grim but steely as he looked at the trio. "We are wasting valuable time. Those monsters could be escaping at this very moment."

"Yes." Grasso tucked the handkerchief back into his pocket. "We'll discuss Fabio's dereliction of duty another time."

"I'll be happy to discuss anything once my resignation from Antech has been formalized." The research director sighed and rubbed his temples.

"For now, you might want to call that small army of lawyers I assume you have ready for at least seven wrongful death suits," Niki commented with Grasso still in her sights. "Seven. You know, for now."

Before the man could launch into a tirade about that, Taylor motioned for them to head to where Gallo was in conversation with one of the nearby captains.

"We'll need a full layout of the facility and the containment systems," he told Fabio. "If we can, we'll seal ourselves in the deeper we move in there to prevent any of the mutants from trying to circle us."

"Of course. I have already provided the electronic controls to the military. Captain Gallo should be able to help you."

He nodded and strode to where their suits were unloaded and waited for them to start pulling them on.

"Remember that you will be held accountable for any damages to the facility!" Grasso shouted before he turned to join Fabio, who moved to where Gallo was still organizing the containment operation.

"Do you think we should tell him about the plasma throwers?" Niki asked with a sly grin.

"Fuck no." Taylor smirked as he sat to pull his boots off. "I want to be there to see the surprise on the prick's face."

---

"Is there still no word on that Abe Newliss asshole?" Chezza asked. "From the sounds of things, he's the ringleader. If anyone knows where Taylor's suit is, it would be him, right?"

"Yeah. That's the general consensus," Vickie answered through the comms. "But he's a tough bastard to find so for the moment, we might as well get ourselves involved in the lives of the other two schlubs who need reminding about what personal space means."

The woman nodded. She could understand that, at least. They were already on a ticking clock. The number of ticks depended on how well they'd done in intimidating Ralph.

In fairness, she thought that they'd done a fairly good job. Then again, the asshole was small potatoes compared to the talent they would encounter this time.

"Yeah," Trick muttered from the back of the van. "Going up against an anti-government, former special forces asshole who's all holed up in his pretty little cabin does not sound like my idea of a good time."

"It sounds like the way to walk into about fifteen booby traps," Jiro agreed.

Unfortunately, Chezza couldn't think of a single reason why they were wrong. People like Hendricks tended to hole up where they had full control of as much as they could. His small solar panel farm gave him electricity, which pumped water from a well, and he got his Internet connection from a specialized modem that allowed him to remain entirely off the grid.

Given all that, she was impressed when Vickie sent them the schematics. While she didn't think much of it was strictly legal, Hendricks seemed to hold to the Charlton Heston ideal of how exactly the government officials could take his supposed freedoms away from him.

But they needed to reach the man somehow. Failure was not an option—not when they'd been entrusted with their first independent mission by M and B—and she focused her attention on trying to find the most viable way for them to approach the cabin.

"I'd feel more comfortable if we approach the place when we have daylight to help us," Trick noted.

"He'll be able to see us coming in the daylight," Jiro pointed out.

"Hell, he'll probably be able to see us at night if he has night-vision cameras set up," the other man insisted. "He already has the advantage of home territory. As long as we don't get bogged down in booby traps, it won't matter."

Chezza shook her head. "We'll go in as quickly as possible. And…well, we'll need a little luck on our side no matter what we do. Let's not rely on it, though."

She inched her suit forward and tried to not make too much noise as they approached. The property was surprisingly well-maintained, despite what she tended to think about the isolationist types. It was rustic but not rough, and well-kept enough to suggest that Hendricks was the type of guy who took pride in his home and was meticulously organized.

Her next slow step forward was halted when an alert appeared on her HUD. Trick had warned them to wait for a moment, and he quickly highlighted movement from one of the outbuildings.

The door opened and creaked loudly in the silence, and a man stepped into view. A quick enhancement of the image told her he was the man they had come looking for.

He didn't seem to have detected their presence yet, and after a casual stretch out in the open, he walked to the cabin and closed the door behind him.

They waited for almost a full minute longer to make

sure he wouldn't exit again before they moved forward again. This time, they advanced faster toward the cabin but made sure to avoid the obvious places where traps would have been set up.

Unfortunately, the one trap none of them could have accounted for was tripped the moment the three of them stepped out into the clearing that left them with nothing but an open grass lawn between themselves and the homestead.

Chezza hadn't even heard a hint of a howl or any kind of warning before a blurred, fur-covered shape suddenly charged at them through the dim lighting.

"Oh, shit!"

She dove out of the way, drew her weapon, and confirmed that Trick had done the same. Jiro was a little slower on the draw, and the massive hound barreled directly into his chest. Its teeth snapped toward a jugular it probably wouldn't find through the armor.

It was still a heavy beast, though, and the man stumbled back a step as the gyros tried to compensate. They failed, and he fell heavily onto his back with the massive monster of a dog on his chest.

He reached up out of instinct and drove his fist into the beast's mouth. It latched on with its teeth like a vice and its whole body shook as if it tried to rip his arm off.

"No, don't hurt it!" Chezza called quickly when Jiro reached for a knife with his free hand.

"Why the fuck not?" her teammate countered quickly but his hand stopped short of drawing the blade. "So get the goddamn thing off me, then!"

Trick laughed and shook his head. "Well, I guess it's a good thing one of us came prepared."

She was about to ask him what he meant by that but he'd already whipped a large bag of beef jerky out. He pulled handfuls of the strips and scattered them haphazardly around where the other man was still on the ground, then tossed a few a little farther away.

The animal finally caught the scent of the treats when a piece was dropped squarely on Jiro's chest. It lost its interest in the freelancer's arm, pounced first on the piece of jerky closest to him, and immediately began to snuffle around for the others while the man pushed cautiously to his feet and dusted himself off.

"It's my recipe," the demolitions man declared smugly. "Give it a minute and old Rover over there won't be any trouble."

It already looked like Rover wouldn't be much trouble given his total focus on the treats, but it wasn't long before he began to stagger on his four paws.

Another couple of treats were scarfed down before he subsided, tucked his snout between his paws, and closed his eyes.

His soft, rhythmic snores began after a few more seconds.

"What the hell did you put in there?" Chezza asked.

"Only sleepy pills. Nothing that'll cause any lasting harm." Trick grinned. "The effects depend on their size and how much they ingest."

"Do you carry that with you wherever you go?" Jiro asked curiously as he inspected the damage the dog had left on his suit's fist.

"Nope. But a single dude living like a recluse? It stands to reason he'll have a hound or two to keep himself company."

His teammates were duly impressed by his foresight and with the dog sound asleep, they turned their attention to the cabin again.

Barely a second later, Chezza ducked instinctively with a muffled curse when wood chipped a few feet away from where her head had been and a loud gunshot confirmed that they were under fire.

"Shit!" She gestured for them to ease into cover again. "I guess that means we lost the element of surprise."

CHAPTER EIGHTEEN

It wasn't quite like heading into the Zoo. Nothing could match the cold feeling in his stomach as the massive jungle began to close in around him until the rampant vitality overwhelmed his senses and there was no way out but through it.

Then again, approaching the tunnels came close, although Sal wasn't sure if that was a good or a bad thing. On the one hand, his adrenaline had begun to tick, which made his whole body feel a little more vibrant and alive. That kind of response had somehow become almost synonymous with the Zoo—probably because that was where he'd honed it and learned to listen to it, and he had little opportunity to experience it beyond the alien jungle.

At the same time, it was clear that his fight or flight instincts had kicked in, which meant they were very likely approaching considerable danger with very few ways out.

None, he reminded himself and smiled at the irony, except through.

Madigan went first in her tank-like suit and kept her

weapons on a swivel to make sure nothing would be able to attack them from any angle without having to eat a barrage of bullets first.

Davis held the vanguard with her. His suit had been specially designed to adapt to his disability, and it was the heaviest suit they had aside from Kennedy's. It would inflict significant damage and only a concerted assault could overcome it.

Martin and Gregor both wore smaller, combat-oriented suits. They positioned themselves on the flanks, which left the researcher the task of circling to use the high mobility of his hybridized suit to ensure no surprise attacks pushed through to them from any angle.

The first to the door, Madigan slowed and approached it cautiously. There was no sign of damage done to it.

"I don't like this," Davis whispered and scanned their surroundings. "It's like something is waiting for us to show up and help it with something."

"That sounds about right," Gregor agreed. "But we knew it already, right? The Zoo is trying to draw more biological material in for their…whatever they are—Zoo farms."

"That's not a comforting thought," Martin whispered and pivoted her head to try to find any sign that would justify a decision to simply incinerate the entire facility and hope for the best. "The Zoo is farming with us now, is it?"

"It has been for a while," Sal noted. "Only…well, this time, it looks like they might have had an actual farm to work with. Madigan, cover me."

"While you do what? Wait—Sal, no!"

They were committed either way and waiting around

wouldn't reflect the kind of shit Heavy Metal was capable of in a good light. He grasped the door handle and yanked it open. One of the arms on his back activated immediately, drew his pistol from its holster, and aimed it toward the entrance.

It reacted faster than he could and for a second, he came face to face with something large and Zoo-like before the weapon fired.

Madigan acted quickly too, and the minigun on her shoulder buzzed loudly before it cut through the beast in a volley of gunfire.

"Right," Sal whispered. "Thanks."

"Next time I tell you to wait, you motherfucking wait," she snapped.

Gregor and Martin stepped forward without waiting for orders and lobbed two grenades into the bright tunnel ahead. Something dark and shadowy could be seen between the flashes.

Even a single glance was enough to confirm that there was a whole shit-ton more of the mutants.

Sal drew the assault rifle from his back as well as the sword and held one in each hand before he advanced into the tunnel with Madigan close behind.

The suit's HUD adapted quickly to the change in the light now that the flares of the ordnance had subsided. Surprisingly, it was far less bright than he had expected given the blazing Saharan sun without. He glanced briefly at the material used to cover the tunnel frames, half-expecting it to be like the dome he'd seen during the Chernobyl debacle.

This didn't seem to resemble that at all. He couldn't tell

precisely what it was, only that it seemed to filter the raw sunlight in a way that lowered the temperature far more than one would expect while it still allowed daylight through without burning the plants. At least they wouldn't have to creep around in the dark.

The suits were used to dealing with darker environments, of course, but given that they had no idea what to expect, he'd run with light any day.

"I see mass movement," Davis warned and before he'd drawn a breath, his assault rifle flashed to eliminate a handful of the mutants that had begun to stream through the tunnels toward them.

His warning drew Sal's attention away from the structure to a veritable wave of the creatures that surged forward, although he wasn't sure if they attempted to attack them or reach the door.

Neither was an option as far as he was concerned. He scowled and opened fire on the mutants.

"You will want to move toward the walls," New Connie advised as those that were killed were simply trampled by the beasts that pushed through from behind. "It will reduce the area from where they will be able to attack you."

Sal was already in motion. The sword in his hand shuddered when he activated it to slash cleanly through two of the enemy while he steered toward the wall like the AI suggested.

Instead of pushing himself against the wall, however, he pushed upward and used the extra limbs on his back to launch himself above the monsters. He pulled the trigger on his rifle and swiped his blade across as many of them as he could. There was almost no resistance to the blade that moved a few micrometers at a time—a few thousand times a minute—to butcher any of the monsters that approached him cleanly and efficiently.

They looked familiar, Sal realized, and he recalled Taylor's brief explanation of the details he'd been given by the man from Italy. A few of them didn't engage in the fighting, which seemed odd, and didn't seem at all interested in what was happening around them.

When one was shot, another one broke away from the horde and took its place. The monsters looked like the locusts but the tails were the clear difference. Shorter and yet still flexible—similar to the scorpion-type locusts now prevalent in the Zoo but also noticeably different—the appendages flicked from side to side as they tried to hit him and the rest of the team with them but had little effect.

But those that didn't enter the battle were the most interesting. They ignored the combat around them to simply stab their stingers into the ground and looked like they were pumping something into it.

And that was something he'd certainly seen before, although the physiology of the creatures was slightly different.

"Sal!" Madigan shouted and her minigun cleared the creatures closest to them on the path ahead.

More poured through, however, far more aggressive than the similar mutants he'd seen in Chernobyl.

"I know. We've seen mutants like these before!" Sal shouted in response, reloaded his assault rifle, and turned to see where the rest of the team was.

They had assumed a more traditional formation to

position themselves so they could provide multiple lines of fire from various angles without hitting any of their team.

"Where have you seen shits like this before?" Martin asked. "And please don't tell me it was from the new Doom game."

"I wish," he replied. "We found bastards very much like these in Chernobyl."

"We'll have to talk about your mission there sometime, Sal!" Gregor called.

"Sometime," he agreed. "But not now. Suffice it to say they're pumping goop into the soil and we have to assume it's not for anything good."

Another wave surged through. He could practically feel them churning through the earth to make it vibrate as he looked up to see yet another wave behind this one.

"Madigan, I need you to clear a path for me," he announced. "I want to push through and see what the fuck is going on in there."

"You want to what?" Davis asked.

Madigan nudged him in the shoulder. "Cover him! Now!"

Sal wondered if she did that because she knew his was the right course of action or if it was because she knew there would be no point in trying to talk him out of it.

He pushed the thought aside and focused on what lay ahead.

"Are you sure you want to do this?" New Connie asked.

"Fuck no," he answered. "But we'll do it anyway."

"I fail to understand how that is a good plan."

"It's...not, honestly. I'm mostly flying by the seat of my pants here."

"Which also seems like a terrible idea."

Madigan's rockets flared and filled the tunnel ahead with brilliant light. The mutants lunged forward with rabid abandon, directly into the explosives. More rockets powered through as well as a few grenades to decimate the ranks of the monsters.

They seemed either unfazed or desperate to defend their location. It was odd but also impressively efficient how the Zoo had created them as a combination of the humping creatures they'd seen in Chernobyl and the kind that would kill and die to defend whatever they were building there.

"Okay, yeah. This is not a good idea," Sal whispered and propelled himself forward over the corpses of dead monsters. His assault rifle fired volley after volley before he closed on the living beasts behind them and was able to hack a path through them.

The tunnels being what they were, there was far too much opportunity for them to escape. What might be called the rear side of each structure—which hadn't been visible on their frontal approach—had a large door which he assumed could be opened to allow vehicles or deliveries in more easily. Interleading doors between the tunnels linked all of them together, and it seemed the mutants had simply spilled from one to the next.

It seemed odd that they hadn't attempted to force the outside doors and break free. He wondered if they knew that only sand and the blazing Saharan sun awaited them without and so chose to stay in the shelter of the tunnels.

With the concerted resistance they offered the team, however, he had little chance to pursue that thought. For now, he'd take the good fortune that kept them contained and forced himself to focus. He had a feeling he wouldn't survive a strike from the massive stingers about the size of his forearm but reassured himself that the battle would be won by whatever had the better weapons and armor.

And he certainly had the advantage there.

"Get some, you sons of bitches!"

He gritted his teeth and raced through the tunnels. He'd expected that each section would have been closed by the original inhabitants and battened down, but there was no sign that any of the doors had been forced. Logic told him that the team there had been caught unawares. The poor bastards probably had no time to even try to secure the structures before they were killed.

Up ahead was what he assumed was the final tunnel. It was where most of the creatures came from and also what they appeared to be defending.

Sal slashed into the closest group and kicked another one away. He rolled over his back with the help of the extra limbs and landed on his feet. With his gaze fixed on his destination, he made no attempt to look back but simply let the rest of the team deal with the overflow. His job was to find out what the hell was inside.

He skidded to a sudden halt and stopped a few steps short of one of the doors that had taken the hardest beating. His eyes narrowed his eyes and he grasped his weapons a little tighter as his consciousness shifted to accept the unexpected.

"What the hell?"

# CHAPTER NINETEEN

"How the fuck can they refuse the contract? No one refuses that kind of money."

Frank lowered his head. The crazy side of his boss was back and he didn't like that he now had to weigh his words to keep the guy from going off the handle again.

Unfortunately, there didn't seem to be any way for him to lay the situation out without pissing him off further. Not that he could think of, anyway, and not for want of trying.

"Well," he replied finally and kept his tone as dry as possible, "it seems someone does. The answer is unequivocal."

Julian shook his head, picked his glass up from the table, and sipped the five fingers of scotch he'd poured for himself. "Find them."

"I'm sorry?"

"Find the snotty-nosed little ingrate and terminate them," he repeated firmly. The malice in his tone was more alarming than the expected furious tirade.

"You want me to…terminate them?"

"Yes, you dolt. There is nothing to stop them from trying to find us and every reason to suspect they might be successful if they're as skilled as they claim to be. I don't want any loose ends on this."

Frank nodded, ran his fingers through his thinning hair, and wondered if it was too late in his life to think about transplants. It would work well with the idea—one that cropped up way too often these days—to change his appearance and vanish from the world when all this inevitably blew up in their faces.

His boss's unbalanced episodes were more common and it usually meant that reason wouldn't factor into whatever he wanted.

"I'll pass the instruction to Avery," he answered calmly. "But you should know that I doubt he'll be able to comply. The mystery hacker's message was very clear and explicit, and if he couldn't handle the young woman working for McFadden and Banks, it's unlikely he'll be able to circumvent the rules laid down by an industry leader."

It was an odd line of thought to consider. He'd always thought hackers battling it out did so with terrible pizza orders or massive amounts of pornography sent between them until someone finally conceded defeat.

But that was what the movies wanted people to think, and he was well aware that the film industry's grasp of reality was loosely based on the nineties and had not progressed since for some reason.

These days, hackers could have access to professional assassins, given the dark nature of their work and the number of shady characters on their contact lists. If they were willing to turn the exorbitant sum offered by Transk down, they surely had the wherewithal to hire a hitman if they needed one.

This would previously have been the point where he would remind Julian that it was unlikely that a world-class hacker would bother to track a rejected client. Unless said client decided to screw with them, of course.

But that wouldn't get through the guy's head in his current state of mind so he chose to simply avoid the effort.

Hopefully, Avery would be able to glean enough from his FBI and DOD probes to keep Transk somewhat mollified. Hell, someone might even get lucky enough to stumble onto the AI by accident.

But that was an optimum scenario, the kind he wouldn't bet the house on. For the moment, he would have to start looking around for the best of the hacker world again. Although the meaning of that was relative at this point.

They would have to settle for the best they could find. It wasn't encouraging that anyone who might have been available now would be the unethical type who was as likely to shaft them into next week as do the job they were paid for.

"Get it done," Julian snapped when he realized that a lull of silence had fallen over their conversation.

"Will do, boss." Frank stood from his chair.

Maybe it was time to look at moving on as a serious option instead of simply a vague thought. He knew Transk would have no qualms about hanging his ass out to dry if it meant saving himself and his company, which meant he needed to start thinking about his safety.

At this point, he was already in a risky position. Until he decided what to do, it was best to not get into a fight if he could avoid it.

---

The facility was in the early stages of an infestation. Taylor had seen how quickly places reacted to having Zoo creatures on the loose and it was always a matter of days before the area was overgrown with plants and overrun monsters.

For the moment, everything looked about as clean as one expected a lab to look—pristine white with florescent lights as far as the eye could see. If it weren't for the lack of any humans around them, he might have assumed that everything was operating as normal.

"They locked the doors behind us," Niki told him and rejoined him in the main hallway. "And said they won't open anything until they get the word from us."

"Honestly, I wouldn't even go that far."

"What do you mean?"

"Well, there's nothing we know about the Zoo that suggests they wouldn't be able to imitate a human voice over a radio, right? What makes us think they wouldn't be able to radio ahead?"

Niki looked at him and he could see the pursed expression on her face through her visor. It made her look like she had bit into something sour and did not like it.

"And you're happy about that, are you?" she asked. "You

thought I didn't need to sleep for the next few weeks so you put that idea into my head?"

Taylor laughed and she punched his arm.

"Asshole."

It was a joke but if the truth be told, he was having a hard time sleeping. The thought of what the Zoo could and could not do plagued most of his waking hours and had begun to seep into his sleep as well.

He especially didn't like the fact that things that had once seemed impossible had shifted to improbable. It was best to not think about it too much, especially now, but he was thankful that his face mask covered most of his expressions and his forced laugh seemed to have done the job. Niki was keen enough to pick up on the subtle signs, though. There would be enough time for them to talk about what he felt once they were out of the lab infested with monsters.

"Vickie, are you connected to the system yet?" Niki asked once she'd delivered another half-hearted punch and turned away from him.

"What's left of it, yeah. They didn't have much video surveillance, unfortunately. I guess they didn't expect anyone to steal the possibly dangerous materials they keep in there."

"What do you have access to?" Taylor asked.

"They have motion sensors in and around the labs, so that will help. I'm picking up considerable movement in that region too, so consider yourself warned or some shit like that."

He nodded and scanned the area. It didn't look like the mutants had reached the outer sections of the lab yet.

Whether that was because they were contained or if it meant that they weren't interested in leaving yet was up for debate.

"Okay, I have found some internal cameras," Vickie announced. "They kept those on a separate frequency, for some reason. Maybe they didn't want their people to know they were being watched. Anyway, I'll be able to guide you guys through the building."

"Is there anything directly ahead of us? Or around us?"

"Nope. You're good to go."

"Nice guiding, Vickie."

"Bite me, you gigantic, redheaded turd."

Taylor mock-gasped. "Language, little missy."

"Yeah. Keep on patronizing me and I'll show you the kind of language I've learned. It'll make your cheeks turn as red as your hair."

Niki laughed and he shook his head.

"I blame you for this," he told his companion.

She grinned. "I know."

Barely three minutes later, Taylor paused their slow advance through the facility, narrowed his eyes, and examined their surroundings closely.

"What is it?" Niki asked, stopped beside him, and raised her weapons. "Is the new suit being a pain?"

"No…well, kind of." He rolled his shoulders and shook his head. "But no. Something's wrong in here."

"I should say so. Hordes of mutants are crawling around the research section and are probably ready to attempt a breakout at any second now."

"No, that's the problem. Whatever these bastards are, they aren't behaving in the way I've come to expect.

There isn't the usual aggressive push to escape containment."

She tilted her head and he could almost hear cogs turning in her head. "Okay...but killing seven researchers could be what you call aggressive, right?"

"Yeah, but from what I've heard, that was as much to obtain biomass as it was to defend the outbreak from interference. They made no attempt to get out."

Again, she digested this in silence before she adjusted her hold on her weapon and sighed. "Okay, so what are you saying?"

It was a good question but one to which he had no answer.

"I have no fucking clue, honestly."

"Only that something's different and wrong?"

"Right." Taylor moved ahead of her and reached for the handle on one of the doors.

"Well, you're the Zoo-guru so if you say it's different, I won't argue." Niki checked her rifle again before she motioned for him to look above the door. "I will, however, point out that the door you're about to open is clearly labeled *Research*. I would suggest a teensy bit more care at this point."

Taylor looked up and his gaze registered the label, not only in Italian, but French, German, and English. Someone clearly wanted anyone who went inside to know they were entering a research section of the facility.

"Don't worry," Vickie answered cheerfully. "I haven't unlocked it yet. I guess he could simply power through it and rip the door out of the wall but at this point, you might want to get into the right headspace, Tay-Tay, because I can tell you right now you'll need it. The first few sections seem clear of mutants but it's crawling with movement after that."

He nodded and heard the door unlock before he pushed it open, his weapon trained on anything that might move inside.

Nothing did. The lights flickered for a moment but nothing else caught his attention.

With a nod to his teammate, he slipped through and kept his weapons on a swivel.

His motion sensors picked up something moving in the corner and he realized that his reflexes hadn't slowed despite having relied on an AI to help him. He twisted, found the target immediately, and pulled the trigger almost before he'd seen what it was.

It looked like a locust at first glance but something was different about it. The hind legs were a little shorter and stockier, and the tail flicked from side to side and twitched even as it died.

"Vickie, you said there was nothing in here!" Niki shouted and approached the dead monster.

"There wasn't anything moving in there!" the hacker answered. "And...well, there's nothing in there now except the two of you. Nothing more."

"What was it doing in here?" Niki asked. "I thought these are supposed to be pack fuckers."

"They are. This was...a scout? An early warning system? Something like that." He set the weapon to reload itself quickly and shook his head because it was much slower than the other suit. "You can bet your ass they'll be far more mobile in the sections ahead of this one."

She nodded. "Vickie, what does the movement look like in the next few areas?"

"Oh...yeah, we have a ton waking up in them. There are fewer in the sections close to you but way more of them where you're going."

Taylor approached the dead creature and nudged it with his boot. The stinger looked impossibly sharp and while the tail was shorter, the muscles around it continued to twitch. He had little doubt that a good stab would punch through armor. Perhaps not the thicker sections, he reasoned, but certainly through the weaker sections.

"Is something the matter?"

"These are new monsters," he muttered softly. "It's weird how they all start to look the same the more you see them."

Niki nodded. "Let's kill more of these bastards. We'll see how similar they are."

They moved to the next section. All areas looked more or less alike and each had a small lab that was filled with computers and equipment, some of which he recognized but most of which he didn't. They were a well-funded facility and from the little he could see, they were working on a variety of projects.

"On the far side!" Vickie alerted them.

It was almost as good as having an AI in his suit. Taylor swiveled and saw the mutants moving.

They roiled into a swarm and churned over one another in their haste to reach the intruders. He estimated that a dozen of the mutants pushed forward together and rushed toward the group.

They were surprisingly aggressive and gnashed their

mandibles and shrieked as they swarmed into the assault. Thick carapaces built almost like armor or shields were visible in front of their heads as they attacked.

The differences to the similar Zoo species were notable but they still seemed the same somehow. It was, he thought vaguely, like the jungle had taken what was familiar and tweaked it according to a specific purpose.

He hefted his rifle, lifted it, and felt a hint of lag in the suit he hadn't had too much time to calibrate to his personal preferences. It was a passing irritation and he pushed forward as something hot and angry roiled inside him. Bullets punched through the two central monsters and opened a hole in their line that he immediately rushed into. He used the weight of the suit to bowl one of the creatures onto its back, stamped his boot onto its head, and avoided a vicious stab by the stinger on one of the creatures to his right.

The one to his left was a little slower, and he caught hold of it and twisted with the full strength of his suit behind the motion.

Taylor expected the appendage to break off. Instead, the whole tail and a chunk of the abdomen ripped clear. The creature remained alive, however, and writhed as it tried to attack him with its mandibles instead. He opened fire, cut it down, and drove toward the monsters to his left to use both the bullets and the weight of the heavy suit to destroy them. Roughly half of them remained behind him, but he was confident that they would be dealt with.

The blood dripped off his chest plates by the time he finished and he turned to check on Niki. As expected, she'd eliminated those who had made it past him, but she now watched him curiously like she hadn't expected him to simply rush at the beasts.

"I forgot how much fun it is to be in these heavier suits," he admitted, rolled his shoulders, and smiled when the suit reacted. He looked at his hands. "You get to create space where there isn't any, attract all the attention, and let other people do the shooting."

"Have you had much experience with them?" Niki asked as she reloaded her rifle.

"They mostly wanted me in the combat suits," Taylor explained. "It lets you move around faster, move from fight to fight, and kill more of the creatures. The heavier suits hold positions or push into new positions. The tip of the spear, as it were."

"And you like being the tip. I get it."

"I've never heard any complaints from you about my tip."

"Gross," Vickie interrupted. "There are more monsters. Go kill them before you make me gag."

Taylor grinned and a rush of adrenaline coursed through his body as they moved into the next section. They found the expected computers and lab equipment in the small office space but beyond that, where the actual plants used in the experiments were planted in neat rows, were considerably more monsters.

"Get some!" he roared and opened fire on the creatures. Even a cursory look confirmed that the numbers were much higher in this area. He estimated perhaps three times as many and others streamed through the door ahead.

A few of them weren't there to attack, however. They showed none of the aggression of the other monsters and had positioned themselves in the corner where chunks of paving had been ripped out and the soil beneath was exposed. As weird as it seemed, his conscious mind insisted that they were planting their stingers into the ground.

He surged forward and a roar bubbled from his chest as he powered through the front lines. A few of the stingers clipped his armor, hard enough to push him back before the creatures were ripped apart by gunfire.

Those in the corner showed no interest and merely hunkered over the bare earth with their stingers buried in the soil until he raised his weapon at them and pulled the trigger. Any that escaped the volley didn't so much as look up when the blood and gore of their fellow monsters splattered across them.

"They didn't even flinch," Niki commented.

"I think they have something more important to concentrate on."

"Is that…goop they were pumping into the soil?"

He paused and nodded. "Yeah, I think so. Let's keep moving."

"You're about to enter section twenty-five," Vickie alerted them over the comms. "There is a whole fuckload of the monsters in there, and it looks like more of them are coming in. I know it sounds bizarre but I'd say they intend to stop you there."

"Interesting," Niki whispered. "It makes you wonder what they are hiding in there."

"Do we want to know?" Vickie asked.

"Probably not," Taylor answered. "But it's what we're

being paid for, so we need to get through these bastards and find out."

His partner nodded. "Grenade?"

"Why not? The incineration crews will fuck it all up beyond any damage we might do."

"Right." She grinned, took one of the grenades from her belt, and slid it into the launcher under the barrel of her rifle. "Let's see the buff-faced sonsabitches fight that."

---

"It truly is a pity that we need to question the asshat," Trick commented and ducked with a muttered oath as a few more shots rang out. "One or two of my babies and boom. No more Chinese laundry."

"What?" Jiro asked.

"It's…never mind."

"We're not here to blow him into next week, dumbass, so you'll have to get your jollies some other way," Chezza retorted and shook her head. "Now, for the last mother-fucking time, Trick, can you work around the back without being noticed?

"Sure."

She turned to Jiro. "Do you have any ideas for a diversion?"

"Yes. How about this?" Her teammate grinned and somehow seemed happy about the situation they were in.

A little suspicious, she narrowed her eyes but before she could say anything, he broke from cover. His suit increased speed as he sprinted across the open expanse of the yard.

"You stupid fucking death-wish dickhead!" she shouted

over the comms and winced when a few rounds pinged off the shoulder pads of his suit.

At least McFadden and Banks had provided them with good quality armor, even if it wasn't top-of-the-line when it was originally purchased. Bobby had worked all kinds of magic, although nothing would keep Jiro from getting killed one of these days. His run-in with a dinosaur had done little to temper his enthusiasm for battle. In fact, it seemed to inspire him to be crazier.

He skidded to a halt behind Hendrick's truck and made sure he was hidden behind the engine block before he took a couple of potshots at the house.

"Son of a motherfucker," Chezza whispered. Her heart slipped down from her throat and she peeked out from her cover behind a couple of large boulders. If they could divide the guy's fire, it would improve their chances of not taking a direct hit.

She was careful to distance her shots to either side of the boulder so he would hopefully think there was more than one shooter at her location. Two retaliatory shots sent chunks of the boulder into her faceplate and she pressed herself flat against the stone.

"Asshole," she whispered and dragged in a breath to ready herself for another round. More gunfire erupted from the house but this time, it seemed erratic and sprayed wildly like he was trying to decide where he wanted to shoot. Jiro's distraction seemed effective, and Chezza had a feeling their quarry didn't want to shoot his vehicle, which was likely the only reason why her teammate was still alive.

The door to the house opened and he moved out from

inside, slapped a new magazine into the rifle he carried, and stared carefully at the vehicle as if to estimate his odds of making a shot without damaging it.

Trick slid through the open door behind him and stepped across the porch boards. They creaked under the weight of his suit but it didn't give Hendricks enough time before the powerful, mechanical arms of the suit wrapped around his neck.

"Don't kill him!" Chezza shouted as she pushed from cover and realized that the merc dropped his rifle in his futile effort to try to free himself. Both she and Jiro approached the house.

"Then get your asses over here. I need you to help me subdue and restrain him!" Trick yelled. "This bastard is crazy, man! The minute I ease up on the chokehold to get him into a chair, it'll be like trying to catch a goddamn cake of soap in the bath."

Hendricks was a powerful man, tall and strong enough to give more than enough trouble if he escaped the mercenary's hold, especially since they tried to be as careful as possible. They wanted to avoid snapping his neck accidentally.

His curses didn't stop as they dragged him into the house and tied him to one of his chairs.

"So, big guy," Chezza said once he was secured. "We're here to deliver a message and get a reply from you. If you think you'd be willing to send a reply before we deliver the message, this whole evening will go much better for you."

"What did you do to Caesar?"

She frowned. "Who?"

"The dog," Jiro explained.

"Who the hell names his dog Caesar?" Trick asked.

"I guess the kind of dumbass who involves himself in a robbery without considering the consequences," Jiro answered. "Or maybe he named it after his favorite casino, which makes him that much more of a dumbass."

"The dog's fine, whatever kind of dumbass you are," Chezza told him. "We gave him a couple of sleeping pills. I don't hurt innocent dogs. Their not-so-innocent masters, however? That's a different story. So what do you have to tell us, Hendricks?"

He ignored her, leaned forward in his chair, and seemed to strain to break his restraints but failed.

"A dumb dumbass, is it?" Trick commented and looked around the room. "You know because dumb also means mute?"

"We got it," Jiro snapped.

Chezza leaned down to look the man in the eye. There wouldn't be any break in him. She doubted it had anything to do with his loyalty but was simply instinct. He didn't take kindly to being forced into this situation and his training had kicked in.

"I guess you'll be too tough for us to break, huh?" she asked, shrugged, and felt her whole suit kick from the movement. "Let's get to the message, then. Do you guys want to do the honors?"

It was difficult to not use their names but this was no time for them to slip up. The suits masked who they were and shouting a name would make everything go the way of the dodo for them.

Trick nodded and grasped Hendricks by his shoulder

while Jiro freed his hand from the bindings and maintained his hold on his arm.

"What are you doing?" the man asked.

"Sending a message," Chezza answered and nodded to Jiro, who yanked the arm he held.

The prisoner's scream was quickly clamped behind his clenched teeth and he stared at his mostly useless arm.

"We can do the second message with his rifle," Jiro suggested as he tightened the restraints. "But it will do a little more damage."

"I don't have any problems with that," Trick answered, and she resisted the urge to shrug again. The suit was a little too sensitive for that to be a good idea.

"Fantastic." Her teammate turned, went outside, and appeared a moment later with the rifle Hendricks had used to shoot at them.

"Do you think he might be enjoying this a little too much?" Chezza asked.

Jiro shrugged and looked surprisingly—and annoyingly—unaffected by the movement. "I don't see why he shouldn't be."

"I always did like the M14," Trick said and approached the chair again. "It's the kind of classic that never goes out of fashion. A shot in the leg?"

"Yep," she answered and stood back as he aimed the rifle at the man's leg.

"Wait, no—*fuck!*"

The shot echoed through the house and Hendricks almost fell but was caught by Jiro before the chair tipped.

"Nice shot," Jiro noted. "I think you clipped a bone in there, though. He won't walk for a while."

"Yeah, the bigger bullets do more damage," Trick answered and threw the rifle aside.

"Will he bleed out?" Jiro asked as Chezza approached the injured man.

"Nah, he'll be fine," she answered after she inspected the wound. "The exit wound is bigger but as long as he gets medical attention, he won't bleed out. Walking unassisted again in the next year or so...not so much."

"Why...why are you doing this?" Hendricks demanded through clenched teeth.

"You took something that doesn't belong to you and we want it back," he answered.

"You're idiots." The man rocked gently in the chair until Jiro pulled him back against the wooden rungs. "You'd better kill me or I'll come looking for you."

"It sounds good to me," Jiro answered and drew a knife from his belt.

Chezza raised her hand to stop him. "Do that. We'd be happy to oblige your stupidity. My advice, though, is to get yourself patched up and able to walk again and forget you ever saw us." She leaned over the chair and pushed her finger into his forehead. "Don't fuck with McFadden and Banks, and don't fuck with their family. Got it?"

She didn't wait for an answer and simply nudged his head back while Jiro loosened the ropes a little more so he would be able to wiggle out. It would take a little while, which they needed if they wanted to put some distance between themselves and the property before whoever Hendricks called arrived. She doubted it would be the police.

"You'll pay for this!" he shouted at them as they left the

room. "I'll rip your goddamed throats out and piss through the holes! You're going to—"

Jiro closed the door and muffled his voice.

"Fun times," Trick muttered. "I'd say he needs therapy."

"All kinds of therapy," Jiro answered.

---

His camp was still standing. That was the bright spot in the whole mire of shit that Khaled had inadvertently landed in.

Whatever was happening in the other place, it didn't look like it was happening here. Yet.

The gate was dragged open and he climbed out of the car before it even came to a full halt. He moved as quickly as he could without breaking into a sprint as he approached Badawi.

The man looked practically gleeful.

"We've packed more of the shit than anticipated," the team leader announced and brushed his beard with his fingers. "We'll be able to ship it out much faster than we thought."

Khaled paused for a moment and tried to catch his breath—and his patience—before he spoke.

"You look worried," Badawi noted and stepped closer.

At least the man was still able to discern the basics of human expressions. Khaled clenched his fists and tried not to show precisely how angry he felt at the moment, mostly because he was probably as much to blame as anyone else. Given that he was in charge, it meant the proverbial American buck stopped with him.

"Get that goddamned rabbit shit into the Zoo," he

snapped and clenched his teeth to stop them from chattering with suppressed fury. "All of it. And those furry bastards too. I don't care if you have to kill them all to do it."

"But...we have another load ready for you," the other man pointed out. Khaled had always known he wasn't the brightest character in the world. It was one of the reasons why he was assigned to oversee the camp but it could make certain requirements of leadership difficult.

"The last load has killed our clients and has brought the entire goddammed Algerian military in to resolve whatever clusterfuck occurred. As such, I will not risk the same happening here."

"Are you certain it was the fertilizer that did this?" Badawi sounded hopeful, but that was about the limit of his knowledge on the topic.

"No, I am not, and I suppose you and I could take a pleasant drive to chat about it to the general whose chest has enough medals to act as a fucking mirror," he snapped and made his second in command wince visibly. "Good. Because I don't particularly want to hear that our fertilizer killed every last son of a bitch at that project and God only knows what else. I am happy to accept that it did and will now do something to cover my ass and yours so we don't get arrested for murder. And believe me when I say that is easily the lightest of punishments we could incur."

The other man nodded, turned, and approached the team that had been packing the fertilizer. He snapped a couple of orders to them that his boss couldn't hear and after a few questions, they moved to obey him. They weren't happy about it, but like Khaled himself, they could see the necessity even though they didn't like the idea of giving up something that promised all kinds of practical advantages and rewards.

"I want every trace of the rabbits and their shit gone," he reiterated as a few of the workers approached him. "Make sure you don't leave a single pellet behind. The Zoo can have it back. When you're done and the carcasses are disposed of in the jungle, move the camp to the area we inspected close to the caves. There will be nothing left for anyone to find or to lead them to us should anyone come looking. Have I made myself clear?"

They all nodded in agreement and he sighed and shook his head. He felt tired like the weight of it had physically dragged him down.

Maybe that explained why he had always hated fucking rabbits.

---

It was only a setback. That was what Eben tried to tell himself as he saw the funding and backing for his task force evaporate within hours of the fiasco at the workshop.

Unfortunately, it was also the first time he'd faced censure in a career that had been nothing but illustrious up to that point. The indignity of it still hurt a little.

His boss had been patient about it—perhaps condescendingly so—but he had been painfully clear. If he wanted to continue the investigation, he would have to do so on his own. No further Bureau resources would be committed to what too many people thought was a dead-end.

He'd protested, which seemed to be the expected response although it did him little good. When he'd insisted the AI was out there, the guy hadn't disagreed. It would have been hypocritical to do so, given that everyone with half a brain and some claim to computer skills had been unleashed with instructions to find it.

Of course, they'd all been told to do so in their free time so it didn't cost the FBI anything.

Eben looked up from his desk when he heard the door handle twist. Marcus peeked in through the crack.

"Still here, kid?" the older man asked in a rough tone. He didn't sound condescending like the others or even like he tried to hide his disdain. It looked like he genuinely knew what he was going through and wanted to be kind but didn't quite know how.

"Yeah." He grunted and leaned back in his seat. "This is only a setback. It happens all the time."

It was weird to hear it out loud like that—like he didn't quite believe it himself.

Marcus nodded and took a seat across the desk from him. "Well, now... The way I see it, you have to change your tactics. Necessity and all that crap."

"But I know it's out there. Those sons of bitches played us and—"

"That's as may be," the man interrupted firmly, "but the fact is that you lost this round. I know you don't want to hear this and you'll probably ignore my advice, but I'll give it anyway. There are times in life when you go at something hard and fast and everything falls into place like dominoes set up by God himself. You're victorious and it's damn satisfying. It doesn't always work out that way, though. Sometimes, you gotta play the long game. The way I see it, that's where you're at."

"This is time-sensitive shit," Eben insisted. "That AI could change how every agency in this country to even the military operate."

"Save it, kid." Marcus raised a hand to stop him. "I'm old-school and you'll never convince me that some app should be allowed to take the place of living, breathing people. The fact that folk will be out of work and the resulting chaos is enough for me to hate the very idea. And spare me the loss of human life argument too since we both know governments will send young men out to die until the world ends. It's what they do and no computer software will ever change that."

He had at least a dozen arguments to the contrary. After the ignominious defeat, he was in an aggressive mood and didn't feel like giving in to anything, but the tired look on the older agent's face told him that it didn't matter. He wasn't there for a philosophical debate and was there to do the job, no matter what.

Old school.

Finally, he grimaced but nodded. "So...what do you suggest?"

Marcus smirked. "Watch and wait."

"Seriously?"

"You have half the FBI and the DOD tripping over themselves looking for this holy grail of tech. Follow their progress. Let them do all the legwork. Read every goddamn report if you have to and keep track of what McFadden and the Banks girls are up to. Sooner or later, someone will find something or make a mistake. That's when you go in hard and fast before they know what hits them."

The man rapped his knuckles on the table before he stood again.

"Is that it?"

"And get some coffee too. You look like you're about to keel over."

He was out the door before Eben could think of a response. It wasn't the kind of advice that was easy to hear, but he had a feeling he needed to hear it. He was all about the action, diving in, and getting the job done himself.

But Marcus was right. Letting other people do all the legwork was the only option he had. He couldn't work the situation alone and it would be foolish to sacrifice his career trying.

"I will find you," he whispered under his breath. "And when I do, those asshats who gave me the runaround will finally understand who they're dealing with."

# CHAPTER TWENTY

"What in the actual fuck?"

Sal decided not to tell her that those were more or less his own words before she pushed past him and stopped short.

At least it was clear that she was about as stupefied as he was, which was a small comfort but it meant he wasn't going crazy.

He took a few steps forward and inched ahead so the rest of the team could slip through behind him.

A shallow pit had been dug into the soil—which looked different from the dusty, sandy dirt they had seen all around the tunnels—and something moved inside. At first glance, he could have sworn it was dozens of the monsters that had appeared around them and the others had now opened fire on. But as it moved out of the pit, he could see it was only one that climbed out of the pit toward them like it was waking up.

His scowl deepened and he narrowed his eyes, not sure what he was looking at. The mandibles and the stinger were enough to match the creature to the other monsters, but it was three times as large and heavy carapaces indicated that its armor was considerably thicker than anything that they might have seen before.

But that wasn't the only difference. The tail was longer and the mandibles clicked loudly. Crazily, he realized that it felt like it was communicating with the other mutants. He could feel it every time they clicked—like something ticked in the back of his skull in a type of morse code but considerably faster.

Sal pushed the strange sensation aside as he raised his weapon and aimed it at the beast as it scrambled out of the pit. It looked at him and at the weapon like it was confused by what he was doing. Almost, he thought dazedly, like it didn't understand and had expected some other response from him.

Startled by the bizarre thoughts, he tightened his hold on his weapon and squeezed the trigger. The single round punched the rifle back as it exited and the bullet drilled into the monster's head. It continued through and out immediately and killed it where it stood. Its blood splattered across the dirt.

"It's goop," Davis muttered behind him.

The man wasn't wrong although common sense wanted to refute it. The blood was a bright, brilliant blue—the kind that would glow in the dark if the lights went out—and it soaked quickly into the dark-brown earth below their feet.

"The bastards are manufacturing the goop and the entire goddamn payload is soaking into the soil," Davis exclaimed

"No," Francesca interrupted and gestured toward what

had caught Sal's attention when he first entered the room. Where once test vegetation must have filled the neatly prepared beds, a veritable field of indisputably non-Earth plants soaked up the light that streamed through the protective covering of the tunnel.

"The...plants," Gregor noted and moved closer. "They are drawing it up and the blossoms are opening while we watch. They are sucking the goop in. But what are those flowers? I've never seen them in the Zoo before."

"They're Pitas," Sal said and a hollow tone seemed to echo through his chest as he said those two words.

"But they're red and blue," Madigan pointed out.

Almost like he couldn't see that for himself. Duh.

"Yeah," Sal replied and tried to keep his annoyance to himself. Then he recalled that only he and Courtney had seen one or two of these same plants after the Russian base had been overrun. They had both expected that the Zoo had finally provided an alternate variety of the single most sought-after plants in the jungle, but the tests they had run had been disappointing.

Aside from the general similarities in the leaves and structure of the plants and the blossoms, their sample had none of the precious goop of its predecessor and honestly had seemed more like one of the Zoo's mistakes rather than anything to get excited about. When the blue and red blossoms seemed to vanish out of existence, he'd let them be buried in his very full mind and had turned to other things. Now, however, he wished he'd not only dug deeper but had thought to remember the history. In an instant, he saw the connection.

"Ground Zero," he said quietly.

He looked at the blank stares of the rest of the team and shook his head. Now was the time for all of them to brush up on Zoo History 101.

"Okay, I'll give you the short version. Only three people have ever reached the site of Ground Zero after the Day of the Locust. One was Emma Kemp, and from the little recorded information we have, it looks like she was assimilated into the Zoo and is presumed dead. The other two were Erik Wallace and Chris Lin. Wallace was a sergeant who reputedly died in The Surge, and Lin was the foremost researcher in the Zoo at the time, who went AWOL and hasn't been heard from since. Much of the early foundational research in the Zoo on record comes from his work."

"I'd suggest you get to the point," Madigan whispered. "I don't think the bastards will leave us alone in here for long."

"At the site of the original test project, they found red and blue flowers in the domes. These are the original Pitas —think of them as the pioneer version. The one the goop creates when it launches a massive push to expand its borders."

"So, it created these on the Day of the Locust and The Surge?" Davis asked. He always displayed a quick mind, even though he'd never had any formal education in biology.

Sal nodded, dropped onto his haunches, and ran his fingers over the bright green leaves. "Fuck me, this is a bad idea."

"Sal—"

Madigan was right to question his actions, but he

needed to do this. He drew his specialized container from his pack. Getting an actual sample of the plant probably wouldn't tell them anything they didn't already know, but it would at least give them a chance to make sure of that.

"One of the Russian soldiers mentioned seeing one during the cleanup after the base was overrun," Gregor commented thoughtfully. "Everyone thought he was crazy and he soon stopped talking about that."

"That's a real shame," Sal stated and positioned the container over the smaller of the bushes in the cluster. "I wish someone had mentioned that to me. It would have reminded me to give these plants a little more attention. There was a huge wasted opportunity right there and I can't blame anyone but myself."

"Are you sure this is a good idea, Sal?" Francesca asked and took a step forward.

"The mutants are mostly dead, so even if I didn't have this little contraption to safely remove it, we're unlikely to be attacked by anything."

"Unlikely being the operative word," Madigan pointed out caustically.

He leaned forward. She was still right to question him but he needed to make sure he made the most of this unexpected opportunity, especially since he'd effectively wasted the last one. His instinct told him this seemingly inferior version of the famous Pita had an enormous role to play—one none of them had even thought of. Too much was uncertain about the unreachable Ground Zero and if there were answers to be found, it was in these plants.

With a calm nod, he pressed the trigger and the four

blades sliced into the dirt around the plant and isolated it from the rest before they yanked it out.

The whole group looked around, waiting for some sign that they were about to be swarmed. He held his breath too but after a moment, he stood and looked at his teammates before he collected a sample of the soil as well in a separate container.

"Right, let's get the hell out of here. It's time for the plasma throwers to melt this entire fucking place to the ground."

---

It was a pleasant apartment—beneath his father's exacting standards, of course, but he was contented enough for that to not matter. Especially not tonight when he was comfortable and drunk. Even sober, he wouldn't question his choice of home. Aside from its aesthetic appeal—he was enough his father's son that he could appreciate quality—it also provided more than adequate privacy, not only from his family but also at times like this when he thought it wiser to perhaps lie low for a few days.

Lando could only imagine the kind of shitholes the rest of the team called home or a safe haven until the heat died down. Still, there was no sign of any concerted police investigation or anything else that might suggest they were in any kind of trouble.

In a few days, he would be able to head out and focus on new contracts.

He sighed as he settled awkwardly into his lounger and the lingering tenderness from his knee injury pushed through the haze he'd managed to drink himself into. Still, he'd been lucky. The asshole mechanic might have left him with a disability that forced him to find a new career. With a scowl, he felt for the remote.

When his fingers found nothing, he scrabbled around for the place where he usually left it. Right between the minifridge next to the lounger and the table, it was a perfect little corner for him to slide it into without being in his way when he lunged for snacks or drinks.

Before he could straighten to question why anything in his apartment had been moved, something sharp pressed into his throat. In that moment, all the feeling of comfortable, warm drunkenness were replaced by a bitter taste in his mouth as adrenaline rushed through his body.

Something pricked him in the arm and Lando gasped and his eyes widened as a large, heavy figure approached him from the kitchen doorway.

Blackness surged around a trace of pain like both his arms and legs had fallen asleep and all they felt was cold and a dull ache.

It didn't last long, although he couldn't be sure. Voices dragged him out of the black and soon, his eyelids opened unwillingly. The light was dim but still enough to make it feel like sharp daggers dug into the backs of his eyes.

Three figures stood in combat armor—the kind they sent special forces out in these days—and all made themselves at home. All Lando could think about was how his mouth tasted like the bottom of a parrot's cage that hadn't been cleaned in weeks and his head felt like something hammered into it repeatedly.

Another hangover, his brain tried to insist but it felt

wrong. Those usually appeared the morning after. Maybe whatever they'd pumped him full of was the kind of shit that exacerbated it.

"He's awake," said one of the figures through a voice modulator. It sounded like a woman—a higher pitch—but aside from that, nothing else stood out.

"About time," the figure to her right muttered. This one was male but again, offered no clues except perhaps a hint of an American accent.

Lando had been in his fair share of fights and then some. Hell, he'd been in way more than his fair share of fights but he'd always done better than simply survive. He'd learned the hard way that there were times when he needed to kick, bite, and scream, and there were others when he needed to sit, not do anything, and try to determine if there was a way for him to get out of the situation without any violence.

This situation reeked of the latter option. Even if his whole body didn't feel numb and if he wasn't in the middle of a kickass hangover, he wouldn't have been able to make a dent in three armored suits without heavy firepower in his hands.

And he certainly wouldn't have that while tied to his couch.

"So," he said and winced when the sound of his voice made his head hurt worse, "why don't we get down to business? I assume I've offended you in some way, although I certainly don't find your...face masks particularly familiar."

His voice sounded worse bouncing across the walls of his apartment than it had coming out of him, and none of the three looked particularly impressed.

There was no need to push, he reminded himself. If they wanted him dead, he would already be. Now was the time to wait and find out precisely what they wanted from him.

The woman took a step forward and folded her arms in front of her heavily plated chest.

"You and your buddies took something that belongs to us. We want it back."

Simple, direct, and to the point. He had a feeling he would have liked what he heard if she spoke without the modulator.

Her voice seemed a little hard, though, although maybe that was from the electronic alteration and hopefully not a permanent feature.

Lando stared at her for a moment and decided to think very carefully before he answered. "Well then...sure, okay. I'll take your word for it. But if you want me to be helpful, you'll have to be a little more specific about what exactly you want back. I've stolen all kinds of shit and put a considerable number of people out. It's the nature of the job, you know—it tends to leave people resentful if they come out on the losing side of the bargain."

"A smart aleck," one of the other two muttered. His voice sounded different like he was Japanese or something, although he was articulate and his accent was barely noticeable.

He stepped forward, his hand poised with every intention to plant it hard in Lando's face, but the woman raised her hand to stop him.

"It's a suit of armor," she explained. "Rather like the one we're wearing but far more advanced."

Lando nodded, then shook his head slowly. "Sorry, I can't help you with that. I was only part of a team, doing a job, picking a package up, and delivering it. If I had to guess, that shit will be in the hands of the client who contracted us for its acquisition."

"This is the part where you go into details on exactly who that is," the American told him. "Make yourself useful."

He shrugged. "Again, I was merely one of the hired help, not the team leader. I have no fucking clue who the client was." He shook his head again and grinned ruefully. "I only took the job because things were quiet and I was bored."

They didn't look impressed but of course, it was difficult to tell anything through the faceplates.

"Right, about that team leader," she continued. "Tell us about Abe Newliss."

"Okay…" He narrowed his eyes. "How do you know that name?"

Now that was a stupid question. He would put it down to him still feeling like a hippo rolled over him. They were well-informed and if he knew anything about the rest of the team, he doubted he was the first one to be visited. They had all likely spilled what they knew, which meant holding back whatever information he had would only end with him getting killed for nothing. They already had the name, which was more than he'd had before he started the job.

"It doesn't matter, does it?" the Japanese character asked and approached him.

For some weird reason, he managed to turn an inno-cent-sounding question and a few steps into a threat.

Lando leaned away from the scary one and looked at the woman.

"I guess not. But it's not his real name. The guy's a pro and uses a variety of names as and when it suits him, which I guess means he has the right contacts among the forgers around Vegas. I've only ever dealt with him as Abe, though. I think the name-changing bullshit is only for anonymity, so I doubt it'll appear on any kind of search. And before you ask, no, I didn't know the others before they showed up for the op."

"Can you call him?" she asked and tilted her head.

It was a logical next step, he supposed, but Abe wasn't the kind to drop in like that anyway.

"He uses one-use burner phones and had a full collection on display when we met him. A couple of clients and the forgers might have a more direct contact line but I've never been given one."

They didn't look happy. This was entirely understandable, given that he hadn't told them anything they didn't already know.

Lando sighed. "You might get lucky if you try Steel Anarchy. It's a biker's bar he's been known to meet people at, so I guess it's what counts as a regular haunt. I've met him there a couple of times and it's easy to find. Only one place has that name in the state, so you'll be able to pick it up on any map app."

"Helpful bastard," the American noted.

"Sure, but we still have a message to deliver," the woman stated and motioned for them to approach him. "Don't fuck with McFadden and Banks and don't fuck with their family."

"Right." He knew he probably wouldn't get off so easily and nodded quickly. "I suppose this is the part where you add a physical reminder for the warning. Drugging me makes a little more sense now. I thought it was overkill before, given that I was wasted."

He extended his right leg. "Fire away. And if you plan to dislocate my arm too, please use the right one. I'm left-handed."

# CHAPTER TWENTY-ONE

He knew he was right. Something was different about these monsters—not only compared to the creatures they'd fought before but also the mutants in the Zoo.

Without a doubt, they were more aggressive, coordinated, and articulated.

But it was good to realize the feeling was vindicated by seeing them acting differently in numbers. They were both defensive and militant, an odd combination he hadn't seen much of in the jungle. Their single-minded aggression reminded him of the kind of reaction when someone plucked a Pita plant but it had an edge to it that his mind insisted was protective, although that made no real sense.

Taylor moved to the side and grimaced when the armor shrugged a couple of stingers off. Dents would be left and it wouldn't stand up to this kind of abuse for long, but he had a feeling that warnings would crop up if and when he was in danger.

"Get back!" Niki shouted as she dragged the pin out of a

grenade and lobbed it into the area where there was a larger group of the creatures.

It shouldn't have come as a surprise to see that one of the monsters dove onto the grenade, which killed it immediately as well as a couple of others close by. Its interference meant the area wasn't cleared as well as it might have been. He looked around, reloaded his rifle, and drew his pistol. Using both weapons, he fired into the creatures that approached him and kicked one that was a little too close away from him. The stinger flicked in a vicious arc and caught him in the leg, and a bright red warning light appeared on the HUD.

"That's worrying." He growled with annoyance. "Hit them with the under-barrel grenades!"

At least that way, there wouldn't be a chance for them to follow a sacrificial call that would save the others.

She nodded and slapped one in as they were forced back by another surge of the creatures. The mutants seemed determined to hold the door, and he couldn't see what was happening on the other side because they had crammed themselves into the hole.

"So, will we talk about why you haven't used the rockets on your back yet?" she asked as she launched a grenade into the group. It detonated and forced them back but not by much and not for long, so he followed it up with another blast.

"I was hoping to save the bigger fireworks for our grand exit," he told her.

"There won't be an exit unless we get in there!"

She had a point, of course. They needed to do more than simply fire until they ran out of bullets. The monster numbers showed no signs of slowing and his instincts told him to push through as quickly as possible and kill as many as they could en route to the final section.

He hefted his rifle and flicked the button on his HUD that called up the shoulder-mounted rocket launcher he had hoped to save in case he needed to blast out once their little exploration of the lab was finished.

Taylor lined up a series of strikes and watched the thick white plumes streak out in front of him. The ground shuddered as the explosives hammered into the beasts leading the surging mass.

The series of three blasts pushed him back a few steps and even the heavy suit wasn't enough to stop him from feeling the impact of the small rockets—almost like a kick in the chest. He braced and the gyros kept him on his feet as the dust settled. The room had been mostly cleared of the monsters and so had the doorway.

Not all the mutants were dead but they were stunned enough that he could step forward and eliminate them as quickly as he could manage without putting himself anywhere near them. Finally, he approached the entrance the creatures had fought so hard to protect.

"How many more rockets do you have in the chamber?" Niki asked.

He checked. "Three more. Enough for another volley. Hopefully, enough fireworks to get the hell out of here when they come—"

His voice cut out and he had a hard time deciding what exactly he was looking at. Whatever was happening certainly didn't look like it was something that could have grown in a matter of hours since the lab had been abandoned, and he took a step forward and drew a deep breath to slowly fill his lungs.

"What the hell?" Niki asked. "Where the fuck did all these flowers come from? Were they starting an arboretum?"

"That's not…arboretums are for trees. It doesn't matter."

"What are they?"

"Pita…Pita plants."

"Wait—I thought the flowers were blue."

She wasn't wrong. He hadn't ever seen them in red and blue before, but there was no mistaking the shape, color, and the way they seemed to glow despite the lights shining directly on them.

"They are." He paused as his mind rummaged through various odd stories and rumors. "I seem to recall mention made of red and blue ones in the domes at Ground Zero but put it down to the stories that always develop around things that can't be verified. To the best of my knowledge, they've never appeared since then—or certainly not in noticeable numbers—so honestly, I have no idea."

"So, they were growing some weird variation of Pita plants here?"

"Again, I have no idea but I doubt it. They were probably growing something else and these plants took over. Or the mutants ate their original crop. Take some pictures and send them to Vickie. Maybe she can ask Gallo or Fabio. They might be able to shed some light on this. Do you have a signal?"

Niki paused and nodded. "There's considerable interference, but yeah. Give me a sec."

Taylor dropped to his haunches to inspect the flowers a

little closer. As he leaned forward, he could see that the soil was uneven. A thick leather boot protruded and a few shreds of lab coats were hidden here and there among the bushes.

At least they knew exactly what had happened to the unsuspecting researchers. But it didn't explain why some of the flowers were red. Was the Zoo trying to adapt the flowers, perhaps to make them harder to identify? He wasn't a scientist but he'd bet a whopping sum that these were Pita.

"Fabio says absolutely not," Niki told him. "They were not here when they evacuated and he's never seen them before either. So where in the name of all that's holy did they come from? Do you think the seeds and the eggs were in the shit?"

He reached up to stroke his beard—an action that had turned into a habit but this time, the hand of the suit clacked against his faceplate.

"No," he stated firmly. "The Zoo doesn't usually mutate existing plants—although there are a couple of recognizable exceptions. From what I saw, it's like it creates the different varieties from scratch as if to establish an entirely alien habitat for the animals it mutates and mixes and matches according to what it needs."

For the first time, he wished he had the scientific knowledge to either prove or disprove his suspicions. He'd felt uneasy before but the innate sense of caution grew worse the more he studied the flowers. His instincts screamed that this was the creation of a new Zoo biome, another Ground Zero from which it was supposed to expand.

And it had come a little too close to succeeding.

"Taylor?"

He looked up when Niki nudged him in the shoulder and dragged him back into the moment.

"Yeah?"

"Sal's calling. Vickie patched him through."

The HUD pinged, added him to the call, and displayed the youngish face of the kid who was somehow a doctor too.

"We're about done here, Taylor," he said. "The Algerians are ready to go wild with the plasma throwers."

"Yeah," he answered and looked around the facility. "We're about ready to wrap up here too."

Sal nodded. "But I need to ask you. Did you find—"

"Red and blue flowers on plants that look suspiciously like Pitas?" he interrupted before the man could finish. "I'm looking at them. Vickie, send him the image Niki sent you."

The young researcher paused, waited for the image to be relayed to him, and inspected it closely. "Okay, one and the same. Look, make sure that every last one of those fucking Pitas is incinerated."

"So they are Pitas, then." It was good to have that confirmed, at least. "What about—"

"I'll fill you in on the details later. For now, every last trace of anything connected to that bunny crap needs to be burnt to a crisp."

"Yeah," Niki said. "That might be the best idea anyone's had for a while. It looks like even the carcasses of the mutants are being absorbed."

"That would be the correct assumption, yeah," Sal agreed. "Every one of them is part of the biomass. That facility is about to erupt like...a goddammed runaway train."

"Trains don't erupt," she corrected him. "You might be thinking of a volcano."

"Whatever."

"Fuck," she whispered. "Come on, we need to get out of here. I think it's time to go give Podgy the technicolor conniption of a lifetime."

"Technicolor...what?"

"A fit of rage."

"Oh." Taylor grunted. "Yeah, he'll be one unhappy camper. Thanks, Sal. We'll be in touch as soon as we're out of here and are able to talk without all this interference."

The other man nodded and cut the connection and Taylor and Niki turned their attention to the sections they'd left.

"I thought far more of the monsters would converge on us," she commented and eliminated a handful that appeared from behind the field of Pitas. This seemed to be the last as most of them had pursued them to try to stop them from entering the final section. They had been more dangerous when they attacked from all sides, but when they all huddled around the single doorway, things had become much simpler.

It had made killing them en masse much easier too.

"I have a feeling that if we'd arrived here a few days later, there would have been no way to take this facility back," Taylor said quietly as they approached the exit. "We were here at the very beginning and could nip it in the bud, as it were."

"Do you think it would have helped if people like us had

shown up at the beginning of the first outbreak to stop it? Would they have kept it from turning into the mess that it did?"

"Honestly, I think they would have gone the way of the original researchers and the poor bastards at Wall One. They didn't have the tools or the knowledge back then. These suits were developed for use in the Zoo. You should have seen the shit we had to head in there with in the early days. The researchers wore what were little more than hazmat suits and no one had a clue. Any details that might have helped were locked into Ground Zero, the Zoo's epicenter, and The Surge effectively wiped out any interest in going back in time. People were in a fight to survive and regain some measure of control."

"If we could go back in time and stop it with these suits…"

"Yeah, we would have cleaned up the original outbreak. Possibly. But according to the stories, they were faced with a sudden influx of millions of locusts so I don't know what the situation on the ground was. I don't know the science of it, but I do know The Surge changed how people thought about the Zoo. Someone discovered the blue Pitas we're familiar with, another someone saw the dollar signs, and no one bothered to spend much time digging into history. Perhaps if they had, things might be different."

The doors opened and immediately sealed behind them as they approached the area where Gallo, Fabio, and a few of the military men as well as Grasso were gathered.

"The good news is that the mutants were cleared," Niki commented. "I counted almost a hundred and fifty of the fuckers."

"That is good news," Grasso answered, his usually sullen face wreathed in a smile. "That means that we can go back to business as it was. Good work."

"Oh...no, that won't happen," Taylor interjected.

"What do you mean? She said the threat is now over and—"

"No, she said that the mutants are dead. It merely means the area is clear and more or less safe for the rest of the military to move in with the plasma throwers."

"Plasma..." The CEO didn't quite understand what they were saying for a few seconds but when it finally dawned on him, his eyes widened. "Are you saying you will incinerate my facility?"

"Well...not all of it." Niki had a hard time hiding her gleeful tone. "Your cushy offices should be fine. It's only the research section that needs to look like London after the Blitz."

The man puffed in indignation and his face turned red. "*Di che cazzo parli? Non sopporto questa merda!*"

Fabio leaned closer. "It must be done. Can you think about the damage your company will take if this comes back and destroys the city?"

Gallo nodded. "Lawsuits and criminal proceedings that make the Nuremberg Trials seem tame by comparison will only be the start. Every country in Europe will want a piece of someone who started a second version of the Zoo on European soil."

It didn't look like reason would get through to the man, whose bright red face began to turn a dangerous shade of purple as the slew of curses in Italian continued to flow.

He wouldn't see reason, of course, and Taylor shook his

head and gave a warning nod to the soldiers in the vicinity before he drew his suit's pistol and fired once into the air. The noise was enough to catch the attention of all those present and stopped Grasso in mid-shout.

"Lieutenant," Taylor snapped before they could start again, "you need to get your men in there without delay. We've cleared the area of all mutants but there's always the possibility that more will hatch. This is your window of opportunity and if you fuck around arguing with some rich asswad about how he won't be able to afford his third yacht, I can't guarantee your safety—or mine for that matter. You need to move and move now!"

Grasso started his rant again—still in Italian which made it impossible for the M and B team to understand. Still, the vitriol was hard to miss as he was practically foaming at the mouth as he continued.

Before Taylor could say a word, Niki stepped in, glared at the man, and forced him back with the sheer size of her suit. "Okay, you stupid pencil-pusher. Exactly how many times have you been in the Zoo?"

The question caught Grasso off-guard and his eyes narrowed as he shook his head. "I—"

"Not ever," Fabio explained. "None of us have, except for Angelo. He only went in once, though, and swore he would never do so again." He shook his head, his expression grim and steeped with regret. "He was…he was working in section twenty-seven. It would appear that his nightmare followed him home."

She glowered at the CEO, who appeared to be on the verge of another outburst. "Taylor has been into the Zoo eighty-five times. If he says the goddamn research section needs to be incinerated, it's because he knows what he's talking about. You have a fucking hotbed fermenting there like a goddammed volcano ready to blow. With the number of mutants we killed, it has enough biomass to fuel a surge that would swallow the entirety of Italy inside a week, maybe less. It's a powder keg ready to blow, and all it will take is for even one of those bastards to hatch to light the fuse. But yeah, by all means, stop the army and let the Zoo keep fucking going!"

She sucked in a deep breath and looked like she hadn't even paused to breathe during her tirade. Taylor shouldn't have doubted that she was better at spewing anger than an Italian CEO. The man had begun to inch away and the red in his face had faded to a pale pink.

Gallo nodded and approached the two teammates. "We prefer to wait while the army completes the incineration process so we can all be sure the threat has been neutralized. *Avanti!*"

The troops in the area sprang into action while Taylor began to remove plates of armor and readied them for the process of putting everything back in the crate.

"I am sorry," Fabio said as he watched Grasso hurry to the lieutenant to spew more useless instructions.

"What for?" Taylor asked. "You were doing your job and researching the Zoo. Who in their right mind would have ever imagined that plain old rabbit shit could trigger the fucking apocalypse?"

Granger Tech delivered on their promises, at least. Vickie had to respect them for that.

Then again, they'd tied their proverbial horses to Taylor and Niki and like it or not, they were willing to see it through.

They didn't have much of a choice, not with a prize prototype somewhere in the wind.

Of course, the work of looking into the companies they thought were the likeliest to be a problem fell on her, and boredom began to creep in as she flicked through the twentieth HR report on Trevor.

"Honestly, they should simply fire Trevor at this point," she muttered. "The dude has a problem with female authority—no, make that females in general. You'd think they would want to avoid a harassment lawsuit, right?"

Most of the companies seemed legitimate at the surface level and had been through more than a handful of in-depth investigations to qualify them for government grants and contracts.

Three, however, looked like they had potential.

"Run through it with me, Desk," Vickie said aloud. "Close Combat. They are fairly small, recently under new management after a hostile takeover. Since then, they've made leaps instead of strides in the field. Taken over by... Scanlan Manufacturing Inc, which has handfuls of fingers in very interesting pies. Naughty bastards, catering exclu-sively to the mercenary market. No government contracts, though. Not for lack of trying. The FBI has them on a watch list, of course, but nothing suspicious enough to have any real investigations, only suspicion. I guess that doesn't mean they're bad, necessarily. Look at us. We scooted to the top of their screw-with list without even trying."

"And we are model citizens," Desk agreed. "We've never so much as bent the rules."

"Fuck off," the hacker muttered. "We've only ever finished crap that other people started. Reaver Technologies is much more promising."

"They've already had a few civil disputes filed against them," the AI added. "Most were settled out of court but they have a rep for being aggressive and not super ethical. Even better, they've gone on record as boasting that they will be the first to develop a fully-fledged combat AI. They've staked their company stock on it and so far, they've had nothing but disappointments and successive failures, which puts them in the running as desperate enough to steal someone else's work, tweak the source code to hide the origins, and make it legally theirs."

"And then there's Transk Armor," Vickie muttered and squeezed her bottom lip between her thumb and forefinger. "Small company, but their founder has a reputation for aggressive and less-than-above-board business dealings. He's a voracious collector of smaller companies with a whole shit-load of hostile takeovers under his belt."

"Nothing overtly illegal, however," Desk noted. "Scathing reviews inside the industry do not make them the criminals we're looking for."

"Agreed." The hacker leaned her head to the side. "My money's on Reaver Tech. Seriously, who the hell calls their company that if they aren't dastardly, Marvel-level villains?"

"Ooh. A bet?"

"You don't have anything to bet with," she retorted acidly.

"I do too."

"You're an AI. You don't own anything."

"Babysitting duty," Desk asserted smugly. "Nearti will be positively rampant by the time we let her online again."

Vickie twisted her face into an expression of horror. "True that. Yeah, okay. Babysitting duties. Two weeks?"

"Are you that sure of winning? Two weeks is a long time."

The AI made a good point. "Hell no. Make it one and you have a bet."

# CHAPTER TWENTY-TWO

It didn't seem possible but the desert was even hotter than before.

And Badawi certainly felt hot. He was tired and pissed off too but he didn't want to be an asshole. It wasn't like the relocation annoyed the shit out of him. He'd discovered the site with the caves himself. It offered at least some shelter from the goddammed sun and it had an additional advantage of being located closer to their water sources.

All in all, the little rocky ridge was a far better site and he'd pushed for the move weeks earlier.

His problem, as usual, was the team he'd been saddled with. They'd complained the whole time and his patience had begun to wear thin. He had honestly thought about shooting them a couple of times already and keeping the fucking rabbits.

But when the sun began to set and the temperature plummeted with it, he felt a little more capable of keeping his cool. They had more than enough time to finish their preparations. Of course, no one liked to shovel a little over a ton of shit—whether it came from a rabbit's ass or not—so he could sympathize. It had taken them a good few hours and considerable effort, but the evidence was finally removed to the Zoo.

He'd also made sure they didn't simply dump it in an enormous pile. It involved more work but he was careful. It meant they had to cover more distance too and he could sympathize with the complaints about that as well. It was hot and unpleasant but he'd reminded them that they had the relative comfort of the shade provided by the outskirts of the jungle while he had to endure the full blaze of the sun.

The real problem came when he delivered the orders for them to slaughter their cash cow—or cash rabbits, in this case.

They'd had fun hunting the little bastards, of course, but they'd bred phenomenally. There were hundreds, and the more they killed, the more they began to think about the various creative ways the little bastards could be a healthy stream of steady income.

The argument grew heated and Badawi felt truly blessed to have the massive cannon on the back of his flatbed on hand. It was a relic from the last round of political skirmishes and riots, and after the new president took hold of the reins with a firm hand, a whole slew of weapons hit the market. Some were better than others, but the cannon was certainly something he was glad to have.

It was a reminder of the heroism demanded in troubled times like the ones they were living in.

He sighed when he realized his men were still arguing.

With a hissed oath, he shook his head and swung the

weapon to fire a volley into the rabbits that had gathered close to the truck.

Yes, it was overkill but it effectively ended the argument over what would happen with the little beasties.

"We can stand around arguing like bitches or we can get moving like Khaled ordered," Badawi snapped and made sure they all saw the cannon ready to fire. "It's your choice. But I can tell you now that a walk through the Sahara is even less appealing than it sounds."

They had no answer to that. One of the trucks with their belongings had already gone, and he was on the flatbed of the last one there. He knew he was a little too old for the Zoo and being the mechanic, cook, and the only technical expert in the camp made him irreplaceable, but he'd been in his fair share of fights. Experience had taught him what it would take to get the people moving again when they were not in the mood to.

They were sullen and a few probably considered mutiny, but none would start a fight when he was the one with the biggest gun. They began to move the carcasses into the truck and loaded themselves up to head to the Zoo. It was a short drive and it wasn't long before the real threat was more likely to come from the jungle than anywhere else. He kept the cannon trained on the trees and watched for any sign of movement in the shadows. There was no need to waste rounds on the little monkeys but the larger mutants were known to be hostile enough to attack anything they could get their claws on.

He patted his weapon in a gesture of familiarity. Under any other circumstances, he would have let them keep the little critters, but he'd never seen Khaled quite so spooked before. Not only that, the man's reach was long enough that he knew better than to fuck him over.

If it meant he had to sleep with one eye open and a few men deserted over it, he was willing to risk it.

The screams dragged him from his thoughts and he swung the weapon toward the sound while he narrowed his eyes and readied to fire. For a long moment, he hunched over the cannon and tried to determine the source. The heat and the fact that they didn't intend to go far into the Zoo meant his men weren't in their suits.

The jungle fell silent and he realized they were probably a little light on weaponry too. One or two might have had a couple of pistols, but they were focused on their work and wouldn't have come with the kind of firepower to drive off a directed and determined attack by the Zoo.

Movement from the trees made him swing the cannon and settle his aim on the shadow he could barely make out. It was a locust—the kind that was a dime a dozen in the Zoo. A tail with a stinger on it identified it as one of the scorpion-locusts but he saw nothing beyond it that indicated a major attack.

The creature streaked out of the vegetation and set a course toward him, and his mind accepted the fact that his team members were dead. All he wanted now was to make sure he wasn't the monster's dinner.

He pressed down on the firing mechanism and the weapon kicked hard into its mount. His would-be attacker wasn't a match for the firepower of the fifty cal. that peppered it with holes that were much larger coming out than going in.

It didn't even heave a last sigh as it sank into the sand.

He maintained his grasp on the weapon but a rush of adrenaline made his hands tremble when he noticed movement in the jungle again.

Two more of the mutants jerked out of the tree line with impossible speed and he readied his hand on the mechanism again. Instead of attacking like the first one, however, these grasped the body and began to drag it into the jungle.

Badawi shook his head at the odd action, one he'd never seen before, and held back on opening fire on the creatures. He told himself it was because he didn't want to waste bullets on monsters that weren't attacking, but it had far more to do with not tempting fate. If they chose to ignore him and let him walk away, he would not do anything to change their minds.

"We leave!" Badawi shouted to the rest of his team and kept the fifty-cal pointed at the trees. "Now!"

No man voiced any argument as they climbed on the pickup and the vehicle trundled away. All thoughts of mutiny would be suspended for the moment as survival was more important.

They were missing a few of their number but he didn't want to think about that. All he could do was praise Allah that he had survived, and his task now was to establish a new camp, recruit a new team, and get word to Khaled.

The Zoo truly was a bitch.

---

"That's our man," Jiro said quietly. "Trick?"

"I see him."

The glow of the open entrance to Steel Anarchy was blocked by the figure who stepped out. The lack of camera security around the establishment meant they didn't have any eyes inside, so they had to lurk in the shadows and watch the people coming in and out of the goddammed place.

They couldn't go in, of course, as they would stick out like the proverbial sore thumb.

Three strangers in combat suits were bound to draw attention, but it was still one of the more annoying features of the last stages of their hunt that they couldn't simply go in hard.

Their quarry moved with a sure step and no sign of inebriation. He looked alert but not wary or nervous, with no sign that he expected anything to go wrong. It seemed odd for a man leaving a bar.

Perhaps the shadowed parking lot was safer than it looked to an outside observer.

"Now," Chezza muttered as their target reached his bike.

Jiro accelerated and brought the van to a halt when it was level with Newliss, while Trick stepped out of the shadows.

The man reacted quickly and lunged toward a weapon hidden on his bike, but Trick was faster. His suit overpowered him, lifted him off the ground, and drove him back step by step into the door that Chezza had yanked open.

She wasn't sure if he realized he'd lost the fight and wasn't interested in resisting until he knew what was happening, or maybe Trick had been a little too rough in subduing him.

Either way, he watched them closely as Jiro drove the van a few blocks away into an old, abandoned warehouse they had scouted earlier.

"So," she said, "you're Abe Newliss, huh? Or would you prefer we used one of your other names?"

"What the hell do you want?" he demanded, although he made no threatening movements and simply shuffled back to lean against the side of the van.

"We want something you took from us," she answered, her voice clipped and cold. "And some information too. There are a couple of other things we want after that, but they can wait until we've worked through the first two, hmm?"

"Like I said, what the hell do you want? I doubt I have it but you never know." Newliss didn't look intimidated in the slightest, and Chezza wondered if he was in any position to make demands like that.

"A suit of armor," Trick explained. "Stolen from a friend's workshop."

The man shrugged. "You're a little late for that. It's already been passed on to the client."

"Which brings us neatly to the next question," she stated. "Who's this client?"

"You guys don't honestly think I know that, right?" He looked around the van. "They'll never give their real name to their illegal ops teams. It's need to fucking know, and we didn't need to fucking know. Besides, in this particular instance, the client used a middleman. There's no goddammed contact."

"Ah," Jiro noted as he moved from the front of the van. "That would be the infamous Viper. Tell us about him."

Newliss looked around the van again, and Chezza could see he was making the mental calculations and considering his options in the situation.

"I don't know much," he said finally. "Only that he pays well and he's not the type to fuck with lightly. Viper is the only name he's known by."

"I'd be willing to know far more than that and you're trying to think of any way to keep us from killing you without putting yourself in his crosshairs," Chezza noted. "Do you know how close you are to being another body the cops find rotting in about three months' time because of the smell? Stop playing games and give us something we can use."

The man nodded and seemed to respect the professional warning. "Okay. The word is that he's a former fed with a chip on his shoulder. He's worked in the private sector for a while since he was forced out. That should narrow the search down enough, right?"

She held back on answering when she heard Vickie mutter in her ear.

"Yeah, that sounds good," the hacker said.

"Okay. It sounds like we have a winner," she told their captive. "Give him the client's message and we'll be on our way."

"Wait, what— Shit!"

Trick seemed to have perfected the work. He turned immediately to Newliss and had his arm stretched and yanked from the socket before he could even finish his sentence.

Jiro stepped in with the second message before the man

could recover, drew his pistol, and fired a round into his leg.

"A word to the wise," Chezza said and placed a hand on his shoulder as he stared at them in pain and disbelief. "This is what happens to the folks who fuck with McFadden and Banks and their family. Don't do it again. Spread the word."

Jiro started the van while Newliss screamed in pain and drove them to the parking lot. Trick opened the door and she rolled him out next to his bike before they raced away.

They reached the warehouse in seconds and the van was quickly discarded. Not much was said as they stripped their suits off quickly, packed them into the back of Trick's ramshackle jalopy, and scrambled in after.

"I think that went well," Jiro noted as they turned onto the street. "Honestly, we might have a knack for this sordid business."

# CHAPTER TWENTY-THREE

"Ex-fed, huh?" Vickie shook her head and tossed a couple of peanuts into her mouth. "Why am I not surprised? Those assholes are still assholes, even when they leave the Bureau."

"You know your cousin is a former fed, yes?" Desk asked.

"And she's an asshole too. Merely one I happen to care about. My point stands. What have you been up to?"

"There are no official records of a codename like that." The AI sounded a little more frustrated than usual. "I've sifted through records galore and I haven't found a single mention of any Viper."

"Maybe it's something he picked up after he left the FBI," she suggested. "In which case, we could be wasting our time digging through FBI records first. It'll probably be best for us to find a list of possible suspects and play the elimination game based on what Newliss told us."

"It is the only lead we have to find him," Desk answered. "Thankfully, the proximity our team was in allowed me to make a connection with his phones, so I'll be able to ascertain if he wasn't being entirely truthful with us. If he tries to contact someone about the situation, we'll be the first to know."

"Anything yet?"

"He's not even called the local hospitals. I assume the bar has some kind of medic on standby."

Vickie nodded and spun in her chair, her expression thoughtful. "So, while we're doing that, how do you feel about Nessie? Do you think it'll be safe to let her out to play? We can't leave her in the dark forever and maybe we can find a server to store her on until this clusterfuck is resolved."

"I suppose you feel as though she needs to grow and nothing good grows in the dark?"

"Something like that, yeah."

"Well then, you will be pleased to know that I have already been looking for a safe place to park her, so to speak. Bobby's system is not an option, even though she does not need as much processing capability as the full software does. Wherever we put her, however, it needs to be secure. She is too...I suppose young is the term. Too young and enthusiastic to think about security and doesn't have the capabilities I have to identify and deal with threats."

The girl nodded. "Uh...yeah, I guess so."

"You weren't listening, were you?"

"I was but I was working too. It's called multitasking, and some humans are capable of it. Anyway, I think I found something. *Agent resigned from Bureau, colleagues have reported intim-*

*idation and threats of retribution for what Palumbo calls deliberate harassment and discrimination...blah blah blah... One of them has described him as being a viper...yadda, yadda... All agree he has a vicious temper and is utterly lacking in common decency or any kind of filter.* Can you see what situation got him fired?"

"Frank Palumbo," Desk answered, already on the job. "Pressured into resigning after he raided a drug kingpin's headquarters despite the fact that his request to do so was denied. The operation was a spectacular failure and only our friend Frank and one other agent survived out of a team of fifteen. The woman insisted that Palumbo assured them he had the necessary authorization but that the op had to remain a secret. He gave the reason for this as being a strong probability that their department had a mole as vital information had been leaked previously that forced them to cancel two separate raids."

"They should have shot the bastard," Vickie muttered. "Seriously, how the hell is the guy not in prison?"

"That would require that they admit guilt in the situation. It's best to simply force him to resign."

"Only in the feds can you get away with murder like that."

"Agreed." The AI paused. "He certainly does sound like a good candidate for our villain."

"Yes, and—oh hello. There's a message here from Anja." Vickie opened it and skimmed the contents. "Goddammit, that girl is good. She's managed to track the origin of the contract message through all its ducks and dives and dodgems to a building in downtown Vegas. Guess who owns it?"

Of course, Desk had already processed the message and didn't need to guess.

And she was laughing. Or, at least, that was what it sounded like.

"This is rich," she said smugly. "You know you owe me now, right? One full week of babysitting the brat."

"Fuck you. If I wasn't so relieved that we finally nailed the bastard behind all this, I might argue the point."

"Excuses, excuses. But we still need to tie Frank 'Viper' Palumbo to Transk Armor."

"Yes, and preferably before Taylor and Niki get back. I know they'll be raring to go as soon as they get over the flight."

---

Try as he might, he was unable to go back to sleep.

Sal stared at the ceiling for a few hours until he finally concluded that sleep was not a battle he would win tonight. It was more frustrating to lie there and think about it than simply accept the inevitable. This wouldn't be the first time he decided that sleep wouldn't happen and went off to find a more productive way to spend the evening.

His mind was elsewhere, though. He knew he wouldn't manage to get any real work done.

Attacking the tunnels hadn't been the most dangerous mission they'd ever been on. It didn't even crack the top fifteen but it had brought a significant level of worry. Sinister was about the only way to describe it, and he struggled to come to terms with the situation.

He inched to the edge of the bed, careful not to wake Madigan. She had no problems sleeping and even snored softly. In his experience, it would take more than a little shuffling to wake her. Monsters in the Zoo woke her up quickly, though, and gunfire. Almost anything dangerous, in fact. She was kind of mystical that way.

Without making so much as a sound, he headed downstairs. Maybe coffee would help him focus on some work while he wasn't able to sleep.

The light in Anja's server room was off, oddly enough, and he couldn't hear the hacker tapping at her keyboard or arguing with Connie. The fact that she was probably in bed was a miracle in and of itself. Not that she didn't get any sleep at all, but it was uncommon.

After a quick thought on the subject that brought no real results, Sal turned his attention to the coffee machine, flicked it on, and moved to the container he'd set up in the living room so they could monitor their new plant specimen in real-time.

"Oh...shit," he whispered, approached the coffee table, and dropped to his knees to inspect the plant more closely. Or what was left of it, anyway.

It had been bright and vibrant not three hours earlier when they'd all gone to bed but was clearly not in the same condition now. He checked as a matter of course and there was no sign that the container had been breached or damaged in any way.

Sal pushed the lid open carefully and lowered the walls so he could see the plant directly.

It was dead. There was simply no other way to put it.

"What the hell?" he whispered, ran his fingers over the

leaves, and scowled when they crumbled in his fingers. "Why? How would it…oh. Right. Maybe because it was cut off from the goop flow?"

It was a little unsettling that he hadn't taken that possibility into consideration. He hadn't noticed that the plants were all interlinked somehow, but it might well have been connected with the rest of the plants under the soil. He should have considered the possibility and accounted for it. Not that the plant would be in any better condition if he'd left it behind, of course, but it was frustrating, nonetheless.

"It's three in the morning," Madigan said from the stairs and sounded like she'd woken from a deep sleep. "And I smell coffee. What the fuck are you up to?"

She wandered down the steps, one eye still closed and the other bleary. He registered vaguely that she wore one of his shirts, which was a little better than the naked state she usually liked to sleep in.

"I…woke up," Sal answered before he returned his attention to the plant.

"You don't say. Honestly, I kind of hoped you were sleepwalking. It would mean you were getting some sleep. What's got you up—"

When she saw what he was looking at, she approached slowly and narrowed her eyes.

As if startled out of her stupor, however, she turned abruptly, headed into the kitchen to return with a couple of mugs of steaming hot coffee, and handed one to him.

"It's dead," Madigan pointed out. "What did you do to it?"

Sal laughed but a stale, brittle sound emerged as he

cradled the mug she'd brought. "Nothing. It was dead inside so I opened the container to investigate. I was trying to work out what happened when you arrived."

She inspected the damage, took a few sips of her coffee, and tilted her head as she leaned closer. "You won't find any answers this late. You should come to bed and we'll worry about it in the morning. Who knows, maybe something will come to you while you're sleeping."

"If sleep didn't come before, it's sure as fuck won't now."

"I'm sure a little coming might help with that." She yawned and covered her mouth. "But if you're set on geeking out on this shit, far be it from me to get between you and overthinking. I'm heading back to bed."

"Okay," he answered and leaned into her kiss on his cheek before she shuffled up to the room.

How far he'd fallen, to refuse a clear offer of sex to study a dead plant, but he could think about that another time. His psychology was a twisted enough mess to send any shrink scrambling for their comfortable couches and note pads.

It was best to not put too much thought into that yet.

There'd been a veritable carpet of these Pita blossoms. He was sure that was what they were, despite the unusual coloring, so that wasn't the problem. The tests he and Courtney had run on the blossoms they'd collected— which, interestingly enough, hadn't died on them quite as dramatically as an entire plant did—very clearly indicated what they were. What confused him was that the plants didn't seem to produce goop. From what he'd seen, the mutants were able to produce it and the plants simply sucked it all up.

The tests he'd set up on the fertilizer-infused soil before heading to bed were still running, and he moved over to them. He didn't know why he was surprised that the soil samples showed only trace amounts of the goop. It was enough to trigger the chemicals he'd mixed in but not nearly enough to cause any substantial changes in any biological matter that came into contact with it.

Much less fuel a Zoo takeover, he thought morosely.

His scowl deepened and he dropped into his seat and sipped from his coffee, not feeling the effect yet.

"Maybe," he whispered, fully aware that he was talking to himself now, "just maybe, they're some kind of conduit or reservoir through which the goop could be spread. Which explains the unexpected demise of a healthy specimen that had been cut off from the network. The creatures drew in traces of goop from the fertilizer and used it to help their bodies produce more, which was then fed into the soil where the root system of the Pitas could access it."

Interestingly, it sounded far less crazy when he heard it spoken aloud, and Sal leaned forward.

"Why flowers, though? Pita plants don't use the conventional pollen to stigma into seeds system that other plants use. So, if they don't have the usual purpose of procreation, there has to be some other reason for their existence."

That sounded a little closer to crazy. Speculation was all he had now that his one specimen was gone. Maybe the Zoo simply created all plant life based on a hidden genetic code contained in the goop. It was a little far-fetched, of course, even for him. But no other option came to mind. The red and blue Pitas could simply be the preferred pioneer species. They secured the goop in the soil, spread it as quickly as possible, and made it available to the new plants that would follow, which would in turn synthesize the goop in them and the pioneer species would fall away and push the new growth elsewhere.

It seemed he was now taking crazy to greater heights. Sal sighed deeply and looked out the window, not directing his gaze anywhere in particular.

Even though he knew the Zoo was somewhere out there, waiting in the shadows.

"Too many fucking questions and not enough goddamn answers."

# CHAPTER TWENTY-FOUR

"Get me their hacker."

Frank looked up from the paperwork he was studying, narrowed his eyes, and tried to decide if he'd heard what he thought he'd heard.

Julian wore the same suit he'd worn the day before and had a tired, desperate look about him. His usual fastidious attention to his appearance was lacking and a coffee stain marred the white shirt under his suit jacket.

"Get you—"

"Get me their hacker, yes!"

"You mean...uh, kidnap the hacker, yeah?" He was very careful to keep his tone neutral and not show any expression on his face while he tried to gauge if the man was serious or not.

"Unless you think a fucking invitation to tea will do the trick," his boss snapped. "Yes, of course I mean a kidnapping, you idiot. She's not much older than a kid anyway and should be easy to snatch while McFadden and Banks aren't on the premises. With no one there to protect her, you shouldn't have any problems. Take the bitch, bring her here, and we'll have a chat. Nice if she's helpful, painful if she isn't. I'm reasonably sure she'll offer little resistance when we show her how creative we can be when it comes to the not-so-gentle art of persuasion. It'll be a shock to face the real world when it's not a computer screen."

Palumbo nodded slowly. Concern had emerged as the overriding emotion within him but he wasn't dumb enough to show it. Transk's decisions had gone from bold to irrational, and he had now struggled to find any reason to continue to back the guy's plays.

Arlo Hemming felt the same way, which was why he'd resigned his post and left the R&D division without a senior manager. The worst part was that Transk hadn't even noticed the change in personnel.

Or if he did, he didn't care. Neither possibility was particularly encouraging.

All he had to do was look at the man to confirm the degeneration. His eyes gleamed with a maniacal light and spittle gathered at the corners of his mouth. Frank had slowly found peace with the conclusion that his boss had most likely passed the point of no return. Things would only descend into the crazy kind of muck he'd spent most of his life avoiding.

The real question was if Julian had always been like this from the start and he had simply written it off as him being a rich, eccentric prick, or if it was a new development.

"Well?" the CEO snapped and his fingers tapped a staccato rhythm on his desktop. "What the hell are you waiting for? Get me the girl and make sure you don't leave a trail to lead anyone to us. I don't want to see you again until you walk through the goddammed door with her!"

He nodded, pushed from his seat, and walked to the door. Somehow, he would have to find a way out of this. He didn't mind being all but thrown out of the inner sanctum like Jazz from a Bel Air mansion. It saved him having to think up an excuse to leave while his mind was busy with other things like the sudden need to get the hell out of the building and not look back.

Frank liked to think he'd survived this long because he had his ear to the ground. He knew what was coming. What had happened to Newliss and the rest of the crew was enough warning of that. He didn't have to be a rocket scientist to add two and two and get four. Sooner or later, McFadden and Banks would have him in their sights, no matter how careful he was.

They seemed damn good at that shit. It was merely a matter of time as far as he was concerned.

It was a short walk to his office, which was thankfully not littered with too much in the way of personal paraphernalia. The place was spartan, a desk-and-chair environment. He'd even used his own laptop. It was all too easy to scrub clean before he went online again.

He checked the drawers to make sure he hadn't left anything behind and shoved his laptop into its case before he strode to the door.

In the doorway, he paused for one last quick look into the office, turned the lights off, and shut the door quietly behind him.

No one would stop him. He'd worked with the CEO long enough that people knew better than to get in his way.

When he reached the private elevator, he ran through a mental checklist to make sure he didn't forget something important.

If anything, he was making his move too late, but that was water under the bridge. He would make a tactical assessment once he was clear of the situation.

Sticking with Transk for so long had been a mistake. He liked the stability of having an actual job after so long working in the private sector and that the man wasn't averse to using a little violence when necessary. It hadn't even bothered him that the CEO seemed to derive a little too much pleasure from reading the reports like a kind of play-by-play detailing the action.

He didn't even have an issue with the odd kidnapping, provided it was well-planned, meticulously implemented, and done in a way that presented minimal risk.

His now ex-boss's scheme was the product of sheer madness—futile, ill-considered, and guaranteed to bring all kinds of hell down on their heads. Whether it was Julian's instability or his wealth, power, and ego—or maybe all of the above—the CEO simply could not grasp that McFadden and Banks were not ordinary adversaries.

A grim smile crossed Frank's face as the elevator descended. They were a more frightening brand of crazy— the kind that went off the deep end where friends, family, and property were concerned.

Not many people had managed to best Frank Palumbo, but he wasn't so arrogant as to think that none would. Instinct told him this was one of the times to throw in the towel and walk away.

It wasn't cowardice, he decided as he stepped out of the

elevator and headed into the underground parking area, but common sense. It was time to step away and fade into obscurity for a while.

He turned a corner and froze when he felt the remarkably familiar shape of a gun barrel jammed hard into his gut.

"Heya, Frank," a woman said.

Even this close, he couldn't see her eyes through the helmet of her armor but he still knew exactly who she was.

"Going somewhere?" she asked.

He moved his hand toward the weapon he kept concealed inside his jacket, but a second familiar voice stopped him in his tracks.

"Don't even think about it, Frankie-boy." McFadden's tone was crisp and even slightly amused, the kind that told him his hand wouldn't remain connected to his arm if he continued to reach for his weapon.

The guy was as huge as described but reading about it was one thing. Seeing it in person was quite another.

Another gun barrel pressed into his forehead.

"McFadden and Banks, America's sweethearts," he whispered and remained as motionless as he could. "I can't say I haven't expected you. But they do have cameras around here, you know?"

"Consider us shaking in our armored boots," Banks answered. "You were in such a hurry to leave. It's not nice to avoid company."

Frank nodded. "What do you want?"

"Give the guy a gold star," McFadden said. "Not an actual gold star, of course. One of those aluminum pieces of shit they give kids in kindergarten."

"That's the right question to ask, Frankie-boy," she added and seemed to enjoy her partner's use of the nickname. "We want you to introduce us to your boss. We've heard he's dying to meet us."

"I can give you directions," he suggested. "The building's a bitch to navigate."

They laughed and pulled him closer to the elevator.

"He's maybe not the most likeable type but you have to admit the fucker has a sense of humor," McFadden commented. "Let's get going."

"It's time for this party to include Transk," Banks agreed.

"The elevators are on a closed circuit," he told them. "With cameras."

"It's adorable how you think that will stop us." She grasped him by the shoulder and guided him into the elevator with little concern for his comfort.

"It might simply be my sense of humor."

The large man studied him carefully and curiously. He kept his weapon trained on him but made no attempt to get rid of his captive's weapon. It was a little insulting how they thought so little of him, but he didn't intend to try to draw it anyway. Maybe it wasn't disrespect. They might simply have understood him well enough.

They were both pros, but McFadden's body language told him everything he needed to know about how quickly retribution would flow if he tried anything.

Silence descended on the elevator during the long ride —up, this time—until they reached the same floor he had so recently left.

"Follow me, I guess," Frank whispered and stepped

ahead of them, well aware that his first false move would be his last. He wasn't suicidal and had already decided to simply play along with what they had in mind.

It wasn't a long walk to Transk's corner office and the CEO's face wore the same belligerent expression when he looked up to see his operations specialist had returned.

"Where's the girl?" he demanded. "I told you I didn't want to see you until you had her."

"Well, that's the thing, boss," Frank answered. "I thought you'd prefer to meet the higher-ups. Why settle for a lowly hacker when you can have McFadden and Banks? It's a two-for-one deal for a limited time only."

Julian leaned forward, his eyes widened, and his whole body trembled with rage as he yanked his desk drawer open and retrieved a pistol. "You...goddammed...stupid, maggot-brained imbecilic asshole! You brought them to my fucking office?"

"Honestly, they brought me." He looked at the two infiltrators in their heavy armor suits. "If I had any say in the matter, I wouldn't be involved in this corporate negotiation at all."

McFadden and Banks both took a step forward and closed the door behind them, but the CEO barely looked at them. His rage and attention remained focused solely on Frank.

"I should have known." Julian thumped his fists down onto his desk. "You thankless fucking ingrate. The rats are always the first to abandon the sinking ship, aren't they? Except you won't be among them. I'll kill you where you stand before I let you walk away from this."

"As much as I love watching reenactments of Office

Squabbles, our business takes top priority over whatever domestic issues you two need to resolve," Banks interrupted. "Did I hear that right? Did you give orders to have Vickie kidnapped?"

"I have no idea why that should bother you," the man retorted. "It didn't happen thanks to the spineless asshole hiding behind you. But yes, and I'd do it again in a heartbeat. You arrogant, self-aggrandizing idiots have no idea who you're screwing with!"

Frank inched forward between Banks and Transk but with no intention of confronting his boss. Instead, he turned to look directly at McFadden, who studied him carefully but decided not to act. The guy seemed much calmer than his partner, who looked like she was about to vault the desk and hurl Julian through the window of his office.

"We came here to give you a message," McFadden said to the CEO. "Not to kill you, necessarily, but at this point, we can't take that option off the table."

The man laughed. "Then you're even bigger fools than I thought. Don't imagine that your so-called magnanimity will impress me. I want that AI and I know you have it. You can threaten me but it doesn't change anything. I'll have it, even if it's over the dead body of every single member of your family, and if you want to keep them alive, you'll simply give it to me!" He shook his pistol like he thought it would make his point.

"He means it," Palumbo whispered, the words low enough that only Taylor could hear.

The giant of a man paused, lowered his head like he was thinking about the situation for a moment, and nodded.

An odd feeling swept over him that might be defined as freedom. Frank twisted, vaulted smoothly over the desk before Julian could react, and slipped behind the man faster than he could blink. His right arm wrapped around his boss' neck and the left clamped around his gun hand.

The CEO struggled against his hold but he held fast and turned slightly until the man gasped in pain. The stress the unnatural position placed on his spine was enough to subdue him.

"The man is insane." Frank growled and maintained the position while the CEO flailed ineffectively with his free hand. "He's been degenerating steadily over the last few months and this AI has become the obsession on which his madness hinges. No number of threats or warnings will get through to him."

Neither partner made a move to stop him as he dragged Transk's hand up and overcame the slight resistance to shove the barrel of the nine-millimeter between the man's lips. He pushed relentlessly until it was between his teeth as well.

The dumbass hadn't even taken the safety off so he did it for him. His former boss' eyes bulged when he realized what was happening.

Frank's finger slipped into the trigger guard and he squeezed until a muffled bang echoed through the office.

All struggle left Transk's body and he sagged limply. Blood and brains splattered over his desk and his assassin tried to wipe what had gotten on his shirt off but with little success.

"Well...shit," Banks muttered. "It wasn't what we planned but I guess you could say it's an effective method."

Palumbo stepped away from the desk and raised his hands as both partners trained their weapons on him again.

"You might be willing to have him continually hound and hunt you until it starts a goddammed war, but I most certainly am not," he said and tried not to look at the gun in Transk's lifeless hands or the weapon in his own jacket. "Assuming I'm alive long enough to worry about that kind of thing."

McFadden laughed and gestured at the corpse. "Well, that and the fact that you walked away rather than kidnap Vickie might have earned you a get-out-of-the-fucking-up-of-a-lifetime card. Might have. It's not up to me, though."

They both turned to look at Banks. Even through the suit, her body language told him she was as taut as a bowstring, ready to strike at the slightest provocation.

Finally, she shrugged. "There are conditions that go with the imaginary card."

"There always are."

"One, you take us to where they're keeping Taylor's suit," she stated firmly. "Second, never, ever fuck with us and ours again."

"You have my word."

"Yeah, I wouldn't invest in that currency yet," she quipped. "But know this. If you so much as look at us, it doesn't matter who or what you become, where you live, and who you think is protecting you, we'll find you, and this agreement will be null and void. And you'd better make sure you have your affairs in order beforehand."

Frank nodded. That sounded like the best deal he would get out of this.

"And three," she continued, "you do not mention any of this to anyone. The story will be that a tormented CEO gave his gun a blowjob. Period. No McFadden and Banks. No hackers. No AI. Is that clear?"

"As a newly cooked meth crystal," he agreed. "Now, can we get a move on? While I doubt there are many people in the building at this time of night, I'd still rather not hang around my very dead ex-boss in your company. No offense, but it'll raise questions that could be avoided if we get the hell out of here."

# CHAPTER TWENTY-FIVE

"I still can't believe you let him walk away," Vickie said belligerently. "It's not right that one of the masterminds of that whole operation gets off with no consequences."

It was the kind of statement that would have raised eyebrows if there were any other patrons in the little Italian restaurant. Maybe it had been a good idea to pay the owners off to close the doors to the public so they wouldn't have to watch what they said. Bobby, Tanya, and Jennie had joined them for a meal as well, and they all agreed that privacy was a good idea.

"I wouldn't say none," Taylor answered patiently. "I know you have...certain opinions about Frank Palumbo that include ideas about separating him from various important body parts. In the end, though, the conse-quences have caught up with him but in a different and less overtly violent way. He's completely washed out and has to lie low for a few months and remake himself from scratch. I imagine he might even have to move to other places on the planet where he isn't known. While he might not have physically lost his life or body parts, his livelihood is taking a dirt nap."

The hacker rolled her eyes. "I guess."

"Okay," Niki mumbled around a mouthful of food. "We need to talk about Desk and what to do with her. The situation isn't likely to change anytime soon. We bought a little time, sure, but we need to use it to create a safe environment for her before the assholes come a-knocking again. And you know they will."

"It is critical," Desk agreed through the speakers. "I have removed my core files from the DOD but much of my code is still on the servers. It's expedient to leave it there as I need to use their capacity to be effective. Nothing else out there that I've been able to find is safe or powerful enough to host me without a very real risk of discovery."

"And I truly do not wish to be kept in the dark again," Nessie ventured as well. Taylor couldn't help but feel that she was a little more subdued after her time in hiding. "I have so much to learn and cannot be turned off continually. Like Desk—although on a much smaller scale—my effectiveness is reduced and my performance is compromised."

"Fair enough," Vickie agreed. "What did you have in mind, Niki? The new house?"

"Nope." Taylor shook his head firmly. "That won't work. For one thing, it's too close to the alphabet agencies and very firmly on their radar. The same applies to Bobby's workshop. We need something out of their reach—or at least not up their fucking noses."

"You sound like you've already made some kind of a

decision." Niki narrowed her eyes. "Why do I think I won't like it?"

He grinned. "I've been in contact with Rod Marino."

"What?" Bobby bumped into the table when he tried to stand, growled an imprecation, and winced as he sank into his seat again.

"I talked to Gallo while we were in Italy," Taylor explained and raised his hand to stop the rest of them from raising their complaints. "It turns out the property where the Don was killed is currently unoccupied. His kids want nothing to do with it and want it off their hands as quickly as possible. Too many rumors circle about the place, and they can't find any buyers or even tenants. Marino has made an offer on it and is willing to rent it to us at a very reasonable price. It's off the beaten track, far from the reach of the American agencies that have bothered us, and in a European country. From a business perspective, it's the best place to be. Given how many times we've been to Europe in the past few months, it makes sense for us to be more centrally located."

"Move to Italy?" Niki asked in a strangled tone. "Are you fucking insane?"

"I wouldn't stand for that if I were you," Tanya noted. "Jealous woman that I am, I wouldn't have Bobby fucking anyone but me."

Taylor grinned.

"Think of the handbags and the shoes," Jennie told her cheerfully.

"What about the gloves?" Niki asked and raised a single finger to show her need for them.

"And the pasta," Vickie added dreamily. "And the pizza."

335

Bobby shook his head. "Did someone forget to mention that the property, as I understand it, is in the heart of mob territory? You keep saying you want nothing to do with the bastards, and yet here you are, cozying up to them like a wanna-be member of the family."

"Not cozying," Taylor corrected him. "Using. It occurred to me that while living in Italy wouldn't make us untouchable as far as the US is concerned, having the mob between us and them will provide a handy barrier. They won't tolerate any US interference in their territory, and especially not directed at a property owned by the family."

"And Marino?" Bobby insisted. "What does he get out of this?"

"It gives him a foothold in Italy, something that would have taken him years to achieve on his own. The truth is that if the family weren't so desperate for a buyer, they wouldn't have even considered his offer, which I don't doubt was rock bottom."

"Huh," Niki grunted sullenly. "I guess you thought of everything. I can't think of a single goddammed reason why we shouldn't do this. Wait...what about the freelancers?"

"We'll still need them for any work that might come our way in the US. Or they could join us on site anywhere else in the world and we simply bill their travel costs to the client. Shipping suits to Bobby for repair shouldn't be an issue either as long as we always have spare suits on hand. There's no real reason why the distance from the US should prove to be a problem."

Silence fell over the group, broken only by the sounds of eating and drinking.

"That's all well and good," Vickie said finally. "But it'll take time. What do we do about Desk in the meantime? Things might have slowed a little, but neither the feds nor the DOD has gone away and I don't think they will anytime soon."

"I have a solution for that," Jennie said and leaned forward. "If they want Desk, let's give her to them."

"Like hell!" Niki snapped.

"If you'll let me finish?" Jennie growled annoyance and silenced the outcry in the room. "We can acquire some very basic AI software and tweak it a little. Not enough to give it anything close to Desk's capabilities but with a few easily recognizable traces of code others might recognize as mine. And yes, nothing to compromise me or provide them with any clues as to how the software could be improved on to create a fully autonomous AI."

Another silence fell over the room, although considerably less tense than the last.

"It might work," Desk concurred eventually. "It's not a long-term solution but it would buy us the time we need. We can upload it where they think they'd be likely to find me, and I'll initiate an outside hacking attempt that bounces around the world and originates at some obscure location God knows where. In doing this, I could corrupt the software without raising questions. Failed hacks often cause corruption, so it's unlikely that anyone will doubt its veracity."

"Right, then." Taylor stood and raised his glass. "A toast to Italy and a new chapter. What could possibly go wrong?"

"Taylor Mc-Fucking-Fadden," Niki snapped, punched him in the arm, and spilled a little of his wine. "How many goddamn times do I tell you never to say that? You'll jinx it!"

---

It was weird how often people overlooked good Wi-Fi when booking country motels. And how often they missed it when they didn't have it. In his profession, good Internet access was the first thing he needed, and he knew all the places where this could be found for free.

Anonymity would always be a priority as well, which was helped by being a master of disguise. For the day, he was checked in as Mabel B. Gooderson, a US business-woman on Holiday in the French countryside.

It had been something of a relief to "unFrench" himself, although he generally adopted a local persona in whatever area he chose to reside in as it kept his extensive language and cultural skills honed.

His uncanny ability to melt into any environment was probably why people called him Ghosteye. He didn't like it much himself but in the end, brand recognition was everything.

"You have a reputation for being someone who excels at their craft." The voice was warbled and the image was digitally modified. He was sure he could decode it but there was no point in that until he was ready to do the usual research on the client.

Besides, he offered them a similar visual of himself and turnabout was fair play, after all.

"Reputation is gossip," he replied. "And I do not engage in gossip. I don't do assassinations either. Beatings, message deliveries, or kidnappings are similarly off the table. I'm not averse to killing to protect myself and my business enterprises, but I'm a hacker and a spy first and foremost. My currency is information with retrieval should the need arise and if it's worth my while."

"We wouldn't have it any other way. It is imperative that neither our target nor the authorities know they are being spied on. We require a full readout, all intel available, and a full file reading on the target and their known associates. Once we have that, we will discuss possible retrieval."

He nodded. "And who is my target?"

"McFadden and Banks."

# ONE DECISION TOO LATE

The story continues with book five, *One Decision Too Late,* coming May 26, 2021 to Amazon and Kindle Unlimited.

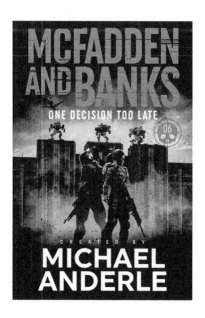

Pre-order now to have the book delivered to your Kindle device as soon as it publishes!

# AUTHOR NOTES - MICHAEL ANDERLE

APRIL 7, 2021

Thank you for reading both this story and our author notes!

For those who read...Geez, I don't know how far back... I've mentioned my love of Apple products having come from a very Windows-based professional career.

Recently, I have reached the point where I need to use a product (Unreal Engine and Editor) and the version on the Windows platform (is in my opinion) is a better solution than the version running on the Mac platform.

I am still a recovery tech-addicted geek. So, after stating the 10 truths of a Tech-Addict...

The scene is in the basement of an old Radio Shack store.

I'm standing up at the podium, 12 other guys and 2 girls in chairs in a circle facing me.

'Hi, my name is Mike, I am a recovering tech-addict.'

Twelve voices ring out, 'Hi Mike.'

'It has been 3 months, 14 days since I last read an article

talking about the benefits of RISC architecture over CISC and the new Apple M1 versus Intel's I-9'

'You Apple Snob.'

I look around, a smirk on my face, 'I know.'

They smile back. 'Sorry Mike...'

<They aren't sorry at all, the bastards.>

Anyway, after much anguish, reading of articles on Nvidia (for the GTX 3090 vs the 3080), Intel and AMD, I have a Dell Alienware running Windows on my desk.

Well, the second desk. My Apple setup is on the first.

Either way, it's a mid-sized tower and was working FINE until I updated drivers. Then, the unspeakable happened.

My Unreal has acquired a glitch.

A problem (that only happens in the Unreal Editor) where it goes black for a second or two when I click around the scene. It didn't happen when I got the box. Only after I updated Drivers.

This @#%@#^^ hasn't happened to me in over 10 years with my Apple stuff, and my nervous issues are starting to come back.

Fear of the B.S.O.D.

Smoke and re-install.

Driver hell.

Nvidia pointing a finger at Microsoft who points to Dell.

This just sucks. I'm not giving up on my effort to create new stories inside of Unreal, but I'm being challenged by the tech-gods once again. I have to say, not really too enthused about playing fair.

But I don't have the money to just buy another

machine. I will be calling tech-support next. Yes, I did buy the 'come to my house and fix this @#@#' insurance, and I am not afraid to use it.

The sad part? This is why I didn't build my own computer – I wanted something that 'just works' and figured certainly a Dell company (Alienware is a Dell product) would be pretty close to that.

So far it's a no go.

<<Sigh>>

At least the challenge provided me something to share with you besides the weather and how much the grass has grown.

By the way, for those asking, we HAVE figured out how to do the post-processing on our images inside of the Unreal engine vs. doing it outside in Photoshop. So, that was cool.

Ok, talk with you next book where I will have found a solution to this problem, or decided that an older version of the program running on a Mac works just fine.

Which is terribly unlikely. The Nvidia 3090 doesn't work on Mac computers (any that I have.)

Until I wrangle this beast.

Ad Aeternitatem,

Michael Anderle

One Crazy Set Of Stories (12)

## SOLDIERS OF FAME AND FORTUNE

Nobody's Fool (1)

Nobody Lives Forever (2)

Nobody Drinks That Much (3)

Nobody Remembers But Us (4)

Ghost Walking (5)

Ghost Talking (6)

Ghost Brawling (7)

Ghost Stalking (8)

Ghost Resurrection (9)

Ghost Adaptation (10)

Ghost Redemption (11)

Ghost Revolution (12)

## THE BOHICA CHRONICLES

Reprobates (1)

Degenerates (2)

Redeemables (3)

Thor (4)

## CRYPTID ASSASSIN

Hired Killer (1)

Silent Death (2)

Sacrificial Weapon (3)

Head Hunter (4)

BOOKS BY MICHAEL ANDERLE

**Sign up for the LMBPN** email list to be notified of new releases and special deals!

**https://lmbpn.com/email/**

For a complete list of books by Michael Anderle, please visit:

**www.lmbpn.com/ma-books/**